SOLOMON'S KNIFE

SOLOMON'S KNIFE

Victor Koman

FRANKLIN WATTS
New York • Toronto
1989

Printed in the United States of America
6   5   4   3   2   1
Design by Tere LoPrete

Library of Congress Cataloging-in-Publication Data

Koman, Victor.
  Solomon's knife / Victor Koman.
    p.   cm.
  ISBN 0-531-15108-5
  I. Title.
PS3561.0452S6   1989
813'.54—dc19   88-34900
                                                CIP

Dedicated to my wife, lover,
friend, and companion,
Veronica,
who, through faith, love,
labor, and courage,
served as midwife to this work

SOLOMON'S
KNIFE

I

A cool breeze blew from the ocean over the hills of Palos Verdes, carrying the scent of salt and clean air with it. Valerie Dalton took a deep breath, held it, let it out. It smelled like the winds that caressed the Rocky Mountains in winter. Fresh and pure. It reminded her of home.

She'd lived in the Los Angeles area for ten years since leaving home to attend UCLA. This was home now, not Colorado. This was where she had chosen to come. This is where she chose to stay.

The man she chose to stay with slumbered in bed, his dark hair tousled, face buried in the pillows. She watched him for a moment. It gave her a certain warm pleasure to know that by rising first to shower, she could allow him a few moments more to sleep. A moment or two more to recover from their late evening of lovemaking.

A lawyer of Ron Czernek's ambition needed all the rest he could get.

Valerie stepped quietly into the bathroom. First stop was the mirror atop the vanity for a survey of the night's damage. She gazed at the flesh around her blue-gray eyes. At twenty-eight, she feared the onslaught of crinkles with an apprehension usually reserved for toxic pollution or nuclear war.

Safe for now, she thought, reaching for her hairbrush. She plucked a few blond strands from the bristles, laid them in a tissue, and balled it up. A light toss sent the ball sailing into the wastebasket.

Two points. She smiled at the thought of how she'd picked up the phrase from Ron. That, and the line about punting. Or was it bunting?

Long nails clacking against the shower tiles, she twisted the hot water on full, waiting outside for the chill to abate. As she slipped out of her peach silk teddy, her thoughts turned to the problems she'd face at work. She wanted to have Shirley fired. It wouldn't look good, though, for a new office manager to flex her recently acquired authority that quickly. Perhaps a discussion with her about her absenteeism. And the condition of her desk.

That's it, she thought as she stepped into the hot, tingling spray. *A quiet, private talk.*

She languished for a precious moment in the swirling warmth of the shower. It became a waterfall off a mountain hot spring. She was successful, comfortable, and in love with a gentle, considerate man. The future lay before her, exciting and sweet. With a smile and closed eyes, she thrust her head into the cascade. Her long golden hair carried the waterfall down her back.

Valerie Dalton was happy. As happy as she'd ever been.

Soaped, shampooed, conditioned, and rinsed, she stepped a few moments later from the shower. The bath sheet felt warm from basking under the heat lamps. She wrapped her hair in a smaller towel, twisting it up and over. *Queena Sheba,* she thought, looking in the soaped portion of an otherwise fogged mirror. Her mother had always called her that whenever drying her. It was years before she realized that Queena was not a first name.

Valerie sat at her vanity. A quick check for water damage to her nails came before anything else. They'd survived.

She had everything timed. Ten minutes for the shower, ten for the hair, twenty-five for dressing and makeup. That left

4

fifteen minutes for emergencies before she gave Ron a last kiss and squeeze. Then he hit the shower, and she hit the road.

When she finished blow-drying her hair to full-bodied, soft-waved completion, she moved on to makeup. Rummaging for that new bottle of foundation she'd bought the other day, she uncovered her Hallmark date book.

Valerie felt a childish glow whenever she opened it. Her mother had always used one and had instilled the tradition in little Val from day one. As long as she could remember, she picked up the giveaway every year while buying Christmas cards. As a child, it had been filled by her mother with important dates. Later, she used it to keep track of friends' birthdays. When she turned eleven, the little book took on a new meaning.

"Now that you're a woman," her mother said, "it's important that you keep track of your friend." She showed Valerie how to put an inconspicuous dot next to the date of her period.

"See?" she said, marking the page on Valerie's date book with a tiny black spot. "No one will know what it means except you."

"And you," Valerie added with a child's seriousness.

"It'll be our secret."

When Valerie turned fourteen, she very daringly chose to use a red pen to make the dots. And she made them just a little bit larger.

Every year at Christmastime she still picked up the date book at whatever card shop she visited. And even though she used her Day-Timer for all other matters of import, she still took a red pen to the page of the date book. Every month. Every . . .

Curious, she opened the book to the page for February. Even though it was the first of March, no spot of red glowed from the previous month's white-and-blue surface. She flipped back to January.

And stared in quiet shock.

She tried to remember everything that had happened in the

last month. Her promotion had so occupied her time that she hadn't given any thought to much outside of her work. If anything, the freedom from aches and cramps had enabled her to handle the transition with ease.

She gazed at January's mark. The third. She counted. Eight weeks. Over eight. It can't be.

She begged herself to remember something. The week or two before Valentine's Day. Spotting, maybe.

Nothing. Nothing at all.

She opened a drawer to check her tampons. The box was nearly full. When did she buy it?

Looking up in the mirror, Valerie saw a different woman staring back.

She missed work that day.

Dr. Evelyn Fletcher's eyes opened three minutes before her alarm went off. Thoughts immediately began their daily churn. Concerns about luteinizing hormones, estradiol, and catheters intertwined with musings over synchronization, scheduling, and budgets.

She rolled naked out of the narrow single bed and, after a perfunctory glance at herself in the bathroom mirror, climbed into the frigid bathtub and turned on the water.

The first blast brought a shudder of cold, followed by a gradual warming. The tub was an antique ball-and-claw design, devoid of curtains and open to the small bathroom. Here, amid brass and porcelain fixtures, mauve and lavender tiles, gray-and-black curtains, she began and ended her working days. The hot water soothed her. The long soak gave her time to think.

Thinking time was what Evelyn cherished most. While soaking in the steaming tub, she paid no mind to her body. It mattered little to her that forty-seven years of life steadily left their tracks on her. The face that lined a bit more with every frown of deep concentration, the hair that turned relentlessly from black to frost, the flesh that would someday slowly surrender to the pull of gravity—these were invisible to her.

The unceasing thoughts continued to buzz within her. Inside, she was eternally young, unaging in her enthusiasm.

After half an hour spent in meditation, the water had become chilly. In that time, Evelyn had reviewed her schedule for the day and given further thought to the ramifications of her research. She turned on the tap to fill a stoneware pitcher with tepid water. A loud, sloshing waterfall substituted for the tub's nonexistent shower. After a few jugs' worth of rinsing, she toweled dry and dressed for the day in her usual clothes.

She favored dark clothing. She'd once commented to a colleague that she preferred primary colors such as white and black. Or blends—gray, off-white, and off-black.

Today she wore black. Only a small triangular wedge showed through at the apex of her lab coat's lapels. The coat—as clean and white as modern laundering could offer—was one of seven that she owned. One for each workday, plus a spare for emergency calls.

With a grunt, Dr. Fletcher hefted a heavy briefcase, filled to its tattered limits with papers, charts, abstracts, and research. Her right hand clutched her black instrument bag. She had never owned a purse on the theory that carrying feminine items would only weigh her down.

As she did every workday, she locked her apartment door's triple set of dead bolts, dropped the oversized ring of keys into her lab coat pocket, toted her burden down to a faded blue Saab that was only half her age, and threw the bags into the backseat. They landed with satisfying squeaks on the torn upholstery.

She hesitated before climbing into the driver's seat. Gazing out of the carport, she saw that the sun had come up over feathery white cirrus clouds. A breeze from the sea blew smog inland from Torrance, bringing with it a fresh smell. Dew from the night before misted on shake roofs, cool night air surrendering to morning's warmth.

It would be a good day.

II

Valerie Dalton stared blankly at the line of men and women before her. She hadn't seen them from the parking lot. Only when she reached the level of the sidewalk leading to the Reproductive Endocrinology wing of Bayside University Medical Center did she realize that some sort of protest was in progress.

The men and women dressed in the casual style endemic in Southern California. Their children accompanied them in an elliptical march along the sidewalk. The signs they carried were neatly printed in bright Day-Glo colors.

ABORTION IS MURDER read several of the signs. END THE SILENT HOLOCAUST read another. One, held by a young woman, said ABORTION KILLS UNBORN FEMINISTS, TOO!

Valerie took a deep breath. She had seen such displays on TV but hadn't considered that she would ever need to cross such a line or even encounter such people.

The continuing orbit brought new signs into view. FERTILITY CLINICS PLAY GOD—GOD IS ANGRY. A small boy carried a sign obviously printed by someone trying to imitate a child's lettering. It read I KNOW WHO MY MOMMY AND DADDY ARE, with a couple of letters drawn backward for authenticity.

They've covered both sides, Valerie thought. *I can't lie my way through.* She let go her breath and walked forward.

"Please don't kill your child," a man in a dark suit said as she passed between the marchers.

"I'm not," she said. "I'm just going for a test." She didn't understand why she felt the need to explain anything at all to him.

A woman stopped to join them. She was older, already gray. She stared at Valerie with a flat, cold gaze. "There are other clinics you can go to. They'll provide the same tests *and* give you any counseling you need."

Valerie pushed her way past the pair. "Please," she said. "I just need a test."

Another woman stepped in her way, smiling warmly. "We want to help you avoid making a tragic decision. We know you don't want your baby to end up like *this.*" She turned her sign around to thrust it in Valerie's face. She stared at the bloody, mangled remains of an aborted fetus. The photograph had been printed in the brightest, most lurid colors. Reds, yellows, grisly black tones swirled through the image.

Valerie's vision faltered for a moment. Her breath hung sickly in her lungs, threatening to drop to her stomach in an elevator rush of shock, as if she were watching a real murder on the evening news.

A firm hand grasped her arm. "Back off!" a woman's voice shouted with military intensity. "You know the rules. You touch anyone *or* interfere with free passage and I'll gladly see you removed from these premises."

Dr. Evelyn Fletcher stared at the assembled group for a long moment before releasing Valerie's arm. "You use laws to keep us from throwing you off our property. Just be damn sure you follow them yourselves." She turned to Valerie. "Come on, miss. The receptionist's right inside."

Picking up her two bags, the doctor led Valerie through the automatic doors. Before they closed, she shot another glance back at the pickets. Her eyes softened from anger to a weary kind of sadness. Turning, she strode silently past the receptionist and into her office.

Valerie always felt uneasy waiting in an examination room. The cool white walls, the antiseptic scent, the indecipherable buzz of voices outside imparted the same sense of mystery and mysticism she had felt since childhood. A doctor's office was like a church. One stepped in from the street into a hushed, different world, with its own unique smells and quiet intrigues. It made sense to her somehow. Priests struggled for the salvation of human souls. Doctors fought for the health of the body. Both listened to their charges with the same inscrutable expression.

Valerie had given up attending church long ago. She tried just as much to limit her visits to doctors. She fingered the wad of cotton in the crook of her left arm. Priests want tithes. Doctors demand blood.

A crisp set of footsteps approached her door, followed by the zip of a folder being removed from the door tray. A long moment of silence, pierced only by the faint sound of pages turning, ended with the sharp crank of the doorknob.

"Oh—it's you." The tallish graying woman who had come to Valerie's aid stepped in. "I'm Dr. Fletcher. Evelyn. May I call you Valerie?"

The doctor extended her hand to her patient. Valerie stood to clasp it, returned the light shake, nodded, and sat down nervously.

"Should I get undressed?" she asked.

Dr. Fletcher shook her head while glancing at the forms in Valerie's folder. "Not for today. First I want to let you know that our test confirms your home test. It's positive, too. You're pregnant." She said it without any congratulatory smile, knowing from the younger woman's demeanor that the answer would not be greeted as the best of news. Valerie's deep breath and slight lowering of the head confirmed her diagnosis.

"What I'd like to discuss with you is your feelings about that and what you'd like to do."

Valerie looked up with wet, panicked eyes. "This is the wrong time. I don't know what happened. Ron and I use the sponge. It's not supposed to happen. I just got a promotion where I work and I can't see my boss just letting me have a few months off to go have a baby which Ron and I weren't planning to do anyway. I mean, babies are nice and all, but we're not even married and we still haven't been to Europe and you can't just go running around Europe changing diapers and expect to have any fun. Not when you have your whole life ahead of you. We both have to work. I can't take any time off. We wanted to have a honeymoon and all that first—"

Evelyn laid a hand on Valerie's arm. "The worst thing you can do," she said slowly, calmly, "is to feel trapped by pregnancy. It won't make anything easier. There are options available for you, especially since we caught this at an early stage."

"I know." She unconsciously pulled her arm away from Fletcher's touch to restore the customary distance between a patient and her physician.

The doctor nodded toward the door. "Ignore those boors outside. They're here once in a while when they can get a reporter to show up." She sat down beside Valerie and took her hand gently. "Whether to keep or end a pregnancy is one of the hardest decisions a woman can make. You have to deal with all the 'what ifs' that arise. And I don't mean the medical uncertainties; a pregnancy termination is a lot safer now than giving birth. I mean *your* uncertainties."

The older woman's voice softened. "When I was about nineteen, I had an abortion. I was a first-year premed student and couldn't be bothered with pregnancy. I regretted my decision almost immediately afterward. I used to wonder what sort of child I might have had. Pregnancy is the first step on the road to forever. If you decide to give birth to a child, it will affect you all your life."

She looked directly into Valerie's eyes with the gentle gaze of hard experience. "The decision to terminate the pregnancy will be with you forever, too, though. It's a rare woman that can put such an action completely behind her and get on with her life." She touched Valerie's arm again with soothing reassurance. "I suffered a great deal of guilt and wondering when I had my abortion." Her fingers tightened. "If there were any way that I could let you make your decision without pain or fear or guilt, I would. Believe me." Her fingers released their grip the instant she realized that the contact unnerved Valerie more than it comforted her.

Valerie gazed at the doctor with puzzlement. "You sound as if I've already made my choice."

"Haven't you?"

She stared at Dr. Fletcher with unchecked surprise. Her eyes lowered just a bit in realization. "Yes, I guess so. I don't think—I mean, I can't have a baby right now. If it had only been a couple of years from now, I—"

"Valerie." Evelyn spoke quietly. "Don't let the *if onlys* sneak up on you. You're pregnant *right now.* You have to decide based on what your life is like right now. You have the right to terminate your pregnancy. It was a hard-won right and the battle"—she nodded again toward the outside world—"is still being fought." She gave Valerie's arm another reassuring squeeze, then turned her attention to the folder. "How does this Thursday sound? You've got a new job, so how about six-thirty in the evening?"

"For—?"

"The procedure."

Valerie felt a strange panic overwhelm her. The bloody image on the picket sign flashed crimson in her mind. "The abortion?"

Dr. Fletcher let go a shallow, disapproving huff. "The pregnancy termination. That's really all it is. If you don't want to be pregnant right now, we can grant your wish. Believe me, there are almost as many women in the fertility program here trying to become pregnant. It all evens out. We try to give everyone what she wants."

After a moment, Valerie quietly said, "Six-thirty is all right."

Dr. Fletcher made a few notes in the folder. "Fine. You

might want to have someone drive you here and back. Are you going to discuss this with the father?"

Valerie nodded.

"Good. It's always best for a relationship not to have any secrets. Can you tell me a little bit about him?"

Valerie took a tissue from her purse and worried at it. "He's just a wonderfully caring man—"

Fletcher cut her off. "I mean his physical characteristics."

"Well . . ." Valerie thought the question curious. "He's tall. Black hair. Brown eyes. He has a beard."

"White?"

Valerie frowned. "No, it's the same color as the rest of his hair."

"I mean his race."

Valerie answered slowly, unsettled by the nature of the question. People didn't *ask* questions like that anymore. Did they? "He's the son of Russian immigrants. You can't get much whiter than that. Why?"

Dr. Fletcher sighed and looked up with a weary smile. "These damned federal forms are getting nosier every year, aren't they?"

So quickly, Valerie thought, driving along the Pacific Coast Highway. *Five minutes for a test, boom—you know you're pregnant. Then you're scheduled for an abortion.* She took a deep breath, urged her yellow Porsche 914 into fourth gear, and raced through the amber light at PCH and Crenshaw. Light aircraft buzzed around Torrance Airport, dancing in the warmth of late morning. She looked out the passenger side of the car to steal quick glances at them. Small airplanes had always fascinated her, though she had never been up in one. They looked like toys, like kites, like wobbly little playthings. She always felt sad when she read or heard about one crashing, as if the people on board had been punished cruelly and unjustly for wanting to have fun.

13

She pulled over to the side of the road to watch the planes and suddenly began to cry.

Ron Czernek listened quietly. Sitting in the corner of the living-room sofa group, he held Valerie in his muscular arms while she told him of her decision.

He was a large man, with black hair and beard trimmed for business and well-tailored suits to match. She had given him time to change into casual clothes and have a drink before telling him about her day.

"I was a little subdued when you left this morning," she said, safely wrapped inside his embrace. "I'd realized that I'd missed my period." She turned to gaze up at him. "I went to the clinic at Bayside for a test." She lowered her head, closing her eyes. "I passed. I'm pregnant."

Before Ron could say anything, she added, "I can't be pregnant. Not right now. Too much is going on with us for me to throw the brakes on and become a mother."

He nodded. Even speaking in quiet, intimate tones, his voice resonated. "You know that whatever choice you make, I'm with you all the way. It's our baby, but it's your body." He held her tighter. "You've got your job to think about. I've got mine. We haven't paid off the BMW yet." His voice caught for an instant. "I'm sure we could make it all work, anyway. I'm with you one hundred percent if you decide to. The classes, being there, everything."

Her body began to tremble against his. He quickly added, "The same goes for the . . . other choice. I'll be with you. The whole nine yards." He smiled and ran a hand over her golden hair. "I'm a lawyer, not a judge. I only want to help you do what *you* want to do."

"I love you, Ron." She pulled herself deeper into his arms. She could smell the scent of a day's work on him. The smoke from the office, the faint odor of self-serve gasoline, the aroma of her lover's flesh. He was eight years older than she, but she felt as if they were high school sweethearts.

She clung to him as she did to her father so long ago. "Please go with me Thursday evening."

"Of course."

They sat together, silent.

III

Dr. Fletcher sorted through the charts kept in a fat, locking file folder on her desk. A cigarette glowed in the plastic ashtray—a giveaway from some medical supply company whose logo in the bottom had long since been stubbed, melted, and ashed into illegibility. The cigarette itself was a Defiant, the brand with the highest dose of nicotine per milligram of tar. She had long ago decided that nicotine was the drug she sought in smoking, so logically she should get as much of it per cigarette as she could while minimizing the amount of other contaminants. She had even convinced some of her chain-smoking colleagues to cut down from three packs a day of low-nicotine cigarettes to her half pack of high-nic.

She took occasional drags on the stick absentmindedly, giving her sole attention to the papers before her. She had someone now. Someone who matched well enough for everything to work. If she could pull this off, it would change everything. *Everything.* The medical advance would be almost trivial compared to the social revolution.

She took another puff and sat back. Valerie Dalton was a superb prospect for Karen Chandler. Fletcher's quick eyes scanned Karen's file. Dark haired, but that's all right; her husband's blond. Gray eyes to her husband's brown. She glanced back to Valerie's New Patient form for the answers she had innocently given to Fletcher's questions.

The father of the child was Caucasian, dark hair, dark eyes. Evelyn nodded. Blood tests rushed through indicated that serologies were negative. Good. Both women Rh positive—no problems there.

She picked up the phone and punched the number on one of the forms.

"Hello, Karen? Evelyn Fletcher . . . Fine, thanks. Do you think you could come to the office at six forty-five this Thursday evening?" She listened for a moment, then said, "Yes. I think we do. . . . Yes. Well, just be here on time and we'll do that."

She hung up the phone, took a final, long drag on her cigarette, stubbed it, and leaned back in her leather chair, smiling.

The Saab sounded better on the short drive home.

Dr. Fletcher lived just five miles from Bayside. The drive, which usually took around ten minutes, was slowed by the presence of a stalled car and tow truck on Crenshaw. She waited out the delay listening to music on the car radio. Whenever the sound degenerated into crackling fuzz, she fisted the dashboard gently a few times to restore it. The rapid movement of the Bach fugue amused her with its contrast to the snail's pace of evening traffic.

Her thoughts again returned to the world of her work. Putting her driving skills on automatic, Evelyn mentally rehearsed Thursday's operations to anticipate any possible difficulties. The roar of anxious engines and the throb of city noise faded as she envisioned the movements of her hands, the position of the equipment, the delicate feel of the tissues she'd be handling. And blood. Always blood.

So much blood. The image on the picket sign haunted Valerie. She had used a different door to leave the hospital, but she could not cause the picture to depart her mind. In bed, she lay beside the warmth of her lover's body and spoke to him in low tones, as if they might be overheard.

"She shoved it in my face. It was awful. It looked like a baby all cut up and dumped and covered with blood." She buried her face in the crook of his arm.

Ron stroked her hair. "Don't think about it. I've read the trespass cases against their sort. They use pictures of third-trimester abortions to gross people out. A seventh-week embryo is probably the size of your thumb. It really isn't anything more than a bit of your tissue. It'll be painless."

She squeezed him tighter. "The pamphlet says we won't be able to make love for six weeks."

His hand snaked around her to touch a soft breast. "That depends on what you mean by 'making love.'"

"Make love to me tonight, Ron. Right now."

With a single fluid motion, he slid easily, happily, hungrily, into her. She clung to him gratefully, just as hungrily, her need satisfied with every movement of their bodies.

Wednesday passed for Valerie like a day spent numbed at the dentist. She tried to concentrate on her job, but the little red square she had drawn around Thursday in her Hallmark date book seemed to be seared into her optic nerve. The image of it followed her at every turn.

She sat in her cubicle facing Shirley, the new word processor they had permanently hired from the temp agency. She studied their contrast. As the new office manager, Valerie dressed in her most conservative cream-colored Oscar de la Renta suit. Her salon tan complemented the color nicely. The dark-haired twenty-year-old's flesh was white as death. She wore a black cowpunk outfit with silver steer-skull bolo and chain bracelets. Even Valerie, who had never been into the club scene, knew that the costume was outmoded. After all, she still read the *L.A. Weekly*.

"Shirley," Valerie began without any preface, "your work here since we hired you from DayJob has not been as good as when you were a temp." She couldn't shake the impression that she was discussing something very minor in light of what would be happening tomorrow. "You've let your desk get cluttered with . . ." She looked at Shirley. Had this girl from Lawndale ever been pregnant, ever had an abortion?

"With what?" Shirley asked, staring at her manager with impatient puzzlement.

"Stuff. Just all those buttons and things. We don't appreciate stickers for groups such as Uranium Holocaust and Stark Fist slapped all over our desks."

Shirley looked out at her workstation, made the sort of face teenagers make when acquiescing to Mom, and said, "Can I just stick them on my Wang?"

Valerie felt an odd sort of flush envelop her. She fought it back.

"Being absent three days in your first month also looks bad. Why don't you . . ." She found no words to complete the sentence, merely sat with her mouth half-open, gazing speechlessly across her desk.

"Are you on something, Ms. Dalton?"

Valerie recovered quickly, saying, "It's been a tough morning, Shirley. Just get back to work and see that you're not unavoidably absent again."

When Shirley had left the cubicle, Valerie took a deep breath and leaned back in her chair. Telling her boss that she needed a second day off this week was going to be tough. She felt a knotting in her stomach that any number of deep breaths would not alleviate. For a moment, the chill thought that there was something *alive* in her making that knot sent an unbidden shudder through her shoulders and back.

She walked over to the vice president's office and knocked, then opened the door.

"Ernie," she said, "I need another favor."

Ernest Sewell sat on the couch across from his desk, legs

stretched out, a sheaf of printout resting on his shins and held from spilling onto the floor by upturned feet. As if reading a scroll, he looked over each page, then pulled up another from the stack below, gathering the remainder in his hands. He wore a rust-colored polo shirt and dark beige slacks that pleasantly enhanced his milk-chocolate skin. Laying the computer paper on his lap, he looked at Valerie.

"If it's another day off, Val, that'll be a problem. How was your doctor visit?"

She took a deep breath. "I may be out on Friday. I have to have some surgery tomorrow evening."

Her boss set the stack of paper on the floor and rose to walk over to her. "What's wrong, Valerie?"

"It's nothing. It's outpatient surgery. Just something I have to take care of right away. I'm sorry that it—"

"Never mind about a thing, Val." He put a hand on her shoulder. "If you need tomorrow *and* Friday, take them both. Just take care of yourself. You're no good to me sick."

Relieved that she didn't have to explain anything further, she returned to her cubicle and telephoned Ron. He was in court, his secretary said. Could she take a message?

"Just tell him that Thursday is on."

The two major crises out of the way, Valerie moved through the day mechanically, performing only the most necessary activities. She tried not to look over the edge of her cubicle at the clock on the wall a few yards away, but every time her eyes reflexively glanced up, her stomach clenched as she realized that so little time had passed. Yet the end of the day caught her by surprise, and she noticed that she had accomplished very little in eight hours.

Knuckles rapped as best they could against the gray brushed fabric that lined the outside of her cramped enclosure. Sewell stood in the opening, clutching a stack of floppy disks in one hand, a thick programming book in the other.

"Your sentence has been served, Val. You're a free woman."

"Thanks, Warden. I just want to finish up the Pro-Dos team roster that Paul gave me."

Sewell hesitated for a moment, his dark eyes gazing around Valerie's office as if looking for clues. His voice softened.

"If it's anything serious," he said, "maybe we should talk."

"What?" Her voice almost cracked.

"You're so full of high tension I'm afraid to bring these disks near you. One touch and you'd degauss them. Is this surgery something serious?"

Under her desk, Valerie's right leg began to shake with slight uncontrollable movements. Her stomach fluttered. Taking a sharp breath that was almost a snort, she tried to sound dismissive.

"It's nothing. Abdominal surgery. A small growth. I hear they do it with lasers now. In and out. You know."

Her boss mulled it for a moment. "If this new position is giving you an ulcer already, take my advice. Self-fulfillment isn't worth it if you kill yourself."

"I'm not killing"—she caught her breath—"*myself*. I'm fine. I'll be back in on Monday. Friday, even, if all goes well." She pointed to her bulging briefcase. "And I'm taking that home to work on over the weekend."

Sewell frowned. "Don't even think of it. I don't want you carrying that in Monday and blowing your stitches or seals or whatever they'll close you up with. Just rest."

"Thank you," she said softly. Realizing that she didn't sound too managerial, she cleared her throat and reached for the briefcase. "I'll need something fun to read in the waiting room. If I need any assistance carrying it, I'll use the hired help."

He snorted a mild laugh and smiled. "Good night, Val."

"Good night, Ernie."

When he had gone, she let out a sigh of tired relief. *It'll be over tomorrow,* she thought, trying to comfort herself as she gathered together her belongings. The briefcase in one hand counterbalanced a stack of progress reports in the other. A series of "Good night" murmurs followed her out of the office area. She made a point of returning each one, even though her thoughts darted feverishly around to her plans for Thursday.

Maybe I should take the day off. "Good night, Marcie." *I can't eat beforehand.* "Good night, Jer." *I'll leave a Top Shelf or two for Ron to heat up.* "G'night, LeRoy." *I wonder if I* will *be able to do any work this weekend.* " 'Night, Faouzi."

She took her favorite scenic route home, up to Malaga Cove, where towering eucalyptus trees swayed in the sea breeze to conceal million-dollar homes. A quick spin past the sea-cliff estates on Paseo del Mar. She had not yet found out which one belonged to Frank Sinatra, but she would keep at it until she did. Every new rumor she overheard mentioned a different mansion, and she thought it too snoopy to ask. Palos Verdes people never pried, and after just three years of owning a small, older house in the Lunada Bay area, she and Ron considered themselves consummate residents. They were not aware whether anyone else considered them so. After all, they were now Palos Verdes people. And Palos Verdes people never pry.

IV

Valerie spent Thursday watching old movies on the VCR. Following the instructions in the pamphlet Dr. Fletcher had given her, she ate a light breakfast—unusual for her, since she generally skipped morning meals. She knew, though, that she'd be ravenous by lunchtime without it.

Wrapped in a mountain-sky-blue satin peignoir she'd just the month before bought at Victoria's Secret, she sat in bed with a serving tray over her lap, the VCR remote reposing in the magazine caddy. She had decided that morning, after Ron had left early for Century City, to pamper herself without guilt. With Daddy gone five years now and her mother still in Colorado Springs, she needed to feel as if she were home from school.

The bloated briefcase sat atop the progress reports in the third bedroom, which they'd converted into an office. Out of sight, out of mind.

Fred Astaire swirled fluidly across the dance floor, with Ginger held gracefully in his slender arms. She watched them move in tones of gray on the screen atop Ron's bedroom dresser. The dancer's death had saddened her more than the usual regret she felt at hearing of the passing of other aging movie stars. She felt that he could have, *should* have, kept dancing forever, that the world had benefited gloriously by his being here and had suffered greatly at his loss.

Her finger punched the remote, stopping the tape and switching to cable. It had been set for "CNN Headline News." Another anencephalic baby had been delivered to a nearby hospital in a recently revived organ-harvesting project. It was to be put on life support. Parents of other children nervously awaited its brain death so that its vital parts might be used to save their own children's lives.

Valerie shuddered at the thought of a baby born without a brain. She'd inadvertently seen a photograph of one on the news but hadn't turned away fast enough: sunken skull, like a doll that had been stepped on, seemingly golfball-sized eyes protruding.

A chill trembled across the backs of her arms and shoulders. What pain the mother must have felt to have gone for so long, gone all the way, and then . . .

She climbed out of bed to change tapes. *Forbidden Planet.* Leslie Neilsen, Anne Francis, and Walter Pidgeon. That will be fun. She hit the Play button and climbed back into bed.

It's better this way, she thought. *You never know what might happen.* She was not certain that she would be a good enough mother to tolerate even a moderately sickly child. She feared that she would not be strong enough to endure a child deformed or dying.

Abortion was best.

She found that she could think of the word without hesitation, without substituting a euphemism such as "pregnancy termination."

She imagined her life spreading before her like a river. She could take any one of an infinite number of streams that branched away. Some paralleled the main flow; others turned sharply away into unknown darkness; still others meandered aimlessly into dry lake beds. A child at this point in her life would break her away from the flow, push her into a backwater, stop the momentum her life had gained.

The M-G-M lion roared. Eerie electronic tonalities filled the room. She ceased thinking about her life, content to finish her egg and back bacon on toasted muffin, drink her orange juice, and watch the Technicolor world of robots, lust, and Monsters from the Id.

There were no children on Altair IV.

The opening and shutting of the front door awakened Valerie from a slumber. At first, she thought it was morning. The outside world was dark; she was in bed. The TV, though, was on. Then she remembered closing her eyes while watching Rossano Brazzi profess his love for Alida Valli in *Noi Vivi*. The tape must have run out, for the TV had switched back to cable.

Ron stepped into the bedroom. "It's five-thirty, Val." He saw her staring at the TV. "Are you okay?"

Valerie nodded sleepily. It always took her longer to awaken from a nap than it did from a full night's sleep. She took a deep draft of water from the Waterford set on her nightstand, sat up, and smiled at him.

"I'm fine, honey. I just drifted off. I'll be ready in time."

He moved to her side of the bed, threw his arms around her, and squeezed with loving tenderness. "You don't have to go through with this if you don't want to."

She returned the hug. "If I don't, you won't be able to say the same thing in the delivery room."

A silence passed between them for a moment.

"Then you'd better get dressed," Ron said, giving her a pat on her backside.

They drove to Bayside in Ron's silver-gray BMW 320i. Valerie wore a loose-fitting cotton sarong skirt in understated forest green purchased just the week before at Banana Republic. The pamphlet told her to avoid tight pants or anything encumbering. Her Costa Brava shirt in the same shade came from the identical source.

Though the March evening was warm and the sun had only

just set, she wore a mock-aviator's jacket of dark olive cotton and still felt a shiver coming on.

Ron had not bothered to change from his charcoal-gray business suit. He drove silently, not attempting to engage her in any conversation. For her part, Valerie stared out the window, watching the planes fly in and out of Torrance, their lights bright and fairylike in the twilight.

As the car smoothly turned off PCH into the parking lot, past the white-and-blue sign that read BAYSIDE UNIVERSITY MEDICAL CENTER, Valerie broke the silence by quietly asking, "This *is* what you want, isn't it?"

He pulled into the nearest available parking space. "I want what's best for you, Valerie. You're not ready to be a mother, and I don't think I'm ready to be a father. Maybe in a few years. We have time to think about it. This will give us time to plan it, save for it, prepare our heads." He killed the engine, pulled the keys, and shut down the lights. "It's your body. You have to make the final decision."

Valerie nodded and stepped out of the car.

They moved quietly up the walkway to the Reproductive Endocrinology Department. Valerie glanced around, relieved to see that the line of picketers had dispersed for the night. A cool evening breeze ruffled the palms and the trio of giant bird-of-paradise plants, brushing their leaves against the office windows on the second story. The yellow-orange light from low-pressure sodium vapor lamps imparted harsh shadows to the dark corners of the entrance. Only a few lights glowed from the windows.

She was so grateful that she would not be walking back to the car alone. She felt that she might have been able to enter the building, moving toward its marginal warmth and protection. To leave it after her surgery, though, to step out into the eerie darkness of a nearly empty, windy parking lot, was something she doubted she could do without a nagging murmur of fear.

Ron held her hand in his warm, firm grasp. The doors opened before them with a pneumatic hiss. Overhead, a tiny red light winked like a knowing, vulgar eye. *We know what you're here for.*

The receptionist, a tired old woman with gray-blue hair and gravity-worn face, checked the calendar, then handed Valerie a clipboard, pen, and form.

"Fill this out, honey," she said in a voice that could sand furniture, "and give it back to me when you're done."

Valerie glanced over the release form, searching for the blanks to fill in. All it required was the date, a few initials, and her signature.

"Wait." Ron took the form from her. "Professional curiosity," he said, carefully reading each paragraph.

"Looks like a standard waiver and release from responsibility," he muttered. "Four pages is probably longer than standard, but if those pickets outside have tried any legal mischief, they're probably trying to cover their asses."

Valerie nodded, reaching for the papers. He held it back to read the last page. He looked up at the receptionist.

"What's this 'waiver of claim to any tissues removed' part?"

The receptionist eyed him with bored weariness. "If you want to take it home with you, hon, you'll have to ask the doctor."

It took a moment for Ron to realize what she meant. Valerie had already turned white at the thought of the nurse's suggestion. She seized the papers from his hands and signed them.

"Thanks, honey." The receptionist's tone was flat, almost mechanical.

"What a gross—" Ron began to whisper before Valerie shushed him.

"You do that every time I have to sign something," she said in a low, clipped tone. "This is a university hospital, for God's sake. They're not going to have me sign my soul away."

"You haven't heard about as many malpractice cases as I

have." He looked up at the receptionist. Her gray-blue hair shimmered oddly in the fluorescent lights. "Excuse me," he said in a commanding lawyer's voice.

"Yes?"

"We'd like a copy of this." He handed her the form.

"Sure, hon," she said without looking up.

They sat in the waiting room. No one else was there. Occasionally, an elevator door would open somewhere nearby, and an orderly or resident would come around the corner to pass through wordlessly. Valerie felt strange, as if she were moving through her paces in some sort of low-grade horror film set in a hospital. Everything seemed to acquire altered meanings. The glance of an orderly, the clatter of gurney wheels against linoleum, the smell of Lysol and formaldehyde.

She put her arm through Ron's and held tightly. His other hand stroked her blond head.

A tan, leggy nurse entered through a door. She appeared to be in her mid-thirties, with deep auburn hair and hazel eyes. She looked as if she should have been in some vaudeville skit as a beautiful yet brainless comic foil. She carried herself with grace and dignity, though, and her icepick gaze belied any sense of vacuity.

She picked up a folder from the receptionist and said, in a voice with just the barest trace of a European accent, "Valerie Dalton, please follow me."

"May I be there?" Ron asked, standing.

"I'm sorry, sir. The doctor doesn't allow that."

Valerie rose, paused, then hugged Ron as hard as she could. "I love you," she said.

"I love you, too, sweetheart. I'll be right here."

"And I'll be right back."

He nodded, a sudden look of concern on his face. He tried to smile. "You do that."

She turned to join the woman. The pair disappeared behind the light green door.

"They never let the man in there, hon," the receptionist said in her tobacco-scoured voice. "You guys just keep fainting."

He gave her a withering glance that went nowhere, since she wasn't looking up at the moment. He sat back and picked through the magazines on the table. *If men spend their time out here,* he thought, *how come all they have is* Redbook *and* Cosmopolitan?

The outer doors opened. Another couple walked in. The woman was in her twenties, brown haired, sweet looking. She wore a loose-fitting caftan in a natural beige tone. Her purse was a leather hobo sack that hung lightly from her shoulder. She was about Valerie's height and seemed imbued with a nervous good cheer. She kept an arm around her escort.

The man she was with was a sort of sandy blond. His skin was sunburned pink, with the characteristic white zone around his eyes that marked him as a skier recently returned from the slopes. An aquamarine cotton windbreaker covered a blue shirt and jeans. He was muscular without being husky and radiated a ready enthusiasm.

Probably do this all the time, Ron thought with minimal charity.

The receptionist looked up and smiled. "Head right in. Nurse Dyer will get you ready."

He frowned, his suspicion confirmed. Preferred customers. The blond man sat at the far side of the room, pulled a paperback novel from his jacket, and calmly started to read.

Ron shook his head. Some people could be too cavalier about it.

Valerie followed the nurse into a larger than normal examination room containing white enamel cabinets and medical equipment.

"Is this where she'll do it?" she asked the nurse.

"Yes. Please undress and put this on." The tall woman

handed Valerie a blue dressing gown. Valerie took it, thanked her, and waited for her to leave before disrobing. She hung her skirt and shirt on a hanger behind the door, put her panties in her purse, and slipped into the dressing gown. The rough fabric was cold to the touch.

She looked at the centerpiece of the room—a padded table with padded metal stirrups, padded metal armrests, handgrips, and headrest, all in dark green.

Is this right? she wondered. *I can't back out now. I'd just be up on that thing again in seven months with a bigger problem.*

She tried to envision being a mother to a crying, demanding baby. She didn't think she possessed the necessary calm patience that child care required. *I could never be like Mom. No one could be that loving and kind all the time anymore.*

The door opened. In stepped Dr. Fletcher wearing a crisp white paper surgical gown, her hair tucked under an equally white cap. She wore light green paper slacks, and on her feet were light green paper shoes. The tall nurse followed, similarly dressed.

"Good evening, Valerie," Dr. Fletcher said with a warm smile. "How are you feeling?"

"Fine."

"Nurse Dyer will assist me tonight. I think you've met."

Valerie nodded. The nurse gazed back with cool efficiency.

"While we're getting ready here," the doctor said, "could you please climb onto the table?"

Valerie sat up on the paper-covered cushion, leaned back, and lifted her legs up to the stirrups with Nurse Dyer's guidance. While Dr. Fletcher pulled on a pair of latex gloves, then slipped another pair over them, Nurse Dyer stepped to the far side of the room to unlock a closet. There, on small rubber wheels, stood a white and gleaming object the size of a small refrigerator. On one side was a control panel with switches, dials, lights, and a small video screen. On the other side was a long, white, flexible plastic tube terminating in a stiff, clear segment with a small opaque ridge on one side.

Nurse Dyer wheeled the device into position a few feet back from where Valerie's legs spread. She hooked a foot to slide a chair under Fletcher as the doctor slipped a mask over her mouth and nose. Dyer pulled a light down from the ceiling, switched its brilliant lamp on, and positioned the beam directly between Valerie's legs.

The rays warmed Valerie like the sun. It brought to her an old memory of a camping trip with her first boyfriend in high school. They had biked up to Flagstaff from Grand Junction. Below them spread the town of Boulder and the endless plains of eastern Colorado. They both disrobed and lay in the sun, its heat tickling parts of them that seldom basked in its radiance.

Valerie let out a startled gasp. The cold touch of a thermometer entering her brought her back to the present.

"Okay," the doctor said, sliding on a pair of goggles. "Hold that in there for a moment."

Nurse Dyer donned two sets of gloves and her own goggles. Silent, well rehearsed, she performed her duties with a practiced efficiency that wasted no motions of her shapely frame. She switched on the machine. It hummed and gurgled. The end of it made a sucking sound for a moment.

"Dulbeco's medium ready," the nurse said. "Pump on. Ham's F-10 warming."

"Buminate?" asked Fletcher.

"Five percent."

Dr. Fletcher turned her attention to Valerie. "Since you're only about seven weeks, Valerie, we're going to use the suction method. This is the latest equipment, and it's very gentle."

"Will it hurt much?" She craned her neck to see what was going on. She saw Dr. Fletcher lubricating the tube with K-Y jelly.

Fletcher withdrew the thermometer. "Thirty-seven point five." The nurse took it from her hand. She grasped the suction tube, bent the hysteroscope into position, and peered into an eyepiece on the end. "Well," she said, "the uterus itself doesn't have too many nerve endings, but it'll feel a little uncomfortable when we dilate your cervix."

She grasped the syringe Dyer pressed into her hand. "We're going to give you a pericervical block. It'll numb you up like Novocain at the dentist's so it won't hurt as much."

Using the fingers of a speculum to open the way, Fletcher guided the needle to its destination and pushed gently. The sharp sensation caused Valerie to twitch.

"Easy," Fletcher said, emptying the syringe into Valerie's flesh. "There. All done." The hypo withdrew. She reached next for the suction tube.

"What makes this device better than the older models is that I can see what I'm doing through this hysteroscope. Here we go."

Valerie felt the cool intrusion of the tube as it slid into her. There was a pause; then she felt a blunt pressure against her cervix. The end of the tube moved slowly around, Fletcher peering head down into the scope like a submarine commander seeking an enemy ship.

"Just relax, Valerie," her soothing voice entreated. "I'm getting it lined up."

A slow, insistent pressure gave way to the pain of numbed tissues and muscle being stretched. Valerie clenched her teeth. If it hurt this much under the painkiller for just a little tube, what must childbirth feel like? In that instant, she experienced an agonizing relief at her choice.

"Relax. Loosen up. We're almost there."

A pain like a fiery knife stab pierced her as a final, firm push drove the tube home.

"Transcervical," Nurse Dyer noted, watching the image on the video screen.

"Now we look around a bit," the doctor said in her most conversational tone. "The uterine walls—I don't know if you've ever seen a picture of one—look like an ocean filled with drifting fronds of seaweed. Nestled in there somewhere is the embryo."

"Go back," Dyer interjected.

"Saw it," Fletcher murmured, gently maneuvering the probe. She continued to speak soothingly to her patient.

"Now what we're going to do, Valerie, is turn on the suction. It's not noisy, and you won't feel any pressure. What we'll do is dislodge the embryo and remove it. This is a very gentle method that doesn't damage much tissue. You'll have a little bit of spotting when we're done but virtually no scarring."

Valerie nodded. She didn't know what else to do. She lay back and stared at the soft green color of the ceiling. A fire sprinkler head hung directly over her, right next to the smoke detector. There was a little brown spatter on the ceiling. She wondered what it was. Could it possibly be blood? How? Maybe it was a water stain. Rust.

She felt something indistinct rip within her. Deep and far away, like a plant being uprooted in the distance.

"Lavage," the doctor called out.

"Cycling," replied the nurse.

"Hold it." She moved the tube around slightly, then withdrew it an inch. "All right. Suction." Her hands held the tube rock steady.

"This is the slow part," Fletcher said in a pleasant voice. "It takes a minute or two to get everything out." She peered and probed gently. "We don't want to leave any foreign tissue in there where it could cause problems."

"Transoptus nominal," Nurse Dyer said, flicking some switches and turning a dial or two. "Capture."

"Okay" was the doctor's terse reply. "Cleaning up."

"Tanking out lavage."

Dr. Fletcher slowly pulled the tube back. "While I have you here, Valerie, would you want me to fix this so it doesn't happen again?"

Valerie looked between her knees at the woman's masked face.

"What? You mean tie me off?"

33

The doctor nodded. "I can do a 'band-aid sterilization' when we're done here."

"Oh, no. I still want to be a mother. Just not right now. Maybe later." She grunted at the sensation of the suction tube's withdrawal. Her cervix throbbed; her vaginal walls ached.

"Then we're done." Fletcher placed the instrument in a small tray on the side of the machine. It was coated with smears of bright red blood. Blood covered the fingertips that reached for cotton gauze.

Valerie did not feel the bleeding. She felt nothing at all now but a dull ache in her abdomen and an impression of finality. There was no going back now. No chance to change her mind.

The gauze rubbed roughly against her tender flesh. Dr. Fletcher removed her goggles, then stripped off her outer set of gloves and threw them in a metal waste can.

Nurse Dyer wheeled the suction device out of the room, switches still on, lights still glowing, a faint hum still emanating from its interior. She used a door that led to a short hallway with another door at the end. Closing the door from the other side, she left Dr. Fletcher to finish up with Valerie.

The doctor lifted her patient's legs out of the stirrups and rotated her to a sitting position.

"That's all there is to it," Dr. Fletcher said cheerfully, stripping the second pair of gloves off. "Expect some cramping and spotting. Use pads rather than tampons until your next period. No vaginal intercourse for six weeks." She handed Valerie three sample packets and a prescription slip. "This is an antibiotic. This one's to control the bleeding. And this one's for the pain. Fill the prescription, take all the medication, and get plenty of rest. Then see us in ten days or so for a follow-up." She turned to follow Nurse Dyer's path out of the room, untying her paper gown and removing her hat to throw both into a can by the door.

"Someone will be by when you're dressed to walk you back."

With that, she closed the door behind her. Valerie stared at the emptiness and listened to the silence. She hurt inside. Pulling on her light yellow panties, she was aware of a growing regret. Without deliberately thinking about it, she pulled a Maxi-Pad from her purse and slipped it into place.

She was free. Free but hollowed. Free of obligation, but burdened with a sudden doubt.

The outer door opened. Ron stuck his head in.

"Val?"

She turned toward him, buttoning her shirt. He smiled with soothing warmth.

"Hi, babe. Miss Tact out there told me I could come take you home. Need a hug and a ride?"

She nodded sadly.

His arms wrapped around her like the warm folds of a thick wooly sweater. Gently, he lifted her from the table to lower her to the ground. She leaned against him, woozy at the change in position.

"I'm starving," she said.

"What should you eat?"

"I don't know. I just don't want anything that bleeds."

V

Nurse Dyer rolled the cart into the short hallway, stopped to close the door, then quickly stripped off her gloves and removed her gown. These went into a receptacle on the side of the cart. Opening the opposite door, she wheeled the cart into another operating room. This one possessed far more electronic equipment and medical implements than the other. On the table, swathed in a paper gown, feet dangling over the edge between the stirrups, lay a brunette with an expectant smile and steely gray eyes staring up at the nurse.

"The doctor will join us in a moment," Dyer said, handing the woman a small plastic probe wired to a computer console. "Hold that under your tongue for a minute." She dressed again for surgery, slipped on a pair of surgical gloves, added another pair, and reached for a second probe.

"Please put your feet up. I'll be taking your vaginal temperature, too."

"I know," the patient said around her oral thermometer, a smile forming like that of a child's around a lollipop stick. "I've been doing this for long enough."

Nurse Dyer smiled. "Right. And tonight's the big night."

Just then, the door opened to admit a smiling Evelyn Fletcher.

"Well, Karen, it's taken us a while, but I think we have a

baby for you." Opening a cabinet on the wall, she dressed for surgery.

Nurse Dyer carefully removed a white cylinder about the size of a two-liter soft drink bottle from the suction instrument. She hefted it as if it were filled with a dense liquid.

"This is the most wonderful moment of my life," Karen Chandler said.

"It won't feel like that when I start," Dr. Fletcher said. "We've loosened you up with the appropriate hormones, but I've got to insert a hysteroscope and microsurgical instruments into your uterus." She snapped on the second pair of gloves. "This will give you a little preview of what to expect in seven or eight months."

"I'm ready." Karen Chandler watched Nurse Dyer carry the white cylinder from one machine to another, similar-looking unit. Sliding the small object into a receiver on the top, the nurse punched a few buttons on the console, switched on the video screen, gazed at dials, and said, "Adding serum to Ham's F-10, seventy percent."

"Check," said the doctor, pulling an instrument tray toward her with one foot. She administered the pericervical block, then picked a sterile tube from an assortment of various diameters and lengths on the tray, lubricated it lightly, and slowly inserted it into Karen.

"Right out of the fridge," Karen murmured. "Can I get frostbite from that?"

Fletcher smiled without distraction. When she reached the cervical area, she slid the hysteroscope into the tube, locked it in place, and gently sought her way into Karen's uterus.

Karen grunted as the probe spread apart her flesh. In a moment, the shock of entry had subsided to a dull, throbbing ache.

"How's that?" Fletcher asked.

"Fine," Karen moaned, taking a deep breath.

"Don't strain," the doctor said urgently. "Just relax. We've got lots of work to do."

Nurse Dyer stared intently at the video monitor. She moved a tube on the machine's side with slow, deliberate motions. A soft sucking noise grew and subsided in concert with the motion of her wrist and the touch of her fingers on the controls. "In place," she said, quickly pressing a button and grasping the tube.

In a blur of rehearsed speed, Dr. Fletcher unlocked and withdrew the hysteroscope, leaving the hollow tube inside Karen. The nurse slid the other tube out of the machine and gently pressed it into Fletcher's hand. With a fluid motion, the doctor inserted the opaque rod deep into Karen's womb.

"Transfer," Fletcher said in a sharp voice.

"Pump on," Dyer replied.

A fluid warmth filled Karen. Liquid pressure swelled in her belly, pleasant and comforting amid the ache of the instruments.

"It's in."

Another jolt as Fletcher removed the device and inserted a combination hysteroscope and laser microsurgical instrument.

Karen Chandler gazed at the doctor's head as she worked intently and silently between her legs. She thought there should be a sign around that read Caution: Baby Being Installed.

She wondered who the donor was. Part of the privacy arrangement, according to her contract, was that the identity of the mother would not be revealed until the child was eighteen years old, and only if he or she asked to know. She hoped her child would someday ask. She wanted the chance to thank the nameless, faceless woman who so generously offered her baby to someone who couldn't produce one naturally.

Nurse Dyer stepped away from watching the work on her monitor to dab sweat from her doctor's brow. Fletcher remained bent over the eyepiece of the hysteroscope, maneuvering the remote scalpel and laser microsuture with intense concentration.

Thirty-five minutes passed during which Dr. Fletcher never shifted from her crouched position, never said a word. Nurse Dyer, watching the progress on the monitor, took over the responsibility of reassuring Karen that all was well.

"The embryo knows what to do," she told Karen. "It's already manufacturing the hormones that will tell your body you're pregnant. But since it's been detached from one uterine wall, we've got to reattach it surgically so that it won't bounce around." She smiled warmly. "You wouldn't want a child that young running around loose, would you?"

Karen tried her best to smile, but the length of the operation was getting to her. She simply stared at the ceiling. Someone had stuck a smiling yellow sun directly over the table. She focused on it, thinking of sunrises and waking up to mother and father and brothers when she was a child. She'd have a chance now to see it from a parent's point of view. If all went well this time. If their terrible past didn't repeat itself.

At long last, Dr. Fletcher said, "There. Transoption complete. Looks good inside." She let go a tense, deep breath. "I took a snip of chorionic villi for genetic testing. That way we can skip the risk of an amniocentesis. We're going to keep you here a few days for observation just to make sure the little one in there is settling in and on the job."

Karen groaned as the tube slid out of her. She raised her head to look at the doctor. "I'm pregnant?"

"That's what you paid for."

She lay back to stare at the bright and silly paper sun overhead. Tears brimmed her eyes. "Thank you, Doctor, thank you. I don't know how I can ever pay you enough for—"

"Just make sure you take every precaution with this pregnancy. I've done all that I can surgically. The rest is up to you and that baby." The doctor remembered something. "Oh—will you want to know what sex it is?"

"No. David and I want to be surprised." She murmured a few more thank yous amid her assurances that she would follow every guideline. Then she allowed Nurse Dyer to unstrap her from the stirrups and help her onto a gurney.

As she wheeled the patient out, Dyer turned to look inquiringly at the doctor. She tilted her head slightly toward the medical equipment.

Dr. Fletcher shook her head imperceptibly. "You take the CV sample to the lab. I'll clean up."

The gurney wheeled out of the room. The doors slammed shut with a muted *thunk*. Dr. Fletcher, alone in the silence of the empty operating room, locked the doors, took several deep breaths, and leaned against a counter. After a moment, she stepped over to the surgical machinery, switched everything off, and pressed a button near the monitor. A videocassette popped out into her waiting hand. She took a case from one of the drawers, slipped the cassette in, and wrote a few notes on the outside. Then she quietly set to the task of cleaning the device.

Cleanup was usually a job left for nurses or surgical technicians. Dr. Fletcher, though, guarded her new machine jealously. No one else besides Nurse Dyer even knew about this night's operation. What *was* known throughout the hospital was that Dr. Fletcher considered the Reproductive Endocrinology Department to be her own private stomping ground. Her success with the fertility clinic gave her the freedom to call the shots.

Even so, she had to be cautious this time. Trust no one. Do all the dirty work. Leave everything spotless.

She had finally crossed the line.

She quietly emptied the holding tank into a container marked with the curving red biohazard trefoil. Out poured a transparent, thickish carnelian liquid. Here and there, suspended in the mixture, floated little deep-red clumps of tissue and clotted blood. She washed out the container with powerful detergents, rinsed it with methanol, and placed it in the autoclave for sterilization. The hysteroscope and microsurgical

40

gear received meticulous cleaning, followed by treatment in a sterilizing bath—they were too delicate for the autoclave.

The customized tubing, probes, and suction hoses were all disposable. She placed them in a receptacle after making note of the specific design she had created on the spot. Each patient would require unique combinations of hardware—notes now could save her time in the future. A future she saw as bold, bright, and terrifying.

The cleanup took twice as long as the operation.

When everything had been returned to orderly cleanliness, Dr. Fletcher glanced at her watch. Nine forty-five.

She could be in bed by ten-thirty if she hurried.

Even in sleep, Evelyn could not escape the consequences of her decision. A dream grabbed her and would not let go. In it she lay—once again nineteen—upon a stiff white table, feeling a young life drain out of her. She was alone, all alone. Not even the abortionist was present. The room became a vast plain that she raced over, flying in her blood-drenched hospital gown. Covered with the sectioned remains of the dead, the plain stretched for unthinkable miles in all directions.

Suddenly, she stood upon a glacier. Trapped within the ice lay hundreds of frozen sacs. Inside the sacs rested tiny, indistinct embryos. Evelyn experienced their patient expectation, longing to help them find a way out of their frozen limbo. Their whispered cries grew audible, distinct.

"You've opened the Door," they said with that portentous significance found only in dreams. "You can free us now."

"Free us now."

"Neither you nor anyone can close the Door," they murmured.

"Can't close the Door."

She realized that she was chanting with them in a mystical rite. White-robed surgeons, arms dipped to the elbows in crimson, chanted with her and the dead-before-life. Scarlet flames appeared on the blue ice.

"Bring us through the Door. Open for us the Gate of Life."

"The Gate of Life," she repeated.

The ice cracked like a thunderbolt.

Evelyn's entire body quaked. She lay in bed staring into darkness. The dim blue light from the alarm clock glowed in the corner of her field of vision. The sheets stuck to her, wet with perspiration.

The Door in the dream, she realized, was a one-way exit from her life as a respected physician. She had crossed its threshold that evening and could never return.

VI

In the weeks after the operation, Valerie knew that her decision had been the right one. She was back at work the following Monday. Ernie Sewell had told everyone that she had taken a couple of sick days for the flu, so she had no need to concoct a cover story. Most people avoided her the first few days back, carefully sympathizing at a distance.

At home, Ron seemed even more loving and tender. As soon as she was able, they took long walks around Lunada Bay, hand in hand, briskly or languidly. They spoke about their future, made plans, looked at larger, more expensive homes around where they strolled.

Her security in her new position grew with every day of accomplishment. She found that she had an undiscovered talent for dealing with the many petty rivalries that surfaced in the office environment. At the end of the day, she and Ron would meet for dinner in Redondo Beach or at the little Italian restaurant in Lunada Bay's small shopping center to share the day's adventures with each other.

When it was finally safe to make love, they did so with an unbridled intensity that was just clearheaded enough for them to use at least three of the many precautions against pregnancy.

That summer, she took nine days of her vacation time right after the long Independence Day weekend and traveled with

Ron through the Bahamas. They took their contraceptives with them.

Over the months, though, she discovered that she would stare for an instant whenever she saw a pregnant woman, sizing her up, estimating her term. For a while this mystified her, until she realized that she was trying to envision how she would have looked had she not had the abortion.

It troubled her to be in an island paradise such as Eleuthera watching pregnant young women, wondering if this one was six months along, that one seven, and was that one exactly six and a half?

In late September she began to wonder when she would have given birth. She estimated that it would have happened some time in mid-October. That's when she stopped looking at pregnant women and started to observe women with babies.

She said nothing about this to Ron, but one day in October he caught her staring for longer than usual at a blond woman with a tiny red-haired baby in her arms. Its little face peered out over its mother's shoulder, watching the world with the stunned, unfocused expression of every recent immigrant.

"Sweetheart?" he said, reaching across the restaurant table to touch her hand.

"Hmm?" She looked back at him, realized why he seemed concerned, then blushed lightly.

"Don't think about what's past," he said. "Whenever you want to, we can go ahead."

Valerie nodded. Her tension relaxed a bit. The woman and child had moved on into the depths of the mall. She smiled with embarrassment. "It's silly. I feel sometimes as if I'm looking for my baby. It's the way I felt when my uncle Lanny died. My mother thought I was too young to attend the funeral, so I never fully accepted that he was dead. I always thought that he had vanished for some reason but that I would someday see him on a local street or in some place far away. Maybe a face in the crowd in a newspaper photograph." Her voice dropped. "I never did."

Ron grasped her hand more tightly. "It's natural to wonder about the way things might have been. Don't let it detract from what we have right now. We—"

"I'm not," she said quietly, looking up into his dark brown eyes. "It's just that if I'd stuck with it, the baby would have been born by now."

Ron said nothing, held her hand. His concern for her reflected in his face.

"I'll be all right," she said. "I sometimes just wonder how it might have been."

"Remember, Valerie, what your doctor said about regrets. They're pointless."

"I know," she said. "I'm fine. Really."

A woman walked past the restaurant patio with three children in tow. The one on her shoulder wailed loudly as the two older ones orbited around her legs in the midst of some sort of disagreement. The woman's face was haggard with annoyance. Bitterness radiated from her like the sputtering light from a street lamp ready to burn out.

This sad vignette comforted Valerie in a small way. The might-have-beens could always be far worse.

The Metagram pager beeped insistently.

Evelyn's hand groped in the darkness over her nightstand. Finding the offending device, she squeezed it until it shut up. She switched on the light to read the liquid crystal message strip.

CALL RE K. CHANDLER

Picking up the telephone, she punched star-zero-one on the glowing keypad and let the autodialer do the rest.

"This is Dr. Fletcher," she said when a young man's voice answered at the other end.

"Karen Chandler's husband called," the voice said. "Her water broke. They're on their way in."

"Page Nurse Dyer. I'm on my way." She rolled out of bed.

Two A.M. on a Sunday morning, she thought. *It never fails.*

The blue Saab roared into life eight minutes later, breaking the residential quiet of the complex. Headlights illuminated the dark alleyway lined with fences and cinder-block walls over which grew ivy and bougainvillea. Even in the bright beams the colors had the gray look of late night.

Evelyn sped through the rear entrance of the apartment building, wended toward Normandie, then turned south. Though she might have had an excuse if pulled over for speeding, she found that she lost more time identifying herself to police than she gained by breaking the limits. At that hour, forty miles per would get her to the hospital in a matter of minutes. And at 2:00 A.M. the lights were all with her.

She slammed the Saab to a halt in one of the reserved parking slots right next to the emergency room doors. The bars were just closing; it looked fairly busy. Two paramedic vans were in the bays, both unloading simultaneously. One man with a minor gunshot wound walked out drunkenly. An old, disoriented woman on a gurney displayed the classic symptoms of myocardial infarction.

She rushed past the receptionist. "PACE" was all she needed to hear as she went by.

The patient assessment center was a large room comprising several beds divided by curtains. Women occupied two of the beds. One, a girl in her teens, looked frightened. Her parents and a boy who didn't look old enough to shave clustered around her, murmuring assurances.

Two beds down lay Karen Chandler, her husband standing

at her side. A fetal monitor strapped across her swollen abdomen sent signals to equipment at bedside. She had obviously taken the time to brush out her deep brown hair before arriving. She looked lovely.

Nurse Dyer wore her lab coat over a pink-and-black miniskirt that occasionally peeked through the button front whenever she shifted around. Evelyn had seen the outfit—and others—before on late-night calls. She hoped the pager hadn't interrupted anything *too* sizzling.

"Dilation four centimeters. Contractions every ten minutes." Dyer's voice had the distinct buzz of someone fighting fatigue and a couple of drinks. Fletcher knew it would not harm the woman's performance but made a mental note to take the fact into account. She was certain that the Chandlers were too occupied to notice.

"Hello, Karen," she said. "Hello, David." Karen wore the all-purpose hospital robe, hiked up over her belly. David wore beige slacks and a rumpled royal-blue cotton shirt.

She looked at Karen's husband. "Remembering your partner exercises?"

He nodded and tried to sound steady. "Ready when you are."

Dr. Fletcher smiled. "I think it's a matter of our being ready when the baby is." She bent over Karen to check her pupils with a penlight. "What time did your water break?"

"Around one," she answered, looking up at the doctor with concerned eyes. "I was asleep, and I woke up and felt this wetness, but it didn't feel like my bladder cutting loose. There weren't any labor pains, so I figured we'd call Patient Assessment and they'd tell us to come in whenever the contractions started. I thought I could just go back to sleep."

Evelyn smiled again, shaking her head. "Whenever the water breaks, we bring you in. If labor hadn't started soon, we'd have had to induce it. If we wait too long, infections can happen." She slipped on two right-hand gloves and gently inserted a finger to touch Karen's cervix. "Lucky for you that things seem to be progressing." She turned to Dyer. "Fetal heartbeat?"

"One fifty and strong."

"That's good." She grasped Karen's free hand and smiled reassuringly. "Everything's fine. I'll be back when you're a bit more dilated." With that, she turned to leave.

It was dawn when the contractions finally came five minutes apart and Karen was fully dilated. They had moved her to the homey environ of their Natural Delivery Unit, where she lay on an old-fashioned brass bed amid soothing Victorian furniture, wallpaper, and curtains. The music they had chosen— one of the Brandenberg concerti, though she couldn't remember which one now—played softly from hidden speakers. At the moment, she had no idea whom they were trying to soothe. The pain overwhelmed her, at times slamming her onto an ocean of agony that crested every few minutes in waves of incomprehensible torment. She tried to describe the wrenching feeling to her husband through red-faced, sweating puffs of breath. Several times she had asked for something to numb the pain, but Dr. Fletcher had reminded her that they could not take chances with the baby.

In his own hell of pain, David watched his wife suffer while he could do nothing but coach her breathing.

"I don't want to do this," she moaned, her face straining crimson and wet. Her fingernails dug into David's hand as a contraction drove pain straight through her.

He did not know what to say. Nothing could stop what was happening. She must know *that.* How to console someone suffering the inevitable who pleads for the impossible?

At last, Dr. Fletcher relented and told Nurse Dyer to administer a mild hypnotic. It did nothing to reduce the pain, but Karen seemed to notice it less.

"It takes the edge off," she murmured to David a few minutes later.

48

"That does it," Nurse Dyer said, looking up from between Karen's legs. "I see the head."

Dr. Fletcher took over, positioning herself at the end of the bed, instructing Karen to scoot toward the edge, ordering David to concentrate on getting her to breathe with him.

"Okay. Push *now.*"

"I can't," Karen screamed. "It's too much."

"Don't worry. You'll make it." She cut a minuscule episiotomy with surgical scissors. Blood flowed on the sheets.

"Breathe like this, sweetheart," David said, panting and puffing like a dog.

"I *can't,*" she screamed, her entire body convulsing. She fell back, exhausted.

"That was good," Fletcher said calmly. "The head's almost through, so one more time ought to do it. Wait until I tell you, then push as hard as you can."

"I can't."

"You will."

The contraction came. David lifted her up and forward by the shoulders.

"Push," Fletcher cried. *"Now!"*

"He's tearing me up!" Her voice became a straining animal grunt.

David cried out, "I see its head!" His voice, ringing in her ear, sounded so full of love and wonder that she began to cry.

Dr. Fletcher gently cradled the head in her hand. "Not yet. Stop straining. The shoulders are next. Coordinate it with the next contraction."

While Dr. Fletcher held the unbreathing baby in her hand, Nurse Dyer battled with sponge and gauze to keep other bodily fluids away from the newborn.

The baby rotated about, cradled firmly in Fletcher's grasp. Another contraction loomed. "Push *now!*" she said.

"Come on, honey," David cried. "Push!"

Wordlessly, Karen leaned forward with David's aid and

pushed as hard as she could. This time was easier than the last. David's voice was near tears.

"There she is! It's a girl! God, Karen, she's beautiful."

"Eleven-oh-seven A.M.," Fletcher said, glancing at her watch. Dyer made a quick note of the time.

The little purple-red, blood-smeared, vernix-coated figure rested in Dr. Fletcher's hands. She gently ran a finger through the baby's mouth to remove the mucus plug. Dyer used a tiny suction bulb to do the same to the infant's nose. Fletcher tenderly transferred the newborn to the belly of her mother.

She took her first breath. Intrigued by the change in procedure, she tested her new equipment with a healthy, hearty wail. Her parents wept with joy seasoned with not a little exhaustion.

Dr. Fletcher gripped the swollen grape-purple corkscrew of umbilical, gently holding tension on it to guide the afterbirth farther out with each uterine contraction. At the same time, the baby received added blood from the placenta, topping off her circulatory system.

Nurse Dyer registered the baby's Apgar score—a nine in her first minute. That was nearly perfect, since out of superstition nurses rarely gave babies a ten. Only the newborns of pediatricians ever received the top mark, and only then because the doctor would worry if her own child were not pronounced perfect. Dyer put down the clipboard to mop the doctor's sweaty brow. That done, she turned her attention back to the baby, placing erythromycin drops in her eyes.

"Now, Karen," Fletcher said calmly, "in births such as yours, the placenta doesn't all come out, so I'm going to go in to get the last of it after you've expelled the main part."

They heard none of what she said. The couple watched the pulsations of the umbilical cord, mesmerized. They gazed at the squalling child on Karen's stomach. It turned from purple to a radiant shade of ruddy pink.

A series of contractions expelled the afterbirth into a shallow tray held in place by Fletcher. The cord collapsed, lost its candy-swirled shape and shiny gloss. Taking her cue, Fletcher used a yellow plastic clip to seal off the umbilical as close to the baby's navel as possible. Nurse Dyer handed the husband a pair of scissors.

"Would you like to do the honors?"

Crying, he took the scissors and allowed her to guide his hand within an inch of the clip. A quick snip severed the cord. Blood pulsed out, dark red, further collapsing the cord into something that resembled a limp crimson noodle. Fletcher put the tray aside.

Nurse Dyer gently snatched the infant away from Karen, taking it to a scale for weighing. She measured the circumference of the baby's head, her length, and fastened an ID tag on her wrist.

"Six pounds, eight point four ounces," Dyer called out. "Nineteen point five inches."

Karen wept happily at the news, taking her baby back to hold her.

"Doctor?" David asked, remembering something from his classes. "Shouldn't you count the veins?"

Dr. Fletcher smiled and reached over for the tray. David watched with curiosity, splitting his attention between the doctor, his wife, and his new daughter. She picked up the end of the umbilical, nipped it between two fingers, and spread the edges back to examine the interior.

"All three are there," she said simply. "Nice to know you're checking every detail."

David let go a relieved breath. His hand squeezed firmly the weak one it held. He was not sure what the danger was, but he knew that three veins was good, two veins bad. Karen had not even noticed the exchange. She gazed lovingly, exhaustedly, joyfully, at the little person on her stomach.

"You may give her a drink if you wish." Nurse Dyer smiled with a warm tenderness.

Carefully, she helped Karen lift the tiny bundle to her left breast, showing her the way to cradle the head and neck. Karen held the child in one arm. David stuffed pillows behind her to raise her into a sitting position. Dyer cleaned the new mother's nipple, which Karen offered to the baby's cheek.

Feeling the stimulation, the tiny light blond head rotated, sensitive lips searching. In a matter of seconds, her mouth found a new source of nourishment and happily began to feed. The room fell silent for a moment.

"Pardon the intrusion," Dr. Fletcher said, picking up a hysteroscope. "As I suspected, I've got some cleaning up to do. Don't mind me." She took only a few moments to examine Karen and remove a few bits of tissue that had remained at the surgical attachment points of the transplant operation.

Karen hardly noticed. David pulled a Canon camera from beneath his hospital garb and shot half the roll. After a few minutes, Dyer announced that nursing time was up and that the baby needed to be cleaned. She poured an inch or two of tepid water into a bright yellow tub and placed it on the table next to the bed. Urging David to observe carefully, she inserted a finger alongside Karen's nipple to break the baby's suction. The baby began to cry, jerking her arms and legs, her eyes tightly shut.

With a sponge almost as big as the baby, Nurse Dyer softly dabbed away the blood, leaving just enough of the waxy coating of vernix to keep the newborn's skin from drying out.

"Now," the nurse announced, patting the child dry with a bright white towel, "you both need a rest, and so does she." She put the baby in a Plexiglas tray under a warming lamp.

David watched Nurse Dyer lay a small green bottle of oxygen next to the baby, a tiny little mask placed about two inches away from her ruddy, drowsy face. "Where's she going?"

"They'll both be moved to the postpartum room. They need to sleep, and so do you. Kiss your wife good night and go home and rest."

He looked at Dr. Fletcher. She nodded in agreement.

"Sweetheart?" he said. "Will you be all right?"

Karen Chandler smiled at her husband. Tears of joy began to

well up in her soft gray eyes. Her chestnut hair, wet with sweat, hung in near-black tangles across the pillow. Blood smeared her abdomen, her belly still large and soft from the ordeal.

She was the most beautiful woman in the world.

David stretched across the bed to hold her for a moment. They wept those misty-eyed tears that survivors of great adventures weep. They murmured the phrases new parents speak that seem to them so momentous and emotional at the time.

"We have a baby," she said.

"A daughter," he said.

"She's beautiful."

"So are you, my love."

Nurse Dyer wheeled the baby out of the room. The little one had already fallen asleep.

"Where—?" David began.

Fletcher removed her mask and goggles. "She'll share the room with her mom but be accessible to the nurses so that Karen can get some sleep."

David kissed his wife with warm, deep love. "Sleep well, darling. I'll be back as soon as I can."

"Rest, David. We'll be all right."

They embraced again. Nurse Dyer returned with a gurney. David helped his wife shift over to it. A last kiss and she rolled away through the door, Dyer pushing gently.

David Chandler watched his wife disappear into the postpartum wing. A hand slapped him on the back with weary heartiness.

"Congratulations, Dad." Dr. Fletcher smiled. Her eyes seemed to hold back a deeper emotion than she revealed in the friendly gesture. "She's a beautiful baby."

He nodded, then smiled widely. "She is. They both are. We've waited so long for this."

"Have you got a name for her?"

"Renata. Karen's grandmother was named Renata. It means 'born again.' "

Evelyn Fletcher raised an eyebrow but said nothing.

VII

Karen awoke to the sound of a baby screaming. The short, high-pitched shrieks cut through her sleep like meat cleavers.

"What's wrong?" she cried, sitting up in the hospital bed, looking around in the darkness. She had been awakened several times that day for breast-feeding, but the baby's cries then were nothing like these.

She looked through the window in the wall at her right. The sliding tray that allowed Renata to be reached either by her mother on this side or the nurses on the other lay open to the nursing area. Renata was gone.

"What's going on!" she shouted through the glass.

"Nothing," one of the nurses said casually. "Just taking a few drops of blood for tests. We give her a little heel stick, that's all."

Renata screamed as if she were being murdered. Karen pressed up against the glass, flattening her face in an effort to see what they were doing to her child. They stood somewhere out of view.

The cries continued. Karen's entire body reacted to the sound. It was as if each scream were fashioned to activate every primordial mother instinct lying hidden in her soul. She wanted to smash the glass and seize her child from the monsters in white.

One of the torturers—an over-thirty frump with a bored expression—deposited the frantic, kicking infant into the drawer, gently sliding it over to Karen's side of the wall.

"All done. Feeding time."

Karen hated the nurses already.

She scooped up her daughter, held her up to her right breast, and offered her nipple to the terrorized baby.

Renata sought out the proffered meal and sucked heartily. An occasional residual whimper escaped past the areola.

Karen waited until Renata had calmed down to examine her tiny feet. They were both still purple from hospital-form ink. A small, round Band-Aid adhered to the bottom of the left heel. She hugged the baby tenderly, cooing to it and whispering soft, loving mother sounds.

When Renata finished eating and fell into a satisfied sleep, Karen willfully ignored the rules. She did not restore the baby to the drawer in the wall but kept her bundled against her breast, sleeping protectively with her.

"Just a little ear infection, that's all."

Dr. Fletcher peered through the otoscope into Renata's tiny right ear. "When you look inside, the eardrum should look silvery and sort of reflective. If it looks red or swollen, that's a good sign that some antibiotics are in order."

"Is it serious?" Karen held the baby tightly. Renata watched the proceedings, blue eyes staring in an unfocused gaze of incomprehension.

"We just have to pick the right antibiotic." She made a few notes on the chart, then picked up Renata's left foot. She stroked a fingernail down the center of the sole, watched the toes flex, and made another note. She smiled.

"Other than that, everything else seems to be in order." She put a finger into Renata's hand. The small, stubby fingers reflexively grasped the digit. "She's got a good strong grip."

Karen smiled and hugged the baby even tighter. Renata gurgled, her mouth curling into a toothless smile as her arms and legs flailed about merrily.

Dr. Fletcher patted Renata's head, stroking the thin covering of light blond hair.

Renata's face became confused, reddened. She fidgeted, then began to cry.

"Uh-oh," Evelyn said. "Changing time."

Karen smiled. "That's one thing I regret about this place." She shifted over to the far side of the bed, lowering Renata into the drawer and closing it. "I don't get to diaper her until I get home."

Fletcher smiled. "Enjoy the opportunity."

That afternoon, Nurse Dyer stepped into Fletcher's office and locked the door behind her. She wore deep emerald culottes beneath her lab coat. No doubt, mused Evelyn, she had a pair of matching high heels to replace the crisp white hospital shoes she currently wore.

"Dr. Lawrence is asking questions."

"Relax." She motioned for Dyer to sit beside her at her desk.

The tall woman pulled up a chair, lowered her frame into the leather folds, and tried to relax. She did not seem to be succeeding. The nurse drummed her blood-red-polished, professionally short fingernails against the brown leather armrest. "The administrator could blow us out of the water if he gets suspicious at all."

Fletcher lit up a cigarette. "Lawrence isn't suspicious. He's just a meddlesome old bureaucrat who confuses irritating the staff with effective management. He's bothering everyone just to look busy."

"He questioned me about the discrepancies on Chandler's reports."

Fletcher looked up. "Such as?"

Dyer leaned forward. "Delivering a full-term infant in just seven months."

"Jesus." Fletcher jabbed her cigarette into the ashtray. "That's so simple. Just direct him to me. That man hasn't touched a scalpel in eighteen years. I'll just backdate the operation and tell him he's confused."

"I think that maybe we tried to do too much. Maybe we should—"

"Should what?" Fletcher stood. "Pull back now when we know it works? Go back to the status quo? Now that we've got the technique? Don't forget why we're in this." She stepped behind Dyer to grasp her shoulders. "Don't forget the goal here. Don't forget the payoff we're finally seeing. Great strides are never made without the risk of stumbling."

"But what if Mrs. Chandler should talk?"

"She won't," Fletcher said, patting the woman's athletic shoulders. "She's got the baby she wanted." The doctor paused, then spoke softly. "I think we should try another one."

David Chandler prepared to run the gauntlet. The day at work—being away from his wife and daughter—had been difficult. The manager of an aircraft fastener warehouse does not have much time for quiet, reflective moments. Roaring forklifts and the constant metallic racket of jostling components make for rattled nerves.

And now he had to face *this*.

"There's the washroom," a stern-faced nurse said. "Put the robe over your clothes so that it ties in the back. Put on the bonnet. Put on the face mask." She handed him a sealed packet. "This is a Betadine scrub brush. Get it wet so that it lathers. Lather up your hands completely, then scrub. Pay strict attention to your fingernails. Not one speck of dirt should be underneath when you're done. Then do it again. Your hands should have a nice orange stain all over."

"Then I can see them?"

"Of course." She looked at him oddly for a moment, then wandered away.

Chandler donned the protective garb and turned on the hot water to perform the ablution. The bright yellow-orange suds coated his hands as the sponge side of the brush worked up a lather. The antiseptic tingled in a small cut on his ring finger that he didn't remember receiving. The Betadine smelled sharply cleansing, very much in accord with all the other hospital smells.

He concentrated on scrubbing his fingernails and cuticles. He plunged his hands into the stream of water to rinse, then lathered and scrubbed again. Drying his hands, he examined the fingertips—now clean and yellow-white beneath the trim nails—and looked up. In the cupboard above the sink sat an open box of scrub-brush packets. David's eyes glanced right and left. No one near to witness the crime. Deft fingers plucked one packet from the box, skillfully sliding it under the gown and into his right front pocket.

He might need one at home. Crime in the service of sanitation.

He slipped on his mask, then paused. He had just touched his pocket and his face. With a self-derisive snort, David Chandler picked up the used brush and repeated the cleansing ritual.

Finally done, the masked man strode purposefully down the hallway, only to stop midway, trying to remember what room number he had been given. The iron-eyed nurse passed by, noted his confusion, and directed him to the room.

Karen Chandler lay in bed in a semiprivate room. No one occupied the other bed at the moment, and the only sounds came from the cries of other babies in the wing. Renata lay in her mother's arms, nursing happily. Tiny fingers pressed against the soft milk-filled flesh.

"Hi," he said, standing in the doorway.

"David!" Her voice nearly burst with affection. "Sweetheart, what time is it?"

"Five-thirty. I came as soon as I could."

"You didn't have to do—"

"I couldn't rest until I saw my two loves." He leaned over the bed to nuzzle Karen deeply through his mask, then gazed at his daughter. Her eyes were closed in a feeding reverie. "How soon until I can take you home?"

"Dr. Fletcher said that she has an ear infection, so the nurse gave her a shot of antibiotics. The poor thing cried for ten minutes after." She stroked Renata's hair. "They want to keep us here another night to make sure her ear's okay."

"I'm sure it'll be all right."

Karen knew it was not all right.

Even though she had been a mother for less than two days, she could tell that the baby in her arms had changed. Its skin seemed less pink. When she put her finger in Renata's pudgy hand, the fingers closed around it but squeezed with less strength. She seemed just as hungry as ever, though she nursed for shorter periods.

Karen told Dr. Fletcher on her afternoon rounds. Fletcher peered into the baby's eyes, shone a penlight through Renata's left ear lobe, then examined both ears with her otoscope.

"The good news," Evelyn said, "is that the ear infection is subsiding. But there may be some complication from the antibiotic. I'll have the nurses take another blood sample."

Karen fought her urge to ask what could be wrong. Silently, she prayed to a God she hadn't addressed personally in years: *Please don't hurt my baby.*

She held Renata close to her all that afternoon, surrendering her only for diaper changes and the blood sample.

Five minutes after Renata had been returned from the blood drawing, Nurse Dyer strode swiftly into the room, pushing a Plexiglas case on wheels. It looked similar to the one that had held the baby in the delivery room.

"What's wrong?" Karen asked, holding Renata to her breast.

59

"Dr. Fletcher will explain when she gets here. Right now we have to take Renata for more tests."

"Where?"

"Dr. Fletcher will explain," Dyer said, all emotion masked. She carefully lifted the baby over to the case, lowered her in, and sealed the lid. Throwing switches and rotating knobs, she turned on heating lamps and increased the oxygen supply.

Renata kicked and screamed for a moment, then weakly relaxed. She had just been fed. The box was warm. Nurse Dyer offered her a fresh Nuk pacifier via the glove box, stroking the clear silicon rubber against her soft baby cheek. Renata turned her mouth toward the faux nipple, sought it out, clamped onto it, and sucked. Intent on nothing else, she drifted off to sleep.

"Dr. Fletcher will be with you," Dyer said, "after she's had a chance to examine the baby."

She wheeled the quietly hissing, softly glowing conveyance out of the room, leaving Karen alone in a silence punctuated by the distant, healthy cries of other children in the postpartum ward.

David held Karen's hand firmly. He stood beside her bed, listening to Dr. Fletcher explain aplastic anemia in laymen's terms. It was all too confusing.

"You *knew* that she could get this from the drugs?" His voice held pain, incomprehension, and a growing anger.

The doctor took a deep breath, trying to project as much calm as she could.

"Bone-marrow suppression is always a risk when we use antibiotics on anyone. Generally, it's a small risk. Aplastic anemia seems to result from unknown, idiosyncratic sensitivities that aren't predictable. We can, however, predict that an ear infection can lead to deafness and further, worse complications if untreated. The benefits far outweighed the risks. Even so—"

"Couldn't you," Karen asked in a subdued voice, "have used something safer?"

"We used the antibiotic with the safest record. I'm sorry that this happened. I want you to know that spontaneous recovery of bone-marrow function can and does occur in these cases."

David's voice was close to trembling. His right leg, foot perched on one of the bed's lower braces, jerked nervously, like some animal ready to take flight out of anger or terror. "Well," he said tightly, "what are you doing about it?"

"We're keeping her in reverse isolation to prevent any opportunistic infections. We're providing supportive care. Intravenous fluids, glucose, proteins, blood transfusions. If not for the obvious problem, a bone-marrow transplant would be the surest solution."

Karen responded to the mention of a problem by placing her other hand on David. He held her even tighter.

"What problem?" she asked.

"Bone-marrow transplants require a very close match between donor and recipient. That's why the donor is usually a very close relative. A brother or sister. Mother or father.

Karen's eyes filled with tears. "I'll do anything to save my baby. What do I have—" Then she saw Dr. Fletcher slowly shaking her head.

Karen's words ceased as if she had been punched in the throat. The sickening realization swept over her that Renata was not *her* baby. She was not the mother. She never had been. And now, when Renata lay in life-threatening danger, she could offer no help at all.

Karen fought against the swirling black faint that pulled her down into the bed sheets. *Needs her mother,* she thought, *needs her mother.* The words choked her soul. David's hands, massaging hers, felt hot and distant. She took a deep breath.

"Where is her mother?" Karen asked with forced steadiness.

Fletcher shook her head sadly. Stepping over to the door, she closed and locked it. She returned to the bed and reached across to close the baby drawer. Her voice was low, understanding, but firm. "You know the terms of the contract. No one is ever to know that the child is not yours. Especially not the donor mother."

Karen stared with incomprehension. "Even if it costs this baby her life?"

"I'm sorry, that's—"

"It's a contract with no teeth," David said. "It relies on our good faith, on our being so happy with the baby that we wouldn't dare risk it being taken away. But that's not the case with Renata." He grabbed Fletcher's arm. "Her *life's* in danger. I don't care what happens to us. I just want her to live."

Dr. Fletcher maintained her low tone. "It's not just a question of custody. I told you that the transoptive technique was experimental. I told you that the donor mother had come in for an abortion. What I didn't tell you is that she thought she *was* getting an abortion. The donor didn't know that her fetus would be transplanted."

The pair gazed at Fletcher in silence. David breathed faster, trying to suppress shock and anger. The doctor made a mental note to watch for signs of hyperventilation. Karen's face paled to the color of the pillowcase into which her head sank.

"You didn't tell her?" she said in a dulled monotone.

"If we went to the mother with this news," Fletcher said, "the repercussions would be enormous. It would put everyone involved into jeopardy." Her voice grew urgent. "The state could imprison us, seize Renata, and ruin our lives. Contact with the donor is *out of the question.*"

She stood to turn her back to them, taking a deep breath and longing for escape. One sick child threatened to demolish all her work, her entire career, which had culminated in the reckless action that had saved Renata's life in the first place.

"I don't understand," Karen said softly.

"What?" Fletcher said, turning around to face them. She sniffed sharply, took a breath, and tried to maintain a doctorly attitude.

Karen searched Fletcher's face for a sign of compassion. "I don't understand why you've done all this. You—you do all this research and study to perform fertility operations. And then you try something that *no one else* has ever done before just to help me have a baby. You must have some overwhelming regard for human life. Then how can you value the life of an unborn child so much that you'll go through all this to save it, yet let it die a few hours after it's born?"

The doctor shook her head. A pressure built up inside her, ready to burst.

"Isn't that," Karen asked, "the mirror image of an abortionist's view?"

Evelyn surrendered to the tears that ached inside her. She wept for the memory of her own lost child, for the fatal choice she had made at an age when her body was that of a woman but her soul was unprepared for a woman's existence.

David watched her stand with her head buried in one hand. He glanced at his wife. She nodded, releasing his hand. He brought a chair over to the side of the bed and helped the woman into it.

"When I was nineteen," Evelyn said, her head lowered, "I had an abortion. I was forced to make a choice no one should be forced to make—to kill a tiny little human or let one night's mistake rule my life forever. Well, I killed it. And it's ruled my life, anyway."

She took a shallow, sobbing breath. Hesitantly, David put his hand on her shoulder. If she noticed, she made no sign.

"All my life since that day I've tried to find a way out for other women. Find a way to protect that fragile, tiny human life while protecting the freedom of the full-grown woman." She gazed up at the man. "Her life's just as fragile, you know."

David nodded. His anger had turned to wonder and concern. He had never seen a doctor cry. He didn't think they could.

Karen's eyes brimmed with tears. She took two tissues from the bedside box and offered one to the other woman.

Evelyn accepted it, smeared at her eyes with it. It didn't bother her; she never wore makeup. Karen dabbed at her own eyes. She wanted to reach out and hold the woman, but she was beyond her grasp.

"I made a desperate choice in helping you." Fletcher's voice lost all trace of dispassionate medical calm. "Now I have to make another choice that could undo everything we've achieved."

"I'm sorry" was all that Karen could say. They sounded like the emptiest, least helpful words in the human language.

VIII

This was the day she had hoped to avoid. She knew it would happen; she had simply hoped to put it off indefinitely. Infinitely.

A doctor has many difficult moments, moments she wishes would never have to occur. Regrettable moments that deal with unavoidable death or grieving relatives or angry patients. The standard, rehearsed words of comfort or confrontation can usually calm a tense situation, but even if not, the parting is generally professional and permanent.

Evelyn Fletcher, M.D., Ph.D., took a long drag on her cigarette, set it in the ashtray, and watched the smoke curl up past the cone of light from her desk lamp into the darkness of her office. In this situation, she was facing the end of her medical career. Words would be useless.

She had endured another crisis just as severe years ago: the day she had to tell her boyfriend that she was pregnant and had decided on an abortion. Words could change nothing then, either.

Ian Brunner was another premed at UCLA in the late 1950s when the world took a breather between Korea and Vietnam, between the Air Age and the Space Age. Between D day and Dealy Plaza.

He sported a crew cut, skinny tie, and spoke of medicine as

a way to make a great living. His only regret was that he had to be around sick people all the time.

Ian and Evelyn were an odd item at the school functions. She dressed like a beatnik in black leotards, black dance shoes, and a black cashmere sweater that hung to her thighs. Her jet-black hair, pulled into a single thick ponytail, reached down to the small of her back. This did not endear her to the more staid eighteen-year-olds in premed. That she carried a copy of Gray's *Anatomy* instead of Sartre's *Nausea* set her apart from the beat crowd, too.

She liked Ian, though, with his conservative trappings that failed to disguise a rebellious streak. If their academic records had not been so superb, their notorious behavior might have gotten them sacked in their first year. Both, however, enjoyed their studies as well as their lives.

That was why she never quite understood his reaction to her announcement. They had finished a chemistry class together and gone for dinner to Ship's on Wilshire, a brisk walk of a few blocks in the cool winter air. She was troubled all the way, not really knowing how to broach the subject. All through the meal she had a sinking feeling that no matter what she chose, things would change between them.

Finally, on their way back, she lit up two Camels, handed one to Ian, and said, "A friend of mine died today."

"Who's that?" he asked.

"A rabbit named Friedman."

She didn't have to elaborate.

He took a long drag on his cigarette. His expression was unreadable. "So what's the plan?"

"I can't have a baby," she said in an apologetic tone that surprised her. "I've got years of med school ahead. I'm seeing someone tomorrow to get—" Her voice caught for a moment. "To get it fixed."

They walked in silence for a long time. Finally, his voice cool and muted, he asked, "Is it mine?"

"Yes."

66

He flicked his cigarette into the gutter. "Are you sure?"

She stopped to stare at him. "Yes. How could you doubt me when I—"

All pretensions of cool adulthood fell away from him in a blaze of anger. "I don't see how you could go ahead and just kill it. *Kill* it! Take a miracle like that and—"

"Ian, I—"

"Don't try to rationalize it. It's your body. Go ahead and get sliced up. Just don't pretend you're not killing our baby."

Without a glance back at her, Ian strode away into the night.

That was the last conversation they had ever shared. When Evelyn visited a Santa Monica doctor the following evening, she went alone, lonely and scared. When the deed was done, she slipped into the darkness to seek out a hotel room nearby. She spent two days there, in bed, coping with the physical and spiritual pain of her decision.

It was in that drab room with its window overlooking the bright and beautiful Pacific that Evelyn first came to realize that there had to be a way out of the horrendous morass of death and guilt that surrounded abortion.

She returned to her classes the next Monday and never slowed down. She entered medical school four years later, concentrating on reproductive endocrinology. If she found out the how and why of pregnancy, she could find a way to free women from abortion.

Studying birth and death would be her life.

It was twenty years later that she experienced her final, crucial insight. Soaking in the antique tub in her small bathroom, she read through a stack of medical journals at a swift but, for her, leisurely pace. Every fifteen minutes or so, she would drain two inches of cooling bathwater and add the same amount from the hot tap. She also added more jasmine-scented bath foam in order to maintain the heat-trapping layer of bubbles that surrounded her.

The effect of all this on her magazines elicited clucks of disapproval from any colleagues who happened to see one of the warped, stained periodicals on her desk at the medical center. Letting a copy of the *New England Journal of Medicine* degenerate to such a condition was equivalent to using the Bible as a doorstop.

Her usual riposte was that she, at least, read the bloody things.

Immersed in the issue of *Microsurgery Proceedings* she held inches above the surface foam, Fletcher quickly scanned through articles until one headline fairly leaped out at her face. It was not a particularly dramatic title: "Some Progress in Vascular Reattachment and Nerve Connection in Transplanted Rat Cerebral Tissue." The body of the article, though, outlined a delicate and egregiously complicated microsurgical laser technique for attaching the minuscule blood vessels and nerve junctions of a rat brain inside the cramped environs of another rat's skull.

One would not expect a rat to survive such cavalier treatment, but the one in the article did. Not only that; it also exhibited a small degree of motor response and ate what the brain's previous owner had been trained to eat. The rat died a week later, succumbing to foreign tissue rejection.

Such an article might not in itself have intrigued someone interested in reproductive endocrinology except that it outlined in fairly rigorous fashion each step involved in the microsurgical process. And Fletcher had just finished reading an article in *Fertility Week* that outlined the latest progress in nonsurgical ovum transfer in the cattle industry.

Adrift in the warm, softly undulating waters of the bathtub, Evelyn laid the magazine down on the stack nearby and closed her eyes. Thoughts and images associated freely in the open frontiers of her mind. This was the time in which her wildest dreams occurred. Not in sleep, that lost, aimless time when unbidden symbols clashed pointlessly in obscure meaning. In

68

the world between full alertness and relaxed bliss lay the realm of focused imagination.

Jasmine drifted into her nostrils. Steam dripped from the mirror and the walls. She was once again in placental warmth, her body supported, her mind free to wander.

Nonsurgical ovum transfer sounded promising for human infertility. It was no answer to abortion, though, because the fertilized ovum could only be removed *before* it implanted in the uterine wall. A woman would have to know she's pregnant less than five days after conception in order to have the egg lavaged out. As a treatment for infertility, it had—as the authors suggested—great promise. To remove an embryo that had already implanted, though, involved cutting or tearing away infinitesimal connections between the embryo and the forest of capillaries in which it nests. Connections that grow stronger, thicker, and more complex with every passing day.

By the time a woman realizes that she's pregnant, the fetus has already made itself at home. Still . . .

She knew that late-second-trimester abortions were sometimes performed in such a way that the fetus survived only to die of intentional neglect outside the womb. Such stories chilled her, just as she was warmed by the apocryphal tale of the woman who changed her mind after such an event and took the living child home with her.

A fertilized egg is viable outside the womb; it can even be frozen and stored indefinitely. A fetus is generally viable outside the womb after the twenty-fourth week or so. But for twenty-three weeks the fetus requires a uterus in which to attach itself. To remove it at any point during those twenty-three weeks is invariably fatal.

Unless one found another uterus, she mused. She sat up in the tub. That had always been her stumbling block. Abortuses were by their nature unwanted. Who would care for them if they survived? Yet another bloated state bureaucracy? She was well aware of the sickening abuses within the government-financed orphanages and mental hospitals. But if another woman wanted it, if *nonsurgical* ovum transfer could solve infertility, then *surgical* embryo transfer could solve abortion *and* infertility at the same time!

The two branches of medicine that seemed so vastly and inalterably opposed fused together in her mind. She closed her eyes and slid to chin depth in the warm waters. The scent of jasmine filled her as a bold new future formed out of darkness. Her career choice now made total sense to her. She would no longer need to justify aborting some pregnancies while initiating others as merely "giving women a full choice." She would become the conduit between the two. One woman's choice to end a pregnancy would become another woman's opportunity to begin one.

It all seemed so sensible, efficient, and—she savored the word—*moral* that she felt an ancient guilt floating free from her as if it were being washed away by the water in which she reposed.

This was the way. She had met her destiny face to face.

"Totally out of the question!"

Dr. Jacob Lawrence stared at her with undisguised contempt. He was fifteen years older than Fletcher and sometimes behaved as if he had been born a century before. As a member of the ethics committee at Bayside, though, his support was crucial to any future research she proposed.

The man with the thinning white hair gazed at Fletcher with rheumy eyes over his horn-rims. "You can't seriously ask the board even to review a request for such a project, let alone approve it."

"I'm not asking for an actual project," she said. "Just a study of the potential ethical questions. Obviously, there has to be a groundwork in animal research before we could even contem—"

"I don't care about the research. Things such as this should

70

not even be open to discussion." He looked at her again, frowning. "You think something like this is even possible?"

Fletcher spoke quickly, eagerly. "The fetus does all the work in a pregnancy. It generates the hormones; it makes the decisions. I'm certain that microsurgical attachment to the uterine wall of the recipient would be sufficient to allow the fetus to gestate in the new envir—"

"All right." Lawrence waved a hand for silence. Fletcher fingered the pencil in her hand; she knew better than to smoke in Lawrence's presence. Bayside's assistant administrator looked down through his spectacles at the pages before him. "I'm not going to leave this up to the ethics committee alone. I'm going to send it to an outside consultant. UCLA has an expert in infertility. I read something by him in *JAMA* last month. Works with pregnant women a lot. Ian Brunner."

Evelyn's fingernails plunged into her hand.

Lawrence rubbed his nose. "Ever heard of him?"

"Yes." She sat back, stunned. She knew what the outcome would be. "But wouldn't there be better qualified people at USC?"

Lawrence cleared his throat. "My dear, I am a Bruin."

And that settled that.

It took Dr. Brunner two weeks to return a twenty-page denunciation, which she never saw. It took an additional two years of tabling and extensions by the ethics committee before they issued their own determination. Quoting liberally from Dr. Brunner's analysis, the committee essentially stated that surgical embryo transplantation was impossible, and even if it weren't, the ethical conundrum posed by using the fetus of one woman as seed stock for another made the entire procedure reprehensible from any viewpoint—ethical, moral, or legal.

"Two years wasted," Fletcher muttered over her coffee.

"What do you expect?" asked the lovely woman across from

her. Adrianne Dyer possessed the kind of body that filled her tight uniform in ways that caught the eye of nearly every male patient, orderly, intern, resident, and doctor. It was not her fault, and she permitted no entanglements to mar her professional conduct.

Fletcher liked the taciturn young woman and sought to transfer her to the Reproductive Endocrinology section. Right now they drank coffee in the cafeteria and discussed the scotched project.

"Hospitals will always be conservative," Nurse Dyer said. "They have lots of money to think about."

"Yes." Fletcher nodded. "Why risk it on saving a few lives?"

Dyer shrugged, tossing her head in a way that sent a cascade of reddish-auburn hair whipping over her shoulder. "So work without their approval and give them a *fait accompli.*"

Fletcher grinned. "That'd sear their stethoscopes." Her good humor faded almost instantly. "I've been doing theoretical work and instrument design, but if I so much as thought about trying, I'd lose my privileges so fast my head wouldn't have time to spin."

"Reword it and resubmit it to a different committee." Dyer took a long draft of coffee while she watched Fletcher through deep hazel eyes. "It's worth the struggle." She finished off the cup. "I'd like to help."

"Thanks. You know about *me.* What brought you to the point of wanting to help a mad doctor?"

Dyer shrugged. "You don't need to suffer a personal crisis to determine what's right and wrong. What you said makes sense. If you have a certain perspective."

Fletcher thought quietly for a long while. Dyer said nothing more, allowing the silence to continue.

That afternoon, Fletcher forced through the nurse's transfer to RE. For the next six years they worked together, hypothesized, tinkered, researched, and conspired together. Though they rarely met outside the hospital, they spent countless days in Fletcher's office in after-hours' discussions. They imagined every possible ramification of surgical embryo transfer. It was Adrianne who coined the term *transoption*. Evelyn considered the word *transortion* for "transfer birth" as an alternative to *abortion*, "bad birth."

"Doesn't roll off the tongue well," Dyer said. "You shouldn't make it sound anything like *abortion*, anyway. Raises too many images." She thought for a moment. "Make it sound more like *adoption*. Doesn't something like *transoption* sound cheerier?"

Dr. Fletcher admitted that it did. "The transfer option. Transoption." She felt as if they had created something entirely new, exciting, and shatteringly important just by uttering a word. They were trailblazers on a new path for medicine, a new, wider road for human rights. The future lay dazzlingly bright ahead.

Now all that might collapse into lawsuits, prison, or worse.

Evelyn struggled to find a way to tell Valerie Dalton that she had a daughter. She ran through possible conversational scenarios in the theater of her mind. None of them turned out well. *Why,* she finally wondered, *after lying all this time, should I suddenly tell the truth?*

She thought out the details, then telephoned.

"Hello?" said the voice on the other end.

"Hello, this is Dr. Evelyn Fletcher at—"

"Oh, hi! You have reached Ron and Valerie's place," said the recording. "We're not in right now, or maybe we are and are listening to see if we want to talk to you."

"Christ," muttered Fletcher.

"But if you wait for the tone and leave your name, phone number, the day and time you called, a brief message, and three character references, we'll consult our attorneys and astrologers and get back to you. But don't get your hopes up. Thank you for sharing."

Fletcher used the time to light up a Defiant, take a few puffs, and frown. If she disliked anything, it was flippant—and lengthy—telephone answering messages.

The phone beeped. "This is Dr. Evelyn Fletcher of Bayside University Medical Center. I'd like to speak with Valerie Dalt—"

There was a clattering noise on the line, followed by a woman's voice. "Hello?"

"Valerie Dalton?"

"Yes."

"Dr. Fletcher. You were in to see me last March."

"Yes, Doctor. I remember. How could I forget?" Her voice was hesitant, curious at a doctor's call at such a late hour.

"I know I'm calling a little late, but we have a minor crisis here that I hope you can help us with."

"What do you mean?"

Evelyn took a deep drag, letting the smoke escape with her words. "We've gone over the records of our blood tests, and yours turned up as having the right combination of factors that could help us save a very sick baby here. What we'd like is for you to come in tomorrow morning for a more thorough screening with an eye toward a transfusion."

"Oh, I don't really have the time to come—"

"Miss Dalton, I don't normally call complete strangers asking for blood. This really is a matter of life or death."

Evelyn only heard telephone static for long seconds.

"What about the baby's mother and father?" Valerie asked.

"The father's unavailable, and the mother's blood type is incompatible. And there are no siblings or other close relatives. We exhausted those avenues before we searched the computer files for a close histocompatibility locus match." She lied, knowing Valerie lacked the knowledge necessary to question her story.

"I really don't know," Valerie said. "I've never given blood before. With all this talk about AIDS and all, I—"

"You can't get anything from *giving* blood." Fletcher paused, her mind racing through logical arguments until she hit upon one. "Valerie—have you had any feelings of guilt about terminating your pregnancy?"

After a moment of quiet, the voice on the other end said, "Yes."

"You might be able to assuage some of those feelings by giving the gift of life to another child."

Silence crisscrossed the wires for long moments. Evelyn knew that if she said nothing more, Valerie would have to make the next move to break the awkward hiatus.

After a pause that almost seemed itself to be a battle, Valerie's soft voice said, "All right. What should I do?"

Mark Landry gazed at the blonde entering the lab and thought, *What a babe!* Wearing a maroon cashmere sweater dress and matching high heels, she looked to be in her mid-twenties. That was all right. He liked older women. His fingers tapped at the counter.

Valerie approached the skinny laboratory technologist—he was the only one in the lab whose life at the moment appeared to be untainted by physical labor. She handed him a slip of paper.

"Here for a blood test and a pint, eh? Sit up here, Ms. Dalton. This won't take long."

She sat on the cot. There were three other people in the room, all hooked up to blood bags. She found it remarkably difficult to look at the people or the apparatus. She kept her eyes focused on the young man.

He was a lanky, freckled surf blond possessing an eager, admiring wolf gaze. She was flattered, but since she was in a situation that involved pain and bleeding, she wished for the entire episode to conclude swiftly.

He recorded her blood pressure, taking longer than normal to fit the cuff on her smooth, tanned arm. He gazed at her eyes—gray in the fluorescent light of the lab—while attempting to make conversation.

"My name's Mark." He glanced at the paperwork. "Uh, is this for donation or autologous storage?"

"Autologous storage?"

"You know—setting blood aside before an operation so you only get your own. Safer, these days."

"No, it's for a baby here. It's—"

"Oh, right," he said, removing the pressure cuff and substituting a stretch of elastic. "Directed donation for the Chandler girl. Her mother was in the center's fertility program. Just born three days ago and already in trouble." He donned a double pair of clear plastic gloves. "I'm going to take a drop of blood from your ear lobe."

"Is she sick because of the fertility program?" She stared at the needle Landry removed from a sealed package, then at the syringe he produced. She took a deep breath, focusing again on the man's angular, boyish face.

Landry dabbed antiseptic on her right ear lobe, then stuck her with a disposable needle in a brisk, practiced motion. Drawing off a crimson droplet into a slender tube, he held the blood over a cylinder filled with blue liquid. The droplet fell, hit the surface, and sank to join a pile of blackish globules at the bottom.

"Congratulations. You're not anemic." He slid a sample vial up the hollow back of the syringe. "Anyway, she got a little ear infection, and they gave her antibiotics. Most kids have no problem, but every once in a while you get one that's sensitive and gets bone-marrow suppression. Transfusions can help. Bone-marrow transplants— Okay, make a fist."

"What?"

"Make a fist and squeeze a few times. I need to find a vein. Anyway—" His thumb felt around the crook of her right arm. "Bone-marrow transplants will probably do the trick. Here we go."

Valerie flinched at the sharp jab of the needle. She felt a flutter in her stomach. Landry pushed the sample vial against the back of the needle until it penetrated the rubber stopper.

"Whoa—careful. Let me get it in there." He poked around gently until the dark red liquid pulsed suddenly into the tube. Taping the needle to her arm, he let the vial fill up, removed it, and quickly attached the long, thin plastic tube from the blood bag.

Valerie gazed at the bag. From the squarish periphery of the large central bag extended several smaller bags connected by tubes. It looked like a squashed octopus. "What are all those things hanging there?"

Landry smiled. "This is what we use for baby transfusions. We fill up the big bag. Then, whenever we need the small amount a baby requires, we can squeeze some into a satellite bag, pinch it off, and use it. That way we don't have to enter the main bag. The blood stays usable longer that way."

During all this, he took the opportunity to scan the sheet she had given him.

"I see you visited Dr. Fletcher a few months back."

Valerie frowned. "Yes."

"Were you also involved in the fertility program?"

Valerie stiffened, almost popping the needle out of place. "You mean Dr. Fletcher's involved in fertility programs, *too?*"

A sinking feeling of embarrassment overcame the young technologist. His brown eyes glanced down at her arm. "I'm sorry. I didn't know that you'd been . . . I mean, some people think it's strange for her to be working both sides of the street . . ." *That's* not right. "I mean, I can understand her trying to maximize women's choices, no matter what they—" He taped the tubes to her arm, squeezed the blood bag a few times to distribute the anticoagulant, and let it hang below the cot.

"There," he said with relief, grasping the sample vial in his suddenly sweaty hand. "Just lie down, relax, and squeeze this every few seconds." He handed her a rubber cylinder. "I'll be back in a few minutes."

He made for the water cooler at the far end of the room and took a stiff drink of Sparkletts. A candy striper noticed his flustered expression and wandered over to him.

"What's up, Mark?"

"Nothing," he said quietly. "I just have all the bedside manner of a meat packer."

He handed the blood sample to the technologist behind the counter, then quickly returned to Valerie's side.

Valerie squeezed and released, squeezed and released. It was the queasiest feeling to know that each contraction sent an extra squirt of blood into the bag. The plastic tube lay draped across her arm. It felt warm and sickening, like a snake that had slithered out of the desert sun to rest on her flesh. A wave of unease bordering on nausea washed over her when she dared to glance at where the tube of dark red blood disappeared under white adhesive tape at the inside of her elbow.

Some people did this every six weeks. Her boss, Mr. Sewell, was a member of the Rare Blood Club and kept arranging bloodmobile visits for the office. She never donated. Now she knew why.

Squeeze. Release. Squeeze. Release.

She reminded herself that this was for a little baby whose life was in far greater peril than hers. She thought about how strange it was that blood—something spilled so easily from cuts, in fights, in wars—could, if gathered carefully, be so valuable to another.

Squeeze. Release. It really wasn't all *that* difficult.

After what seemed to be hours of uncomfortable silence, Landry said, "There we go, that's enough." He pressed the bag a couple of times, causing the tube along her arm to creep warmly across her flesh. It made her shudder.

"Do I keep squeezing?" she asked.

He shook his head, busying himself with removing the needle, putting a piece of cotton over the puncture, and folding her arm back. "Don't sit up. Just hold it like this and press," he said. He took the bag over to the sealing unit, and stamped the blood-filled tubing at regular intervals to create almost a dozen sample blisters. He labeled the bag with stickers that

78

read Directed Donation Baby Girl Renata Chandler, adhering a similar tear-away portion of the bar-coded sticker to Valerie's file.

That done, he brought a cup of orange juice and two chocolate chip cookies to her.

"Here's the payoff."

Valerie accepted them with a grateful smile.

"Just relax," he told her. "I have to deliver the lab results to Dr. Fletcher." He gazed at her with a troubled expression, then rose and walked away.

Valerie wondered if something was wrong.

Landry found Dr. Fletcher in the infant intensive care unit. It looked like any other ICU except that the tubes and wires from all the equipment streamed into a clear bassinet not much larger than a bread box.

Evelyn stood beside the instruments, watching the beat of Renata's heart.

"When did you transfer to pediatrics, Doc?"

Fletcher looked up at the intruder. "Mark, did you get the printout?"

"She's still O positive," he said deadpan. "HLA and serologies will take until six o'clock and Debbie said you'll be lucky to get them that fast." He handed her a manila folder. She opened it up to scan the contents. He took the opportunity to check out the baby.

Renata lay inside the germ-free chamber, hooked to an IV. Aside from her waxy pallor, she looked perfectly healthy. Under the warm glow of the heat lamp, her sparse hair shone blond with the softest of golden-bronze highlights. She lay on her back, quietly staring up at a bunny-and-duckie mobile hanging from inside the top of the box.

Fletcher seemed to study the results with cursory attention. "This will do very well," she said.

"Question," said Landry. "How did you know to bring her in when her tests before and after the abortion didn't include the HLA typing?"

Fletcher closed the folder and looked down at Landry from her half-inch advantage. "Dalton's O positive and so is the baby. I had her frozen sample retested, but the HLA results were ambiguous. Since Renata has a rare HLA, I grasped at straws. If we're lucky, Mark, my 'woman doctor's intuition' will pan out, and this baby'll have a better chance." She clapped him on the shoulder. "And isn't that what medicine's all about?"

"Aren't marrow donors supposed to be close relatives? Mr. and Mrs. Chandler both seem fit."

What a snoop. "Do you have access to their medical histories?"

Landry shook his head.

"Then you couldn't be aware of the mismatched ABO and Lewis factors and Mr. Chandler's history of hepatitis B, could you?"

Landry shook his head again.

"Would it be safe to assume that a closely matched stranger's marrow might, under such circumstances, be preferable to the parents'?"

"Well, yes, but why did you go straight to this woman instead of going through the marrow registry program?"

"I told you," Fletcher said. "Her HLA is rare."

"But—"

"Look, scut puppy." She was tired, worried, and irritated. "*You* stick the patients, and *I'll* do the doctoring. Okay?"

Landry said nothing. Turning, he walked out of the infant ICU, leaving Dr. Fletcher behind in her anger.

He made straight for the file room and its computer.

"Is this thing logged on?" he asked.

The busy record keeper nodded without lifting his gaze from a stack of forms.

Landry started tapping away, pleased to know that he was

accessing the files with someone else's security code. Though everyone did it, he felt he had extra reasons to be secretive.

The screen offered up the files on Karen and Renata Chandler. He scrolled through them quickly, noting within instants that their Rh factors were identical. As Dr. Fletcher indicated, though, their ABOs were indeed mismatched. The mother had AB blood, the baby had type O. A transfusion or marrow transplant from mother to daughter would be fatal. Renata's own blood would hemolyze—clump up and kill her.

No mention existed of the father in either file, so the hepatitis B comment couldn't . . .

Landry looked back at the blood groups. Something was wrong. Mother AB, daughter O.

That can't be, he thought. *Can it?* If the mother was AB, the daughter would have to be A, B, or AB. She could never be O. Ever.

When the realization struck him, he laughed. *Of course! She was in the fertility program. She got someone else's egg.* Landry shook his head. *What a jerk. Valerie Dalton must have been the egg donor. That's why Fletcher brought her in. Nothing super-unusual in that.*

Except, he realized, that Valerie Dalton was unaware of Fletcher's involvement in the fertility program. She was only familiar with the Fletcher that performed abortions.

A sickening sensation churned inside Landry's stomach.

Calling up Dalton's file, he noted with relief that the date of her abortion was March third. Scrolling back to Karen's file, he saw that her fertility operation took place January seventeenth. *Maybe I'm wrong. I have to be wrong. Or maybe . . .*

He printed out copies of the screen pages, then darted over to Reproductive Endocrinology, fifty feet down the hallway.

The receptionist listened to his request. "Well, hon," she said in her raspy voice. "I don't know what good seeing the old appointment books will do. We don't keep patients' addresses there."

"No," Landry said, thinking as swiftly as possible. "But you do keep phone numbers. Just let me look at the month of March. I can find the patient's name if I can correlate the time of the operation to the time of the transfusion."

"I don't know—"

"Look, Mrs. Welsch, if the transfusion *you'd* received half a year ago had turned out to have HIV in it, *you'd* want someone to track you down and tell you, wouldn't you?"

"Why, so I can worry myself to death?" She pushed away on her swivel high chair to the shelves behind the counter. A half rotation brought her face to spine with the appointment book back files. She removed a thick blue canvas-covered binder.

"Here's the first half of the year, hon. Bring it back when you're done."

He thanked her and carried the binder off to the break room. Too crowded. He found an examination room that wasn't in use and closed the door. Placing the binder on the couch, he opened it to January seventeenth. Karen Chandler had a one o'clock appointment. No Valerie Dalton. Then he checked March third. No Karen Chandler, but a six-thirty appointment for Valerie Dalton. He sighed and stared at the page. *It was a stupid theory, any—*

He stared at an entry next to Dalton's. Reaching overhead, he pulled down the lamp and switched it on. The intense white glare brought out every detail of the page. The entry next to Dalton's had been written over an erasure.

Landry angled the lamp to bring out surface details. It *looked* as if the name *Chandler* had been there once. He reached into his breast-pocket pen protector. Taking the edge of a pencil to the entry, he lightly rubbed all over until only the grooves made by the original entry showed as white traces against a gray background.

He gazed at the tracing, barely able to make out a captial *K*, a small *e* and *n*, and the last name *Chandler*. He frowned for a moment, almost not wanting to believe. Then he went back to January seventeenth. Karen Chandler's appointment had been written in over another erasure of another woman's name.

Appointment changes were common, Landry reminded himself. That's why entries are written in pencil. The sick feeling, though, would not go away.

Valerie noted the young man's troubled expression as he returned to check her progress. She sat up with his help and had another glass of orange juice.

"If you had it to do over again," he suddenly asked, "would you have gone through with your abortion?"

Valerie turned to stare at him in shock. "I don't think that's any of your concern. How dare you ask—"

"What if some way existed," he said quickly, his words tumbling out in a rapid, anxious whisper, "for you to have ended your pregnancy *without* harming the fetus? What if your baby were ali—"

The door to the blood room swung open. Dr. Fletcher strode in and scanned the room to see Landry crouched next to Valerie Dalton. He shut up the instant he saw her. Rising up unsteadily, he resumed his work.

Valerie said nothing to the technologist. Her confused eyes watched Fletcher's approach.

"Have them get the blood over to infant ICU," she told Landry, then turned to gaze down upon Valerie. "I want you to know how much we appreciate your doing this to help a little stranger. I hope that we can count on you for subsequent donations."

With the doctor's aid, Valerie slid her legs off the cot and sat up straighter, her left hand still applying pressure to the crook of her right arm. "How often will I have to do this?"

Fletcher sat next to her on the padded table. "There's no way of knowing. Transfusions are adequate in providing supportive care. Sometimes it's all that's needed to help the bone-marrow to recover and start producing blood cells again. There's a surer way, though."

"What's that?" Valerie stared at the floor, unable to look at the doctor.

"A bone-marrow transplant will give the baby what she needs directly. Recovery is almost immediate and generally permanent in most such procedures."

"What do you mean by a transplant?" Valerie asked. She noticed that the floor below had two dark brown spots on the green linoleum. Her blood? Or some stranger's before her?

"It's not the same as an organ transplant. We don't do any surgery. It's almost like a blood transfusion except that we put the needle into your hip or sternum where we can aspirate some bone-marrow. Then we inject it in the baby just like a blood transfusion. The cell colonies swim around in her bloodstream and instinctively head right for her bones. There they set up shop and start manufacturing new cells. And then she can lead a full and healthy life." The doctor put a friendly arm around her patient. "And—if your tissue types match—you could be the one who saves her."

"Does it hurt?"

"I'd be lying if I said it didn't. But dying hurts a lot more. And not just Baby Renata. Her parents have been trying to have a baby for years, and she's their first. Remember what I said about—Well, you know. What I said last night."

Valerie looked up into Dr. Fletcher's sympathetic eyes. "I'd like to see her."

Fletcher's eyes became guarded, her entire expression stiffening imperceptibly. "That isn't really possible. She's in Intensive Care."

Landry, gathering up his equipment slowly in order to eavesdrop, said, "She can look through the observation window." He watched the doctor for her reaction, trying to maintain an innocent, helpful expression.

She shot him a troubled glance, then coolly agreed.

Their steps rang in Valerie's ears like hammers chiseling at glass. She and the doctor walked slowly down the corridors of the medical center, Landry behind them with the blood, passing scores of patients of all ages: the aged, tired ones in Geriatrics; the bright, struggling ones in Pediatrics; the invisible crying voices in the postpartum section; and, finally, a section of near silence.

"Infant ICU," Landry said. He watched Valerie for her reaction as she stepped warily toward a large plate-glass window.

Inside the ICU stood a man and a woman bent over an instrument-laden crib, their backs to the window. The woman's straight dark hair reached down below her shoulders to flip under in the last inch or two. She wore a violet satin robe with matching terry slippers that were expensive enough not to look unfashionable. She shook a rattle over the bubble top of the crib.

The blond-headed man next to her was swaddled in hospital garb beneath which lay gray pants with cargo pockets and a soft green polo shirt. He leaned over the isolation crib, a bright yellow rubber duck in his hand. He squeezed it a couple of times, then let his hand fall to his side.

The gesture of weakening hope caused Valerie's throat to tighten. She swallowed, then stepped to the far end of the window for a view of the baby.

Through the window and Plexiglas she saw a tiny waxen figure. It wasn't pink the way a baby should be. It didn't move and kick the way a baby should. She had seen enough babies in the park just the other week to know what a healthy one did with its time.

"Stay here," Fletcher said to Valerie and Landry, taking the blood bag from the lab technologist.

The woman at cribside looked up when Fletcher entered. She said something to Evelyn as the doctor set up the IV. Then she chanced to glance at the window. Her gaze riveted Valerie's.

Valerie lowered her eyes. The look felt as if it had been one of recognition. It wasn't the look one would give a stranger who was helping to save a daughter's life.

Dr. Fletcher, through the glove box, lifted Renata up in the chamber for a moment to change her diaper. Even from the distance of several feet, Valerie saw the blond hair and blue-gray eyes.

She felt something tighten in her stomach, something else go cold and black in her head. The room tilted dangerously sideways. Reaching out for something to grasp, she touched Landry's wiry arms. They steadied her, guided her away from the room, away from the child.

He helped her to the cafeteria, where he bought her a large orange juice and a slice of chocolate cake. Pointing out that she needed to replenish her blood-sugar levels, he encouraged the stunned woman to eat. After she had finished in mechanical silence, he asked, "Was that your daughter?"

"It's impossible," she said, her voice dull and flat. "I had an abortion."

"You had your abortion the same date and hour that Mrs. Chandler had her fertility operation." Landry leaned forward across the table, whispering with conspiratorial intensity. "Your room was right next to hers. Dr. Fletcher performed both operations. She gave Mrs. Chandler your baby."

"It's impossible," she repeated with weary insistence. "I had an abortion."

Landry kept at her. "They transferred the embryo from you to Karen Chandler. You didn't want to be pregnant. Mrs. Chandler did. Dr. Fletcher has been performing nonsurgical ovum transfer for years. That's where you impregnate a donor woman with a husband's sperm, flush out the fertilized ovum before it's had a chance to attach to her uterus, and place it in the wife's uterus where it implants itself. So the wife's pregnant with a baby that is her husband's but not hers."

"They do that?" Valerie only spoke out of some dimly sensed social reflex that insisted she keep up her end of the

86

conversation. She stared down at the bottom of the orange juice glass.

"They've been doing it for years. But I can see that Dr. Fletcher has gone way, way beyond ovum transfer. Into the postimplantation stage, long after the five-day preimplantation period allowed by nonsurg—"

He reached out to seize Valerie's arm. Her pale head tilted toward the table. Fumbling in his pocket for smelling salts, he eventually found a popper and broke it under her nose.

Other concerned staffers charged toward her, each reaching out with an ampoule of ammonia salts or amyl nitrate.

"It's all right," Landry said. "First-time blood donor."

At that, everyone nodded and returned to their tables, some laughing with relief. Nothing worse than for a visitor to code on them in the middle of lunch.

Her eyes jerked open, her body recoiling at the sharp scent of the salts. The swimming blackish swirl was wrenched from her with unsettling swiftness. Mark put the acrid capsule in the stamped aluminum ashtray between them.

"There," he said. "All better." He gazed at her for a few moments, deciding on what he should do. Finally, he asked, "Would you excuse me for a minute?"

Valerie nodded. Landry headed for the hospital phone. Valerie resumed her meditation on the bottom of the glass. An avalanche of thought and emotion coursed through her.

It has to be true, she thought. *Nothing else makes sense. Nothing else explains* everything.

She gave no thought to the *how* of it all. She knew nothing of surgery or medical science. If someone had told her before that such an operation was impossible, she would have probably agreed without thinking about it. Now, told that it was quite possible, she just as readily believed it with as little thought. Medicine was magic to her, an arcane, occult art that merely *existed,* causelessly, in a world where so many aspects of technology seemed simply to be there when most needed. Or when least wanted.

The *how* did not matter. What mattered most to Valerie was the *why*. *Why do that? Why take my baby? The baby is mine. She doesn't look anything like her parents. She must be mine.* The thoughts cascaded over and over. *Why take my baby when there are donor mothers all over? When there are other ways? Why do something so complicated, so risky, when there must have been safer ways? Open ways, legal ways.*

She was certain that what Dr. Fletcher did must be illegal. Why else would she hide it? A cold anger gestated within her soul.

"Valerie?"

She looked up. Dr. Fletcher towered over her. She stared, speechless, as the woman sat across from her in the same seat in which the lab technologist had moments ago exposed the doctor's crime.

"I'd like to talk to you," Fletcher said, "about the possibility of a bone-marrow transplant, if that would be all right."

Valerie said nothing for a moment, then asked, "What happens to fetuses after they're aborted?"

The question caught Fletcher off guard. It took her a moment to compose her thoughts. "That's not a pleasant topic even for doctors to discuss."

"Try me."

"Well," she said, striving for as neutral and sympathetic a tone as possible, "some hospitals just dispose of the fetuses along with the other bits and pieces they normally remove during operations. Some pathology departments catalog and preserve the interesting ones. Some incinerate them, and some bury them. Some use parts of the fetus, such as the liver, pancreas, and brain tissue, in research and treatment of other patients. There are ethical review boards that—"

"What happened to my baby?"

Fletcher gazed intently at Valerie. The young woman stared resolutely at the tabletop.

"It was cremated."

Valerie's voice nearly exploded. "That's a goddamned *lie.*"

88

People at the other tables turned to stare with the eager curiosity of co-workers watching an assault on one of their less loved number.

Evelyn knew that what she said in the next second and how she said it would either create the worst enemy she could ever have or soften the shock enough for her to *understand.*

"Yes, Valerie," she said softly. "Renata was once yours."

Valerie slammed her fist against the table. A shuddering sob escaped from her.

Gazing around at the gawking onlookers, Evelyn tried to quiet her. "Please, Valerie. Come to my office and I'll explain everything. It's not what you thi—"

"I came in for an abortion," she shouted, "and you stole my baby!" Everyone in the room fell silent and turned to watch in alarm. "Some sort of monstrous experiment! How could you think you'd get away with it?"

Evelyn reached out to Valerie. The door to the cafeteria opened. In the doorway stood a tall man with silver-gray hair. His ruddy face set in an angry glower, he spoke with loud authority.

"*Doctor* Fletcher."

Fletcher spun about to face Jacob Lawrence, the hospital administrator. Behind him stood Mark Landry.

"Would you mind," Lawrence said, "coming up to my office?"

For a moment, sick panic showed in Fletcher's face, followed by a hardening resolve. She stiffly turned to Valerie.

"Thank you, Ms. Dalton. You may go home now. You've done quite enough for today." She followed a silent Lawrence through the doors, leaving Valerie alone in a circle of curious nurses, residents, and miscellaneous employees and visitors.

"What was *that* all about?" asked one nurse, staring coolly at Valerie.

"I knew that old biddy was up to something," said another.

"What do you mean, stole your baby?"

Valerie shook her head and started to push her way through

the knot of inquisitors. Still dizzy from being low on blood, she could think of nothing but escape. Half running, she broke out of the cafeteria into the main corridor. Not knowing where to turn, she headed toward the light streaming in through the windows, found an exit leading to sunshine, and made her way to the parking lot.

In a daze, she walked along aisles of cars until she found her disturbingly cheerful yellow Porsche. She climbed in, slammed and locked the door. Safety. She took a dozen long, slow breaths that were more sobs than anything else. A feeling of terror enveloped her. She started the car and drove away at a reckless velocity.

Valerie locked the front door and collapsed in the bedroom. It was too much to take in at once. Her baby was alive. She belonged to someone else. And she was dying.

Valerie had faced the guilt of an abortion last winter, only to face a new life-or-death choice again. That her actions had led to the death of an unborn child had been a terrible burden. Now, when she should have been overjoyed that the child was alive, she felt a horrifying fear that the mortal choice would have to be made all over again.

The terror, she realized with a shudder, was for herself, not for the baby. She buried her face in the depths of the down pillow and began to cry. For herself. And for what she knew that meant about her.

The tears soaked the pillowcase with each trembling sob. She kicked her shoes off and pulled the comforter over her. Drawing her knees up to her chest, she wept while the same thought throbbed in her feverishly: *Jennifer's alive.*

If it had been a girl, she would have called it Jennifer. If it had been a boy, Bryan. Years ago, she had chosen those names for when she finally decided to have children. Since Ron wasn't the marrying sort, Jennifer Dalton and Bryan Dalton both sounded like good names. She had never understood why some mothers wanted their children to "have a name." That is, a last name other than the mother's. Dalton was a perfectly good name. Jennifer Dalton.

Jennifer Dalton was Renata Chandler. Or was she really? Valerie's frantic mind latched on to the problem in morbid fascination. Who was this child, really? Whose right was it to name her? Did it have any bearing on who she really *was?*

Did it have any effect on Valerie's decision whether or not to help save her life?

A new wave of sobbing brought more tears. She pulled back for a moment to gaze at the mascara and makeup smeared onto the pillowcase.

This isn't doing anything, she eventually determined. She sat up in bed and tried to think things through the way Ron would if he were in court.

One, I was tricked into a medical experiment by Dr. Fletcher.

Two, the baby I thought I'd aborted is alive with someone else.

Three, I'm the only one that can save her life or they wouldn't have risked contacting me.

Four, she's Ron's and my baby. Nothing can change that. Not a name, not a secret experiment with stolen embryos.

Oh, my God, she thought with stunned suddenness. *How many others are there?*

IX

Dr. Jacob Lawrence sought to avoid controversy the way most men sought to avoid death. He didn't think about it much when it wasn't present, but when it seemed imminent, he marshaled every resource to combat it.

Mentally, he tried to envision a way out of the mess caused by the woman across from his desk. To his left sat Dr. Leo Cospe, the staff neurosurgeon. To his right, leaning against the windowpane, stood Shawn Deyo, the medical center's legal counsel. It was time to work on damage control.

He cleared his throat. "Dr. Fletcher, I don't want to be placed in the position of grand inquisitor, but your actions leave me no other choice." He gazed across his desk at Fletcher, who sat stonily in the leather chair. She stared at him coldly.

"None of this would be happening," she said, "if the ethics committee had agreed to discuss the merits of transoption *eight years ago.*"

Lawrence sighed. "We'll discuss it now. I've asked Shawn and Leo to be here as a special ethics subcommittee."

"I have nothing to say." Dr. Fletcher stared quietly into the administrator's eyes with a gaze of arctic steel.

"It would be in your interest," Lawrence said, "to be forthright about all this so that we can head off any publicity that may damage this institution."

Fletcher shook her head. "You're going to get publicity no matter what I say or do. The lid's just been torn off the biggest controversy of the decade." She swiveled to look at the lawyer. "What charges have you concocted for me?"

Deyo, a tall, husky man in a fine gray pinstripe suit, glanced at a notebook in his hand. His voice was rich and deep. "Nothing's concocted, Dr. Fletcher. By *your* actions you've left us with no other choice but to notify the district attorney's office. Bayside cannot be perceived as an institution that condones illegal, clandestine experiments. Some likely charges will be performing experimental surgery without authorization. Failure to secure informed consent for same. Battery. Kidnapping. Child endangerment. Improper disposal of fetal tissue samples—"

Fletcher's voice growled low and surly. "Renata wasn't a tissue sample, damn you. She was a *baby.*" She stared at him with a strange, murderous gaze.

"Well, if you want to go that route, they can get you on the other charges I mentioned." He leaned toward her. "But let me tell you this. The DA's going to get you on something. You ripped a baby out of a woman and sold it. And make no mistake, that's how the newspapers will present it."

Fletcher continued to gaze at him, unblinking. "I saved the life of a child who'd be *dead* now if not for—"

"I suggest," Dr. Lawrence interjected sharply, "that we hold such arguments for the DA and right now just find a way to moderate the impact of all this. Surely you must see the sense in that, don't you, Evelyn?"

Fletcher laughed. "There's no way you can moderate this. You had eight years to consider all the arguments pro and con. You waffled and fence straddled until transoption finally rose up to bite you."

"Evelyn." Dr. Cospe spoke in level, sympathetic tones. He was smaller than Dr. Fletcher, spare and balding. He sat in the chair next to Dr. Lawrence and gazed at her calmly. "What you don't seem to understand is that such delays are an important part of the ethical review process. A cooling-off time, if you will. We're dealing with a procedure that involves a high degree of morbidity and risk to the reproductive potential of two women per operation. It is obvious from your initial proposals that you viewed surgical embryo transfer as some sort of universal solution to the problems of both abortion and infertility."

He leaned one elbow on an armrest to support the side of his head in the palm of his hand. In that position, he continued.

"That was eight years ago, as you noted. In that intervening time, such procedures as *in vitro* fertilization and nonsurgical ovum transfer have solved virtually all problems of infertility. The prospect of safe abortifacient drugs promises to resolve the abortion debate."

"It does *not*," Fletcher said. "It just hides the problem—"

"May I finish?" Cospe's voice never shifted from its soft timbre. "All right, then. Contraceptive technology is proceeding at such a pace that unwanted pregnancies will soon be a thing of the past. Will you admit that at that point transoption will be obsolete?"

"Mostly," Evelyn said grudgingly. "But there'll always be someone who—"

Cospe raised his other hand. "Just let me finish. The reason ethics committees grapple so long with such difficult questions as the right to life of a fetus or of risks of morbidity to the mother is that occasionally the passage of time will make such questions moot. You acted in haste. You chose to perform an operation that in a few years will—in all likelihood—be useless or at least extremely rare."

"Well," Fletcher said, lighting up a cigarette, "it's damned useful *right now*. And if I had done this five years ago and it had caught on, there might be a few million kids alive today who are dead now."

"Oh, that'd be great," Deyo said from a corner of the office. "Think of the population mess we'd be in. The world's over-

94

crowded now. Abortion may be the only thing keeping us from Malthusian disaster."

Dr. Lawrence cleared his throat. "Do you see what overwhelming issues we've had to contend with in this?"

"None of these considerations were in your report," Fletcher said. She blew a puff of smoke in Lawrence's direction. "You're making it all up on the spot." She turned toward Deyo. "As for overpopulation, I've heard predictions of doom every time the world added another billion. Did it ever occur to you that one of the children from those extra millions might grow up to be the genius who'll find a solution to hunger or war? How many potential Einsteins have been aborted in the last eight years?"

Deyo snorted. "About as many as potential Charlie Mansons."

Fletcher narrowed her eyes. "We obviously have two different views of human potential. If an abundance of people worries you so much, you can always rectify the matter, starting with yourself."

"*Doctor* Fletcher," said Lawrence in a strict tone. "There is no need to stoop to insult. The ethics subcommittee has no choice in this matter but to notify the district attorney immediately. To do otherwise would expose this institution to a severe liability."

"Which we may not be able to avoid, anyway," Deyo added. "If Dr. Fletcher's criminal intent can be demonstrated—"

"What crime?" Fletcher asked, stubbing out her cigarette angrily. "Show me where the crime is. Valerie Dalton came in for a pregnancy termination. She received one. Karen Chandler came in to get pregnant. She got pregnant. If there's any crime there, I can't see it. If anything, I made efficient use of lab equipment by recycling the fetus."

"That's enough!" Lawrence picked up the telephone and punched a button. "Sherry? Get me the district attorney's office. Yes. Frawley himself." He gazed at Fletcher. "We'll see what he has to say."

Someone had called the reporters. Lawrence and the others watched from the administrator's office window as two screaming police cars, lights flashing, screeched to a halt in the parking lot. Television remote vans pulled up. Station wagons driven by radio reporters and smaller cars loaded with newspaper reporters and photographers disgorged their loads with vomitous urgency. They had not descended simultaneously, but it was obvious that someone had broadcast word of the DA's arrival.

"Election year," Fletcher noted. "And a slow news day, too."

Lawrence sighed. The reporters headed toward the police cars with the giddy expectation of heirs around a deathbed.

Big trouble was brewing, and the administrator was determined to control not only what he said but what the DA perceived.

"I would advise everyone," he told the other three, "to remain calm and let me handle the DA."

His intercom buzzed. He pressed a button. "Is that the DA, Sherry?"

"*Yes,*" a tinny voice said over the speaker.

"Please send him in."

The door opened to admit Malcolm Frawley, an impressively large man who was once a college football star and radio announcer. He nodded his head of thinning red hair at Lawrence.

"Dr. Lawrence," he said. His voice had the rich, deep tones of a professional orator. "Is this the woman?"

"This is Dr. Evelyn Fletcher," Lawrence said. "Dr. Leo Cospe, Mr. Shawn Deyo." Frawley shook the men's hands. He sat in the chair that Dr. Lawrence indicated. The others returned to their own.

"I must admit, Dr. Lawrence, that your call knocked me off my feet. I haven't heard anything this monstrous since ... well, for a long time. Are you sure it's as you say?" He produced a notebook and a gold Cross ballpoint.

96

"I'm afraid so. I received a call from a lab technologist who voiced suspicions that confirmed some of my own. I confronted Dr. Fletcher, and she admitted everything. I called you only minutes later. You have my assurance that the medical center knew nothing of this." He eyed the DA with earnest intensity. "You must understand that we wish to avoid publicity if at all possible. It's the policy of Bayside to assist in the prosecution of doctors who engage in unethical or illegal practices. An ethics subcommittee has already—"

"Railroaded me," Fletcher said.

Before Lawrence could continue, his intercom buzzed again. This time he picked up the phone.

"Yes?"

He listened for a moment, thanked the secretary, and cradled the phone. His puffy fingers tapped a few times against the black plastic.

"There you have it," he said. "The valiant press decided to interview members of our permanent floating picket line. They naturally found out what's going on up here. Someone just decided to heave a bench through the lobby window."

Frawley nodded wearily. "I think you'll want to issue a statement that my department has everything in hand." He turned toward Evelyn. "As an officer of the court, I'd like to inform you of the following rights. You have the right to remain silent. If you give—"

"If you had any understanding of or respect for rights," she said icily, "you wouldn't be here doing this."

Frawley shrugged. Rising to stride over to the office doors, he poked his head through to signal one of the young officers. He promptly entered with a pair of handcuffs.

"Must you?" Dr. Lawrence asked.

Frawley nodded. "It's for her own protection."

Fletcher held out her hands. "What he means is it looks good on TV around election time."

The DA shook his head with a disappointed expression and

removed his navy-blue jacket, offering it to the manacled woman.

"What's that for?" she asked.

"To cover your face when we go past the reporters."

She threw him a withering glare. "I had reason to be secretive. I have none to be ashamed."

"Have it your way," he said, slipping back into the jacket. "Gentlemen."

The two officers flanked him by the door. He grasped Evelyn by the arm and said, "Keep your head low and walk with me as fast as the boys can clear a path."

The doors opened. The two officers pushed into the throng, politely asking everyone to stand aside, please, as they shoved with hands and forearms against the human sea of reporters. Frawley pushed forward on Fletcher's arm to set up a quick pace.

She resisted. Rather than cowering to avoid the cameras, she held her head high and walked with a slow gait that Frawley found impossible to quicken. He took a deep, irritated breath and fell in step with her pace, tugging at her arm every so often in an effort to make her appear unsteady. She seemed to sense his strategy and to counter each tactic he attempted to employ.

This was the day she had anticipated for so long. Anticipated, feared, and rehearsed for. She was not going to act the criminal's role.

A raven-haired woman shoved a microphone past the officers while her partner pointed a glaring videocam at the doctor. Amid the din of questions, hers rang through clearly. "How many babies did you steal?"

"Our only comment," Frawley said, "is that a complete investigation is underw—"

"After performing three thousand six hundred eighteen pregnancy terminations," Fletcher said in a powerful, level tone, "I managed to save one baby from death. I welcome being convicted of such a crime."

That was enough for Frawley. With a subtle but firm tug at

her arm, he caused her to stumble over her own feet. She recovered, glared at him, and resumed her tall stride.

The cloud of reporters orbiting around Dr. Fletcher encountered a choke point at the elevator. The police cleared out a car, and the four descended.

"I know," Fletcher said, "that it's in your interest to make me look bad before the press. Battery complaints go both ways, though. Don't set the grounds for a civil suit against you when all this is over."

Frawley rubbed his nose and stared at the elevator door. "You're right. That was a lame trick. But don't *you* get your hopes up. You doctor types get so wrapped up in your experiments that you think the rest of the world will welcome you as a god floating down from Olympus. Don't count on it. You're a cold, calculating demon, and I'm personally going to see you raked over the coals for this."

The doors parted before another swarm of reporters. The faces were familiar, if a bit flushed, from the third floor. They continued their questioning with labored breath. The entire knot of people moved outside.

"Were you driven to this by religious convictions?" shouted one voice.

"How much did the parents pay you?" hollered another.

"How do you justify breaking the law?"

"I broke no law," Fletcher said in a loud and level tone. "Except the unwritten one that thou shalt not act on conscience. I delib—"

Something hit the side of her head with stunning impact and exploded in a cloud of brown dust. She stared incredulously at the man who had thrown the dirt clod. A member of the picket line, he carried a sign that read ABORTION IS MURDER—SAVE THE FUTURE.

The attack, caught on video, played for the noon news viewers.

Terence Johnson sat in his cluttered Long Beach apartment,

watching with intense fascination. Surrounded by stacks of law books upon which rested empty fast-food containers from Popeye's, Del Taco, and Gourmet to Go, the twenty-six-year-old man observed the scene with sharp black eyes. His curly almost coal-black hair was longer than was currently fashionable for his profession, and the cramped quarters of his Seventh Street lodgings gave lie to the canard that all lawyers made a fortune. As if any further proof were needed, he wore aging acid-wash jeans that had apparently seen more acid than wash. The T-shirt clinging to his trim frame bore the smiling face of Captain Midnight, urging everyone to drink their Ovaltine.

He scooped up another mouthful of *yakisoba* with chopsticks, set the nearly empty carton on his copy of *Black's Law Dictionary*, and concentrated on the woman's expression. He tried to read her personality from her body language and neurolinguistics.

He might as well have used her sun sign for all the information he was able to glean. He was intrigued, though. Enough to reach for his briefcase, shove a few notes into its crammed interior, slip on a reasonably clean, natural-hued knit sweater, and listen carefully.

The camera shifted to the reporter at the scene. "This bizarre story of medical experiments and stolen babies has only just begun to unfold. Dr. Fletcher will be interrogated further in the DA's office downtown. When further word develops on this astonishing—"

Johnson heard nothing more. He slammed the door running and rushed to his battered white Volkswagen.

"You can't make any of the charges stick, Mr. Frawley." Dr. Fletcher addressed the DA in cool, precise tones. She was calm now, sitting in a comfortable leather French Provincial chair inside Frawley's well-appointed, wood-paneled downtown office. Lawrence and Deyo sat in similar chairs off to the side.

Dr. Cospe had elected to stay behind at the hospital, his stint as a member of the *ad hoc* subcommittee at an end.

The police officers, at a glance from Frawley, unshackled Fletcher and promptly retired to the outer room.

She spent ten minutes silently listening to what the DA had against her, then struck back.

"Any charge," she said, "related to kidnapping, child abuse, child endangerment, or indeed any charge that implies what I withdrew from Valerie Dalton was in any way human will directly conflict with the Supreme Court's rulings on abortion. If a fetus is human enough that you can accuse *me* of kidnapping, then *I* accuse the hospital's other abortionists of murder in the first degree. A charge that others have brought with no results." She glanced at Dr. Lawrence for support; he merely stared ahead at Frawley.

Frawley glared back at Fletcher. "For criminal purposes, a fetus *can* be considered a human being. If you'd shot Ms. Dalton in the abdomen, wounding her and killing the fetus, I could easily charge you with murder."

Fletcher smiled a smile that failed to conceal her contempt. "The problem is that she *asked* me to remove the fetus. And it's alive. You can't have it both ways or you'll be playing right into the antiabortionists' hands. You can't arrest me for kidnapping someone I was legally permitted to kill." She drew her cigarette package and Zippo lighter from her lab coat.

Frawley cleared his throat. "There's no smoking in city buildings."

She grinned, lighting up. "If you really want to get coverage, add aggravated smoking to the charge of fetal kidnapping. The press loves little touches like—"

The sound of arguing voices drifted into the room. From outside the office a policeman thrust in his head to say, "Sorry, sir. There's a guy out here claims to be her lawyer."

Terence Johnson peered inside, waved at Fletcher as if they were old army buddies, and nodded at the DA.

Evelyn looked back at him with a blank stare.

Frawley cleared his throat. "Is he?" he asked.

Tapping cigarette ash into an empty coffee cup, she smiled with wry anticipation. "He said he was, didn't he?"

"What's his name?" Frawley asked her.

"Terence Johnson," the lawyer spouted before Evelyn could react. He let himself in and dropped his briefcase beside an empty chair. "But everyone including Dr. Fletcher calls me Terry." He looked at the bemused doctor. "You really should give a guy a call. I had the toughest time finding you."

"I'll remember the next time I'm busted," she replied, sizing him up with cautious eyes.

He looked to be fresh out of law school, full of energy and spirit. If he had legal skills to match his enthusiasm and ingenuity, he might be worth retaining.

He pulled a canary-yellow notepad from his briefcase. "How much have you told them?"

She reiterated the conversations nearly vebatim. He switched on a tape recorder and took simultaneous notes. Occasionally, he used his Pilot Razorpoint pen to brush a curly lock of black hair away from his eyes, back with the rest of his mop.

"Well," he said, jotting quick, almost unreadable notes, "it seems that you don't have any charges centered around child abuse." He looked up at Frawley, then at Lawrence and Deyo. "What else have you got left to try?"

"We've got plenty. Failure to receive informed consent—"

"From whom?" Fletcher asked.

Dr. Lawrence folded his arms and gazed down his nose at Fletcher. "From the women. You'll naturally point out that we can't accuse you of failing to receive informed consent from a fetus since they are not considered humans capable of granting informed consent. But the women were involved in highly risky experimental surgery. The 'donor mother,' as you call her, faced the risk of—"

"Valerie Dalton faced the risk," Fletcher said, "that any

woman seeking an abortion faced. Pain. Bleeding. Severe cramping. Possible hemorrhaging and loss of blood requiring transfusion. Even the chance of being rendered sterile by the procedure. She signed—"

Johnson cut in. "You don't have to say anything else. I'll handle it from here."

"Don't interrupt me." Her voice was harsher with him than with the DA.

"As your legal counsel, I strongly urge you to—"

"When I hired you," she said in a sharp tone, "didn't we agree that I'd handle this my way?"

Johnson gazed at her silently for a moment. The trace of a smile appeared at the edges of his mouth.

"I was hoping you'd changed your mind," the young man said, bending over his notepad. "Do as you like."

Fletcher turned toward Frawley. "Ms. Dalton signed the proper paperwork that's been approved by the ethics committee."

"I looked at those." Lawrence quickly said to Frawley. "They were nonstandard. Wherever the word 'abortion' had been in the original, the term 'pregnancy termination' was substituted."

Fletcher took a drag of her cigarette and blew smoke toward an empty part of the office. "The committee approved the use of the euphemism six years ago, if you'll bother to look at the revision number on the form. Since they were unaware that any other form of pregnancy termination existed, I was able to push that through. All your doctors have been using it." She began to look as if she were enjoying the exchange. "Nothing in the contract required that I kill the fetus or inform anyone of the uses to whi—"

"The recipient mother ran just as much risk, if not more, from the implantation procedure." Dr. Lawrence unfolded his hands and leaned forward in his chair. "Don't tell anyone who's had more than a week of medical school that this transoption technique is safe. Anytime you surgically attach foreign matter into a healthy human being, the capability of tissue rejection, trauma, infection, and morbidity exists. You had no experimental basis for this procedure. No animal research, not even peer-reviewed experimental protocols for establish—"

"What do you propose to do?" she asked him. "Convince Karen Chandler to press charges against me for giving her what she most fervently wanted?" She dropped the cigarette in the Styrofoam cup. "Go to her. Tell her what you plan to do. Tell her you want to imprison the doctor who gave her what no other fertility program could. Wait for her answer. Then take a good look at the waiver she signed. The language is legal." She turned to Johnson. "Did you review the copies I sent you?"

Poker-faced, he replied, "I'll need more time, but they seem airtight on first glance."

Deyo gave Johnson a curious once-over. Dr. Lawrence stared emotionlessly at Fletcher, drumming his fingers on his armrest. "There are noncriminal ways of handling this, as you well know. The principle of *nonsurgical* ovum transfer was established in 1983, under the most rigorous of guidelines. You've chosen to expand that frontier of research in a clandestine, surreptitious, and completely unprofessional manner. This is clearly a matter for the Board of Medical Quality Assurance. I can virtually guarantee the revocation of your license to practice in the state of California. That would effectively bar you from practice in the United States."

"Fine," Frawley said with a relieved nod. "We'll formulate any criminal charges based upon the findings of the board." He looked at Lawrence. "That should keep things out of the limelight for a few weeks. Time enough for things to cool down." The D.A. relaxed—at least *he* was off the hook awhile.

Johnson cleared his throat for attention. "Is that what you intend to tell the press out there?"

Frawley eyeballed him. "Why?"

Johnson ran his hands through his hair and leaned back,

notepad and pen resting on his lap. "Because the subjects of abortion, host mothers, and radical new forms of fertility are all violently emotional subjects. You've got people smashing up your hospital just on the *rumor* that something strange is going on, fetuswise. What sort of publicity will you generate if you let Dr. Fletcher walk out of here with nothing from you but a 'We'll look into it' statement? Everyone would view your position as a wrist slap or as cowardly stalling." He looked at Frawley. "They'll be knocking in *your* windows tomorrow. Maybe tonight.

"But any of those major charges you arraign her on *I'll* get shot down in pretrial because no judge is going to go up against the prevailing opinion on the nonhuman status of the unborn." He glanced from Lawrence to Fletcher. "The AMA has too much riding on the billion-dollar-a-year abortion industry. And that charge of battery is ridiculous. Dalton *paid* for the operation. She got what she wanted. She wasn't touched without her consent and I'd love to see you try to prove criminal intent to *save* a baby's life."

Lawrence's face turned the color and texture of unpolished granite. Fletcher merely looked at the bookcase across the room. Her eyes seemed to be looking somewhere far beyond the office.

Frawley turned to gaze questioningly at Lawrence. The doctor shook his head resignedly, peering at a poker-faced Fletcher. "All right," the DA said. "It's pretty obvious that you've thought all this out rather thoroughly. You must have figured you'd get caught someday." He sat back in his chair with weary heaviness. "You've committed what I personally consider to be a repulsive medical experiment, and you've covered your ass admirably. I'm turning this over to a grand jury, and I'll let *them* issue any indictments. Until then, you're free to go. And I hope you don't have anything put through *your* windows."

Johnson smiled. "Thank you, Mr. District Attorney."

"And you—" Frawley said. "You just watch your step. If I

have to deal with you at all, just remember that we're both officers of the same damned court."

The young man tried to suppress a sardonic smile. "I'm fully aware of that, sir." He switched off the recorder, putting it and his notepad back in the briefcase.

Evelyn stood and turned to go.

"Oh, Dr. Fletcher," Frawley added. "Don't leave the county of Los Angeles without giving us a call, will you?"

"Of course I won't leave," she said. "I have patients to care for."

"You certainly do *not!*" Dr. Lawrence stared at her in shock. "Your privileges are suspended pending full BMQA review. And I'm going to find a way to sack you regardless of any outcome."

"That's absurd," she said. "Renata requires—"

"Newborn babies are not uncommon in medicine," he shot back. "I'm certain that we—"

"You're certain of *nothing* because you have no *facts!*" Her gaze smoldered for a moment. "I know you view the Hippocratic oath as a joke, considering how you have your doctors ignore the part about never conducting abortions—"

"I took the oath of Geneva," Lawrence said. "It had nothing about abor—"

"—but think of the publicity crisis you'd have if Renata died because I was barred from helping her," she continued without interruption. "Bad for funding."

"Why does it always come down to money and publicity with you?" he asked.

"Because that's what it comes down to with you."

"Until the outcome of the inquest," Johnson interjected, "showing cause for suspension under such circumstances would be diffic—"

"Shut up," Lawrence snapped.

"See you in court," Johnson said with a grin.

After a pause, Lawrence spoke in a quiet, steady tone. "All right. Dr. Fletcher, you may remain on staff under strict supervision and with the stipulation that you desist from any further medical experimentation. Agreed?"

Fletcher nodded eagerly. "I agree. As long as neither I nor Nurse Dyer are required to perform or assist in any abortions."

"Oh, you can rest assured on that point."

"Then," Johnson said, "in the interest of avoiding any untoward publicity until the grand jury convenes, how about showing us the back door?"

X

Valerie switched on the bedroom TV with the remote. The lunchtime news appeared with an image of anchorwoman Sally Lin, who spoke while a piece of artwork hovered over her left shoulder, depicting a fetus and the words ABORTION SCANDAL? at an angle in red.

"—still unclear," the anchor said. "The doctor, Evelyn Fletcher, is head of the medical center's fertility program. She also apparently ran the center's family-planning clinic and performed abortions, thus giving her access to live fetuses. Hospital officials have no comment as yet, but sources reveal that the purportedly clandestine experiment came to light when the baby, delivered by alleged surrogate mother Karen Chandler of Torrance, fell ill and required blood from the alleged real mother, Valerie Dalton of Palos Verdes Estates."

Valerie felt as if a charging bull had gored her. Her stomach tightened, her breath caught in her chest, her heart pounded as if she were being truncheoned every half second. The anchorwoman continued, unaware of the effect she was having on a member of her audience.

"There is no word on how many operations of this nature may allegedly have been performed, but we'll keep you informed on this bizarre story as it unfolds."

The scene switched to the other anchor, Jerry Thompson,

a middle-aged man with gray at the temples. "Now you said 'surrogate,' Sally, but this was actually a mother who wanted to have a child, correct?"

"That's right, Jerry. This seems to be different from surrogate mothering in that the woman who wants to keep the child gives birth to it. I think the term they used was 'recipient' mother. But in both cases the real mother gives up the child. The term we heard used was *transoption*, though our medical expert, Dr. Joseph Schulman, says he's never heard the word before."

Thompson gave Lin a concerned and probing look. "And no word as to why this recipient mother quietly went along with what she must have known was an illegal procedure?"

"No word yet. She presumably wanted a child in the worst way."

Thompson nodded. "And that's how she seems to have gotten it. Shocking story coming out of Harbor City. Something we'll follow up on tonight at six. Thanks, Sally." He turned to face the camera. "And a shocking loss for the Raiders in Denver, as Mauricio Sanchez tells us when we return with sports after these—"

The phone rang. Valerie switched off the TV and picked up the cordless hand unit an instant before the answering machine could intercept the call.

"Val!" Ron's voice was distant but alarmed. "Are you all right?"

"Where are you?"

"I'm calling from the car. I'm at PCH and Beryl. I'll be home soon. I heard your name on the radio. Is everything all right?"

"I'm okay. Just hurry home."

"Fifteen minutes," he said. "I'll cut it to ten."

"Drive safely. I don't—"

Someone pounded on their front door. She walked over to look out the beveled-glass rectangle set in the center.

A man with a microphone gestured at her. Another man

hefted a video camera on his shoulder. Behind them, a van pulled to a stop, its tires screeching and thumping to a halt.

"Ms. Dalton, could you step out here to comment—"

"Oh, God, Ron. They're showing up *here!*"

"Don't let them in!" shouted the tinny voice. Somewhere in the static she heard the whine of the BMW's turbine. "I'm coming!"

She watched as more gangs of reporters, cameramen, and sound engineers trooped onto her front lawn. Curious neighbors gathered at the fringes. So much for Palos Verdes people not prying.

Her stomach tightened and began to heave. She controlled the urge but ran to the bathroom anyway, slamming the door.

It was quiet in the bathroom. The knocking on the front door was almost imperceptible. She turned on the faucet in the sink to drown out the last of it. She sat, numbed, waiting for Ron to return.

Ron hit the left turn from Palos Verdes Drive to Via Zumaya at nearly full speed, ignoring the oncoming northbound cars a few yards ahead. He punched the BMW to full power across the two lanes of traffic and slammed onto Via Zumaya at fifty miles per hour. He took his foot off the gas and downshifted for the turn onto Via Carrillo.

And nearly collided with the knot of vehicles jamming the tree-lined street. Brakes squealed in protest, but the antilock system prevented a skid. Even so, he bumped into a station wagon bearing the call letters of the radio station to which he had been listening.

He didn't give a damn.

He slammed the door and ran to the cluster of a dozen and more Pecksniffs loitering on his doorstep.

"Move it!" he shouted in his deepest, most authoritarian courtroom bass. "Get your asses to the property line or be arrested for trespassing. Now!"

The reporters surrounded him, hollering their questions and shoving for position. Awash in a Sargasso of journalists, Czernek pushed toward the door while fumbling for his keys.

"I said *no comment*. When we're ready to talk, you'll know it. Get off the lawn and find some carrion to circle around."

He unlocked the door, entered, and slammed it forcefully shut. "Val!"

He heard the water in the bathroom and ran toward it. "Honey!" he shouted.

She sat on the small French seat in front of her vanity, gazing in the mirror.

He knelt down to wrap her in his powerful arms. His hand stroked her soft hair, his voice even softer. "I'm here now, babe. Everything's all right. I know just what to do. Give me a couple of hours at the word processor. I have to get something stamped at court before it closes."

He released her almost as quickly as he had embraced her. Seconds later, he sat in their office. Valerie heard the whine and chunk of the computer and knew that she would sit alone once more until he was finished. She gazed at her image in the vanity mirror. Her eyes, she noted, looked older, wearier, less alive than they ever had before. In a robotic daze, she brushed at her hair, only to see that the polish on her long nails had grown dull and chipped over the course of the day. She laid down the brush. To the sounds of running water and Ron's feverish typing, she sat staring at the woman in the looking glass.

Evelyn, alone, took a long, meditative lunch at CoCo's after the interrogation, mulling over the conversation she and Johnson had engaged in during the rush to her car.

"I saw you on TV," he said, riding down the service elevator with her. "I didn't know whether you already had an attorney, but I knew I had to give it a try. And I'd like to represent the Chandlers, too, if you and they won't see any conflict of interest there."

"Are you a specialist in reproductive law?" She was fighting for her professional life, she thought, and here was a kid offering his services.

"I will be by the time we go to trial." The elevator doors parted. "There's really nothing to being a lawyer except the ability to apply clear logic to muddled legislation. Add a good head for research and rhetorical skills and you've got a winning lawyer."

"You need one more thing."

"What's that?" he asked.

"A jury willing to believe you."

She ate her meal slowly, spending more than two hours in the restaurant. She had managed to elude the reporters and she wanted her privacy to last. As daylight began to fade, she paid her tab and used the public phone to call the lab. After fielding questions from a concerned technologist and assuring him that she was all right, she heard the news that managed to lift her spirits.

Dalton's serologies were fine. And—crucially important— her HLA matched Renata's rare type on five points. That was close enough to make a marrow transplant possible. Relieved that at least one good thing had happened that day, she left the restaurant and drove home.

She maneuvered the Saab into the alley behind her apartment, parked in the carport, and climbed out. A buzz in the twilight air, different from the usual noises of the neighborhood, alerted her to a crowd in the front of the building. Suspecting reporters, she looked this way and that. The back entrance was deserted. She headed for the door.

A figure shifted in the shadows.

"Dr. Fletcher?"

The voice startled her. She gasped inadvertently, drawing her key ring to hold beside her as a ready weapon.

"Who are you?"

A man dressed in dark blue jeans and a navy turtleneck

sweater stepped out of the darkness into the yellow light of the walkway. He handed her an envelope. "This is for you."

She reflexively reached out for it with her free hand. The instant her fingers touched it, the bearded man released his hold.

"My name is Ron Czernek, attorney for the mother of the baby known as Renata Chandler. You have just been served on behalf of Valerie Dalton with a civil lawsuit demanding the return of Valerie Dalton's and my daughter, the payment of thirty million dollars in actual and punitive damages, and a permanent injunction against your practice of medicine in the state of California. Have a nice night."

Evelyn stood in the pool of light staring wordlessly at Czernek. She felt like an old woman who had just been mugged. Her fingers shifted the smooth surface of the envelope around in her hand.

He turned to leave.

"I only meant to save a child's life," she said.

Czernek whipped about to stare at the doctor with icy contempt. "And how many lives have you ruined doing so? Valerie's nearly mad with confusion and guilt. She went through the pain of an abortion and had finally learned to deal with it when she discovered that she had to undergo more pain to save the life she thought she'd ended. Why? Because a doctor's little experiment screwed up."

"That's not how it was at—"

"I don't care how it *was.*" He pointed at the envelope. "This is how it *is.* We're taking our daughter back." He waited just long enough for a riposte from Fletcher, received none, and walked into the night. His feet crunched against the gravel and broken glass in the alleyway.

Evelyn unlocked the door to the stairwell and stepped inside. In the harsh fluorescent light she leaned against the wall to examine the brief of the lawsuit.

It was all he had said, naming her, Mr. and Mrs. Chandler,

and Bayside University Medical Center as co-defendants. She walked up the stairs feeling old, tired, and shaken. She had always known that her research would be viewed with hostility by her peers. She knew enough history to realize that medical innovations in any particular age were rarely accepted by the physicians then practicing. Usually the old generation of researchers had to die off, clinging intransigently to outmoded ideas and procedures, while a new generation accepted the new concepts as the norm. That's why it took a generation for practically any idea or invention to gain widespread approval. The thought gave her scant comfort. If how she felt after today's ordeal was any indication, she didn't think she could hold out that long.

The first action she took upon entering her apartment was to throw the blue-backed insult on the coffee table. Locking and chaining the door, she lit up a Defiant and located her patient-address book. Finger stabbing like a dagger, she punched in Valerie's phone number.

The line was busy.

She hit the redial button. Busy.

Probably being interviewed by People *magazine,* she mused.

Karen Chandler sat in the ICU, weeping in David's arms. She had tried not to cry, but watching the blood transfusion a few hours ago had been the first blow. Renata hardly reacted as the nurse tried to pierce a slender vein with the tiniest of IV needles. The blood brought a pink glow to her skin, but it didn't seem to last.

Now Renata slept motionlessly inside the isolation chamber. Minuscule electrodes, stuck with gel and taped to her head and chest, delivered vital information to the machinery against the wall. Except for the electronic musings of the equipment and Karen's sobs, the room was quiet.

The sound on the television set had been turned off, but David looked up to see a silent montage of the day's events: the line of demonstrators outside the hospital; the arrival of the DA; the hospital administrator fending off questions; Dr. Fletcher in handcuffs, walking tall through the clog of reporters; her reaction as a clod of dirt hit her; an interview with the man Chandler knew had to be Renata's father.

Her *real* father.

And finally, the news anchor with an insert behind her that read "TRANSOPTION"—SURGICAL KIDNAPPING? The accompanying artwork was that of a fetus surmounted by a gleaming scalpel.

He watched the image fade, to be replaced by an ad for disposable diapers. He looked away, buried his face in Karen's sweet-smelling hair, and tried to soothe her.

A man in dark blue jeans and a navy turtleneck sweater strode quietly down the hospital hallway toward the ICU.

The phone rang. Valerie, just finished talking with her mother in Colorado, picked up the handset.

"Hello?"

"Valerie, this is Dr. Fletcher."

She felt as if her hands had been plunged into ice water. "Y-yes?"

"I just ran into Ron."

"Dr. Fletcher," she said, her words running together in a breathless plea for understanding, "I didn't want it to come to this but everything seemed so terrible when I heard that my baby was alive and I'd have to give her a transplant and all. It was Ron's idea but we both want that baby to live and wouldn't it stand a better chance with me? I'm her real mother after all and it's not as if we can't provide for her even without that money that he asked for. You know I don't care about the money; I just want her to be all right."

"Valerie, I don't harbor any ill feelings. I only want to know that this suit won't interfere with our working relationship. With helping the baby get well."

"Oh, it won't, Dr. Fletcher, it won't." She sniffed back tears and wiped a tissue against her nose.

"You've got to realize that all this publicity is going to be tough on us. You've got to keep your spirits up and stay healthy for Renata's sake as well as yours."

"I will," Valerie said. "I will."

"Your HLA type is close enough to Renata's that we can do a marrow transplant. Can I expect you to show up at ten tomorrow morning?"

"Yes. Ten A.M."

"All right, Valerie." Dr. Fletcher's tone softened. "Thank you."

"I want my baby to live," she said, choking back the urge to break into tears.

"We all do. Get some rest. Good night."

Valerie said, "Good night," and switched off the remote. She lay back on the bed and tried to think about how all this would affect her, her job, and Ron. She'd need more time off for the appointment tomorrow. *And trials are usually held during daytime.* She wondered if Ernie would understand. He always seemed very sympathetic to her problems.

Her mother had been so sweet, talking to her just a few minutes before. She'd called from Colorado Springs to find out what was going on. She'd heard her daughter's name on CNN and called immediately. They talked for nearly an hour about it all, both crying, Valerie assuring her mother that there was no need for her to fly out—Ron was doing everything he could to take care of her.

The phone rang, startling her back to the present time. She picked up the remote. "Hello?"

"Is this Valerie Dalton?" The man's voice sounded guarded.

"Yes. May I ask who's—"

"I'm a stringer with the *National Midnight Star.* I'd like to check a few facts about the changeling for our next issue. I think we can definitely swing a cover headline, though the royal triplets get priority for the pho—"

"What?" was all that she could muster. A sick tightness gripped her stomach.

"Hey, I'm sorry, but we've already got the color separations done on their photo. We'll do the best we can on interior layout, though. Now, let's start off with vital stats. What's the baby's birth weight and length?"

"I—I don't—"

"You're right, I can get that from the mother. Now, do you suspect that the doctor was in the service of the CIA, KGB, or extraterrestrial forces?"

Valerie stared at the phone in revulsion and switched it off. It promptly rang again. She let it. After four rings, the answering machine took over.

"Hello?" her voice said.

"Good evening," said another man's voice. "I'm—"

"Oh, hi! You have reached Ron and Valerie's place . . ."

Following the tone, the caller, obviously annoyed at having been tricked by the recording, said, "My name is Bobby Roy Jensen, and I heard about you on the TV. I know you must be going through a terrible crisis, and I considered it my Christian duty to offer you Bible counseling during your time of troubled decision. Please call me at Klondike five-four-one-eight-oh. If you need immediate help, please turn to psalm eighty-eight, especially verse te—"

The recorder's thirty-second timer ran out, cutting him off. The phone rang again. This time the message activated on the first ring. Valerie numbly listened to it play through, waiting for the caller's message as if she were tuned in to a radio drama.

There was no message. The caller hung up. The phone rang again a few seconds later.

"I think you're a real sick bitch," said a man's voice tinged with the slur of alcohol. "You and your money-hungry boyfriend. You live in sin and try to kill your bastard to cover up your evil, but you got tricked, didn't you, and now you try to gouge some money out of it."

She listened to the voice in a nauseated, drifting blur of

unreality. The world was invading her bedroom, and it was a world of hate and invective directed at *her*.

"Whaddayou want your baby back *now*," the voice rambled, "after you'd given it up for dead? 'Cuz there's a buck in it? Or is your boyfriend running for office? Your kind makes me—"

When the tape cut off, the caller rang again. At the sound of his voice Valerie reached out to switch off the unit's monitor. Then she walked slowly through the house, turning the switches on all the telephones to silence. The messages would accumulate, but she wouldn't have to hear them.

In the silence, the words of the last message echoed relentlessly in her mind. She'd given up her baby months ago when it was nothing more than a little blob of tissue. Just a *potential* baby. Now that it was real, did she have any right to demand it back? Did the money matter? Why did Ron put that in the lawsuit? She understood that it was a way to make the defendants sit up and take notice, but it all seemed so venal. All she wanted was Jennifer.

Someone knocked at the door. She ignored it. Whoever it was rang the doorbell again and again.

"Stop it!" she screamed. Running to the bathroom, she seized a thick green towel and ran to the foyer. She rammed folds of cloth between the hanging chimes, deadening the sound to the muffled thunk of the solenoids.

The thunking stopped suddenly, accompanied by a flare of camera lights and flashes, a scuffling sound on the front steps, and a familiar voice shouting, "Get the hell off!"

Ron quickly entered, closing and locking the door behind him. He hugged Valerie with fierce intensity.

Through sobs and tissues she told him about their hour apart. He guided her to the bedroom, where he laid her down on the covers and helped to undress her.

"And the really awful part of it was those phone calls." She looked at Ron as he pulled her blouse off. "I don't want to go through with this, Ron. Can't we just let them have the baby?"

Ron helped her under the sheets and pulled the comforter

over her before answering. She could tell that he was marshaling his thoughts for a convincing, logical statement.

"Val, you know I love you and I don't want to put you through any pain. But what Dr. Fletcher did to you is just unconscionable."

He pulled off his turtleneck and jeans, undressing quickly to slide into bed beside her. "Doctors can't be allowed to treat women and children like experimental cattle. She can't go around taking babies as if they were livestock to be sold to the highest bidder. That sort of thinking leads to political eugenics. To breeding and killing programs for the good of the state or the good of the race. Dr. Fletcher may think she has the noblest of motives, but she's really no different from a Nazi scientist—"

Valerie buried her head in Ron's arm and cried, her tears hot and unyielding.

"This will be a very important case, Val. A landmark decision. I *have* to be the lawyer who sees this through, who makes sure it never happens again. Don't you understand that?"

She stopped crying. A drunken voice reverberated at the back of her mind.

"Or is your boyfriend running for office?"

"You'd be famous," she said softly.

"Remember," he whispered, "what my dad always used to say about doing well by doing right? It's *right* to fight for your baby, and we'll be rewarded for it by a jury of good people."

Without a word, Valerie rolled over to stare silently at the wall.

XI

"This will be the easiest case I've ever had." Terence Johnson's voice sounded bright and cheerful in Evelyn's ear. She had only just a few minutes before hung up from her conversation with Valerie.

"I've been thinking about it over dinner," he continued, "and I know that after a few days, when all the facts come out on this, there'll be a broad base of support for you."

Fletcher stretched out on her bed, pulled the covers over her, and curled up with the phone. Exhausted, not looking forward to the marrow job tomorrow, she shared little of the young lawyer's enthusiasm.

"If I had seen any such support among my colleagues," she said, "I wouldn't have worked in secret."

Johnson's voice tutted dismissively. "Doctors are a stodgy bunch. Don't you see how transoption cuts across the traditional divisions? The antiabortionists will cheer you because you've finally found a way to save the lives of all those unborn babies. And the pro-choice feminists will applaud you because you're giving women the freedom to terminate a pregnancy without the stigma of death that has always surrounded abortion. Free choice without guilt. Babies saved without oppression of women. You've brought the world to a new pinnacle of civilization. Single-handedly, you—"

"Since I seem to have taken you on as my lawyer in all this," she said levelly, "what exactly am I paying you?"

His tone returned to earth from its stratospheric courtroom excesses. "Oh, just expenses. The other guy is doing this for the publicity, so can I. In fact, I probably have lower overhead."

"Why?"

"I'm unemployed."

"Unemp—" She cut the word off. "Just what legal experience do you have?"

"Well, I passed the bar last year."

"Yes."

"And before that I worked as a paralegal while at law school."

"And after your bar?"

"There are a lot of amoral and immoral law firms out there, Dr. Fletcher." His voice took on a curiously cautious tone. "I have yet to find anyone who views the law the way I do. It was hard enough to get through law school. I had to keep my opinions to myself and just parrot back what the profs told us. Study section was the place where conformity of opinion really got bullied into— Why am I telling you this? You've been through med school."

Fletcher smiled at the memories of her own run-ins with professors and facilitators at every stage of the hierarchy in her teaching hospital. She rolled over on her side, switching the phone to her other ear. "So you've never really practiced law, have you?"

"I've *practiced* a lot. Now I want to *do* it."

"And your plans for this trial?"

"Character witnesses. Expert witnesses. Convince the jury that transoption is literally a giant step forward in human rights and that all who understand it agree."

Fletcher said nothing for a moment, then, "You know where to reach me."

After she switched off the phone, she stared at the darkness, where the ceiling hung, until sleep enveloped her.

Valerie faced the morning with a dread that approached terror. She lay on the bed, fully dressed, staring at the ceiling, listening to the sound of vehicles stopping in front of her house. She would have to penetrate that wall. And another at the hospital.

Ron stepped out of the bathroom, vigorously drying his hair and beard. "You understand why I can't go with you," he said.

"No," she said without emotion.

"I've got to get the ball rolling on this lawsuit. The other side's probably going to try to stall for as long as possible, taking the full thirty days to demur, so I've got to be ready to get it to trial ASAP. And I've got to assemble witnesses, prepare a strategy for jury selection, rearrange my schedule—"

"I understand. You'll be busy."

"Val," he said, sitting on the bed to lay an arm on her shoulder. His dark eyes gazed at her with firm intensity. "It's good that you're going. If the baby has to have a bone-marrow transplant, I'm behind you all the way. It can only help the case if we cooperate in every way with her medical needs. But we can't let that sap our momentum."

"It's supposed to hurt. A lot."

He hugged her. "Honey, I'll *be there*. You'll be spending the night at the hospital, right?"

"Right."

"So I'll be there after five." He kissed her cheek tenderly. "Just relax and concentrate on saving our little girl."

He escorted her to the Porsche. The reporters flashed pictures, shouted questions, and pointed their videocams. Wisely, they stayed on the other side of the property line.

"How do I get past them?" she whispered.

"Just tell them that you can't comment on the case but that all you're interested in is seeing *your* baby get the medical care she needs." He shut the door with a firm push. "Drive carefully and remember—The press can be our best friends in this."

She pulled slowly out of the driveway. A crush of news-hounds encircled the vehicle, thrusting microphones into the half-lowered window.

"What did you feel when you found out your baby hadn't been aborted?"

"Can you explain what's wrong with the baby?"

"Why do you want her back?"

"What name do you have picked out for her?"

"What do you feel toward the surrogate mother?"

Valerie just said, "I want my baby to be healthy," and rolled up the window.

"How sick is she?"

"Did you foresee your decision to abort having such reper-cussions?"

"How do you feel helping the doctor who did this to you?"

She rammed her foot on the accelerator and peeled away.

The newspaper and radio teams hastened to form a convoy behind her, leaving the TV crews to tape wrap-up segments using the house as a backdrop.

The trip down the hill toward Harbor City unnerved Val-erie. Trying to concentrate on the simple act of driving, she nonetheless kept gazing into the rearview mirror in an effort to observe the cars and vans behind her. She counted six, several sporting the logo of a radio station or newspaper. Curi-ous glances from drivers and passengers in other lanes made her blush with embarrassment and fury.

She pulled into the medical center's north parking lot after a quick survey of the entrance. The line of protesters was longer than ever. Several policemen stood at the periphery, quietly watching the proceedings, making their presence tan-gibly felt with that projected mixture of self-assurance and mortal threat that members of their profession so effectively exude.

As soon as she parked her car, reporters surrounded it, quickly joined by the others from the convoy.

"Ms. Dalton—Why are you here?"

"Is it true the baby needs an organ transplant?"

"Do you think you'll be a fit mother?"

"Did you want an abortion because you weren't married?"

"Why aren't you pressing criminal charges?"

"Can you get us inside to see Renata?"

She found it impossible to move away from her car. They had her surrounded by an impassable wall of polyester and power cables. Her breath stopped. Ahead of her she saw a tiny pinpoint of scintillating darkness appear. It grew, expanding across her field of vision as something drummed in her ears with growing power. She remembered having fainted in the cafeteria and welcomed the feeling as an escape that would temporarily solve her problems.

A huge hand reached out of the shimmering blackness to seize her arm. Another equally massive hand shoved something under her nose. The sharp odor of ammonia brought her to with a startling memory of her mother cleaning the kitchen floor. Just a flash of that lovely, sweet face laboring with a sponge mop and a pail and then the crowds returned.

This time, though, she was in motion.

The beefy pair of arms, clad in white, served double duty. The left arm held her by her right upper arm as the right plowed a path through the reporters, huge elbow out like a powerful wedge driving through the field of inquiring minds.

The arms were attached to a singularly huge brute, nearly as wide as he was tall. Topped with close-cropped platinum hair that curled like the wool of a highland sheep, the face was contorted by the sneering smile of a man who enjoyed this sort of confrontation and probably did not get to see it often enough.

"Move it or lose it," bellowed a deep voice with an unplaceable accent. The speed of their progress stunned Valerie. They glided through the crowd, which—though small—replenished itself from rear to front as they moved.

"You'll be all right, ma'am," the deep voice reassured. "They sent me out to get you. Doc Fletcher figured you'd be bothered by these guys."

The elbow threatened, swung, cut swaths through the reporters, never hitting, barely touching. They all quite professionally avoided getting bruised.

"The name's Mason, ma'am. Johnny Mason." He charged with her toward the line of protesters. "I'll be around to take you back through tomorrow." He turned his head to smile at her. Under a gnarled brow framed by thick silver eyebrows, emerald eyes smiled as his fighter's lips twisted into a grin. "I used to be a movie-star bodyguard before I became an orderly."

He elbowed the chest of a particularly obstinate paparazzo. "It was tough leaving show business, but I knew medicine was my calling."

Mason and Valerie moved almost as one into the thick of the pickets. They all stopped what they were doing to stare at the woman and her burly escort. Most gazed at her, not knowing how to react. Were they to hate her because she had wanted an abortion or support her because she came to save her baby? Or vice versa?

Rather than make a hasty decision, they simply stared.

Valerie saw a few of their signs as Mason rammed through the gap that opened to let them pass.

BAYSIDE UNIVERSITY STEALS BABIES.

ABORTION IS MURDER—TRANSOPTION IS KIDNAPPING.

One sign merely read I COR. 1:28.

There were more signs than she could read before the entry doors swung open to admit the pair into the reception area. They breezed past everyone, Mason leading her into Dr. Fletcher's office.

"Sit down and take a rest, ma'am," Johnny said. "That little girl in there needs you in the best health." He smiled gently and patted her on the shoulder with a thick, soft hand.

Valerie thanked him and lowered herself into the brown vinyl easy chair.

Dr. Fletcher entered a moment later, crisp white lab coat over baggy hospital greens. She looked calm. Without any enmity in her voice, she said, "Good morning, Valerie."

Valerie hesitated a moment before replying. "Good morning, Dr. Fletcher. I—I just want to let you know—"

Fletcher held up her hand. "Please. I understand your position, and I accept it. Let's separate that from why we're here. There's a little baby down the hall who's in great danger. Usually there's enough time for me to confer with prospective donors and give them a few days to think things over. As it is, I'm going to explain the procedure to you and give you only a few minutes to consider.

"A bone-marrow transplant is far easier on the recipient than the donor. What we'll do when we have the bone marrow is inject it into Renata's bloodstream. The stem cells will find their way to her bone-marrow cavities and set up shop, turning out the three kinds of cells she needs. It will take anywhere from two to four weeks, though, for us to be sure that all three cell lines have taken hold and are producing."

Valerie reclined a bit in her seat, unconsciously worrying at the nail on her left index finger. All her nails were in disrepair, opalescent polish chipped and dull, but the left index had cracked near the quick. She levered the nail back and forth gently, without even noticing her action.

"What happens then?"

"Then we'll know whether she'll be all right or whether we have to try again." Evelyn shifted in her seat, craving a cigarette. "The marrow creates the red blood cells, the white cells of the immune system, and the platelets that are essential for blood coagulation. If any one of those three is missing, life is impossible. We already have to keep her in reverse isolation to prevent others from infecting her. Luckily, her infant's digestive system lacks the bowel flora that could turn deadly in such a condition. That's why a transplant is of crucial importance."

"That's why I'm here," Valerie said, puzzled.

"I hope that's why," Fletcher said, "because a bone-marrow transplant is a far greater trial for the donor."

Valerie's nail snapped between her fingers.

She lay on the table in the same small operating room where, months ago, her baby had been taken from her. Entering the room, she caught memories of the operation, flashes of remembrance that caused her to tremble with fear and anger. She steeled her nerves and concentrated on a mental image of Renata lying helpless in her electronic cradle. She stared overhead at the red-brown spot on the ceiling. Its familiar presence comforted her. Amid all the madness of the past two days, it had appeared to her, when she lay down, as a steady, old friend. All the activity that must have taken place in here between March and October had not changed it. Scores of women must have stared up at the ceiling. Had any of them seen it? Could any of them have missed it?

She felt a kinship with all of them, all the women who had given up their unwanted children to Evelyn Fletcher. What were *they* thinking about at this moment, hearing the news of transoption?

As Dr. Fletcher explained it, this would be a simple but slow operation, assisted only by Nurse Dyer and an anesthetist. Nurse Dyer looked different. Valerie realized that the tall woman wore a minimal amount of makeup today. The pants and short-sleeved shirt of hospital greens showed beneath her lab coat instead of a dress. She could not have had a good night last night, Valerie thought, and probably wasn't expecting one tonight.

"Do you and Dr. Fletcher work very closely?" she asked impulsively.

"I'm her right hand," Dyer replied with brusque formality.

"Please roll on your side into a fe—Into a curled-up position."

She curled up as requested, sensing the hostility. "She didn't really do it for the money, did she?"

"No more," Dyer said, "than I presume you're suing her for the money. She did it because it was right. Knees up toward your chest."

Valerie knew the dangers of antagonizing a nurse. Dyer exposed the patient's back, swabbing a small patch high on the back with Betadine.

"How could she be so sure it was right," Valerie asked, "if she never sought the opinion of other doctors?"

Dyer snorted. "If she couldn't figure out on her own whether it was right or wrong, how could any other doctor or group of doctors? She knew at the outset what she wanted. And she worked for years finding a way to do it. That's what nobody seems to see. It's not as if she stumbled onto transoption in an old book and thought, 'Gee, let's try it.'"

"Drugs, anyone?" The door to the room opened, pushed by a rolling cart maneuvered by a smiling older man in greens, surgical gown, and cap. Sallow but cheerful, his face regained decorum when he saw the two serious gazes turned his way.

"Riiight," he said with a pronounced drawl. "Dyer." He nodded curtly in her direction while pulling on a double pair of surgical gloves.

"Bill." A reply just as curt.

"How're you feeling?" he asked the patient as his cool gloved fingers explored her upper spine.

"I'm ready."

"Fine. I'm going to give you a high spinal block. That'll numb you from the neck down."

She could not see what he was doing from her postion, but she heard the sounds of instruments and bottles clattering gently on the tray.

"Okay, Valerie." He pressed his thumb between two vertebrae. "I'm going to poke you right there. It's very important that you don't move. Just relax." He dabbed something cool on the spot. "Juuust relax."

Her first reflex was to flinch, but she resisted the urge. The sting was not nearly as bad as she had feared, but to think about what he was doing made her want to shudder. She thought instead about the clouds rolling in over Lunada Bay in the winter. About the fog that sometimes filled the cove so that one could stand on the bluffs and not see the ocean churning, a scant hundred feet below the cliff. In all of LA nothing was more like a seaside village to her. It soothed her.

Something had gone quite wrong with her hands. They tingled.

"Very good," the voice drawled. Something tugged out of her back. "Let's roll her over."

Nurse Dyer pulled at her legs, though she felt nothing but a sensation of pressure and a vague tingling that diminished quickly into an eerie numbness from the neck down. Looking up, she saw Dr. Fletcher gazing at her. She hadn't heard her come in. Gowned, gloved, capped, and masked, as was Dyer, now, she nodded to Valerie and said, "Remember what I told you. Just relax and think about pleasant things."

Valerie nodded, looking up to concentrate on the spot. It seemed to scintillate a bit. A motion at the side of her head caused her to turn. The anesthetist taped a capsule of smelling salts to the pillow. She was fairly certain that it was for her, but for a moment she wondered.

Nurse Dyer brought forward a cart with the aspiration device. It hissed in much the same way the suction device had. Grasping a large, long needle attached to clear silicone plastic tubing, Fletcher hovered over Valerie's exposed sternum. Positioning the needle squarely on the midline between her patient's breasts, she leaned on the device and gave it a hearty, firm push.

Valerie felt only the pressure of something against her chest. The aspirator make a sucking noise. That was when the pain hit her. She tried to visualize the cliffs on Oahu's windward side where she and Ron had flown kites on their vacation two years back. It wasn't working.

Another shove. Again the needle pierced skin, muscle, and bone. Another gasp from the machine. Another lance of searing agony. Valerie chanced to gaze downward and saw a clump of thick, dark red glop slowly moving halfway up the tube. Needle out, reposition, push hard. She felt no sting but heard the faintest of crunches underneath the sound of the pump. The pain came with aspiration.

How long would this go on?

She felt a panic overwhelm her. There must be some other way to help Renata. She'd donate a thousand pints of blood just to be free of the spike that plunged into her chest every few seconds. Sweat beaded up on her face. She watched the spot overhead waver, turn gray.

A hand stroked at her hair. Looking to the side, her gaze met Nurse Dyer's. Above her mask, her eyes revealed a compassion Valerie hadn't seen before. The nurse's gloved hand tenderly stroked her long blond hair. "Be brave," she whispered. "This is the only way to save Renata. Your daughter's counting on you."

Tears leaked out of Valerie's eyes. Dyer picked up a piece of gauze to dab at them, all the while stroking her head. "You've a great deal of courage," she said. "The courage to do right no matter what the—"

"Gauze," Dr. Fletcher said quietly.

Dyer stopped stroking Valerie and assisted the doctor. Fletcher continued to probe, drive home the needle, and aspirate the bone marrow.

Where would it end? Valerie wondered. Not just the operation. All of it.

The needle punctured her, inches from her heart.

XII

Terry Johnson sat on the brushed gray fabric couch in the reception area of Women for Reproductive Freedom, reading their position paper on surrogate mothering. Before he could get more than a few paragraphs into it, the woman at the desk, who looked as if she had just stepped out of *Cosmopolitan*, said, "Ms. Burke will see you now."

Johnson followed the woman to an austere office that, though spacious, contained little more than a large mahogany desk, executive chair, two conference chairs, and a matched pair of Jackson Pollock paintings. A trio of woodgrain-painted metal filing cabinets stood to one side. There were no book-cases.

Jane Burke stepped in a moment later. She was of moderate height, though she seemed taller due to her high-heeled pumps. They were purple and perfectly matched to the suit she wore. On her lapel, a gold Venus symbol, surmounted by two slender hands clasping, indicated that she was a member of the Sisters Network, a sororal order of female executives. Her brown hair was full-bodied, permed, and businesslike. Behind her aviator-style glasses, she could have been a mid-forties executive at any Fortune 500 company whose old-boy network had relinquished control to the new-woman network.

"What's up, Mr. Johnson?" She sat behind her desk, smiling courteously.

Realizing that she favored brevity, he jumped immediately to the point. "I am representing Dr. Evelyn Fletcher in the Baby Renata case. I'd like to enlist your assistance as an expert witness for the defendants." He paused to await a reply, received none, and continued. "This case is certain to be a landmark in human rights, and I knew you would be interested in having a part in the outcome."

Burke leaned back in her chair, peaked her fingers, and watched Johnson with a cool, noncommittal gaze.

"As a champion of freedom of choice," he continued, "I knew you'd be the person to speak out on this issue from a feminist viewpoint."

"Oh," Burke said with a smile, "I plan to. You see, I've already volunteered to be an expert witness for the plaintiff."

Johnson's jaw dropped. Trying to recover, he stammered in disbelief. The words caught somewhere down inside him and refused to escape in any intelligible form.

"If you're that composed in court," Burke said, lowering her hands, "perhaps your client should leave the country tonight."

"How can you be on the plaintiff's side?" he demanded. His voice cracked at the end in an almost boyish squeak. "How can you be opposed to a technique that gives women a new option in birth control?"

Her smile faded to a glare of undisguised contempt. "A new option? What good has any sex technology done for women? Did contraceptives liberate women? No. They merely allowed men to demand *more* sex of women without the burden and responsibility of fatherhood." She leaned forward, one elbow on the desk. "Women didn't invent contraceptives, you know. Men did. For *camels*. They applied those methods to women with the same lack of regard for their health and well-being."

"Well," Johnson said warily, "I don't know about that, but transoption seems to be a way for a woman to rid herself of a pregnancy while freeing her from the guilt feelings associ—"

"Don't try to convince *me* that this latest medical meddling frees women. Not when I've seen women injured and killed by IUDs, pills, and botched abortions. You won't get *me* to say that it's anything more than a scheme to turn women into interchangeable breeding units so that one womb is no more important than any other." She smiled stonily and leaned back in her chair. "Do you know where embryo-transfer research began, Mr. Johnson?"

"I think you'll tell me."

"It began with *cattle breeding*. And *that* is what this male technology seeks to reduce us to."

"Evelyn Fletcher is a woman."

Burke's glare deepened. "And she's doing a man's work, the traitor. I haven't met a female doctor yet who hasn't been spayed by the act of attending medical school. I'll make sure that she receives no sympathy from the women she's betrayed."

The lawyer stared at Burke for a long moment, his sensibilities rocked by the unexpected hostility. "How—" He stopped to think. "If you consider all medical technology to be anti-woman, why does your organization so fervently support legalized abortion?"

Her expression retreated ever so slightly to one of cautious reserve. "Because," she said, "no matter how it has been abused, abortion still allows a woman to have final, absolute control over what becomes a part of her body—something this transoption madness would destroy."

"I see." He didn't, really, but he knew wasted effort when he stared it in the face.

Burke smiled a crooked, nearly impish smile. "Why don't you trot over to Avery Decker?" Her tone bordered on sarcasm. "Protecting blobs of protoplasm is his holy mission."

"He was next on my list," Johnson said.

Since Jane Burke and Pastor Avery Decker were diametrically opposed on the abortion issue, Johnson expected his meeting with the fundamentalist minister to be much less strained and much more productive than his run-in with the feminist. He mulled her arguments on the drive from Santa

Monica over to Decker's Tustin office. Passing Disneyland's Matterhorn on Interstate 5, its artifical snow resisting the afternoon's heat, he wondered at the woman's position. Was her outlook the norm? Why did she support abortion but oppose transoption? They both ended pregnancy in exactly the same way. Wasn't that what they were after—the right to expel an unwanted fetus? Why should she care what became of it afterward?

His lawyer's mind filed the question away. If he was to meet her on the other side of the lawsuit, it might be worth bringing up. He ran through possible cross-examination scenarios in his mind, trying to anticipate her responses to certain questions, forming his counterresponses.

He missed the Tustin exits entirely.

Five miles of backtracking brought him to the new office building situated under the approach path to the marine helicopter air station. A huge Sikorsky Skycrane thundered overhead, with basso pulsations that rumbled straight through Johnson's guts. The slamming of his car door faded to inaudibility amid the roar.

He watched the copter descend toward the airfield. The noise level dropped abruptly, though a throbbing, ringing sound lingered in his ears.

The building was only two stories high, the offices of the Committee for Preborn Rights occupying the second floor. Johnson glanced at his watch and bounded up the stairs.

"Sorry I'm late," he announced to the elderly woman at the reception desk. "I'm Terry Johnson. I have an appointment with—"

"Yes, young man. Please step right in." She gestured with an age-spotted hand toward a frosted glass door.

Pastor Avery Decker stood when Johnson entered. He extended a chubby hand to the taller, younger man. The fluorescent light overhead reflected from his balding pate, seeming to wink at Johnson along with the minister's twinkling eyes.

"Greetings, Mr. Johnson. I'm Avery Decker; this is James

Rosen." He indicated a young, intense man standing by a bookcase in the bright room. Tall and darkly handsome, he seemed more suited to the Colonial furnishings than did the overweight middle-aged preacher. "Jim's my assistant and legal adviser. I hope you don't mind his sitting in on this meeting."

"Not at all." Johnson shook Rosen's hand, making the usual small-talk introductions.

"Won't you have a seat?" Rosen pointed to a well-stuffed wing chair.

Johnson eased happily into the soft leather recesses. This, at least, was a warmer reception than Burke had given him.

Rosen sat in a chair off to Decker's right. He watched Johnson with a studied alertness that marked him as more of a bodyguard than an assistant. It made sense. Decker was a hated man.

"You know," Decker began, leaning back in his swivel chair and placing his hands in his pockets, "when I spoke to you on the phone, I wasn't too aware of what this whole transoption thing was about. I had Jim, here, do what he does with his computer and search the AP news wire to get us up-to-date." He tapped at a thin stack of printouts on his desk. "I don't like it. Not one bit. I'm afraid the answer has to be *no.* "

Johnson dove right in, unwilling to lose the argument to slow response. "I don't know what's in there, but the truth of the matter is that Dr. Fletcher has found a way to save the lives of fet—of *preborns* and she's being persecuted for rescuing a defenseless victim of abortion."

"And who did the aborting, Mr. Johnson? She didn't just stumble across this 'victim.' She *created* it in the first place. If she had refused to perform abortions, this new technique would be unnecessary."

"Oh, come on!" A strange anger grew inside Johnson. "Women would just go to some other doctor, and the preborns would still be aborted and dead, and the problem would remain. Is that what you'd prefer?"

"We'd prefer," Rosen said, "that all the doctors obey their Hippocratic—or is it *hypocritic*—oath and 'not aid a woman to procure abortion.' A very simple solution—just say *no.*"

"You can't expect that," Johnson said with a sharpness that surprised him. *Why are they acting like the enemy, too?* "Some women will always need abortions, and there will always be a market to perform them. Dr. Fletcher has found a way to give women what they want and yet *save the babies.* Isn't that what you're fighting for?"

Decker cleared his throat and put his hands on the desk, clasping them as if in prayer. "What we're fighting for, Mr. Johnson, is an end to all interference with God's plan. If God had wanted that baby to be born inside of Mrs. Chandler, he wouldn't have needed Dr. Fletcher to act as a go-between. It's not just a preborn's right to life we're struggling to defend here. It's the right to live and be born *according to God's will.* Anything that disrupts or interferes with that plan—be it abortion or contraception or transoption—is contrary to God's holy plan."

"I suppose adoption is evil, too?"

Decker smiled with condescending patience. "I would say that it is the least of many evils, the minimum in a wide spectrum of meddling in God's will."

"You'd outlaw that, too?" Johnson leaned forward a few inches, as if the increased closeness could deepen his understanding of Decker's position.

"We don't seek to outlaw anything," Rosen interjected in a calm, conversational tone. "What we seek is a world in which evil actions are never chosen. We don't fool ourselves that it's going to be an easy, overnight task. Caesar's laws are only a temporary expedient toward the implementation of God's law."

Johnson looked from Rosen to Decker. "And are you the infallible interpreters of God's plans?"

The minister smiled. "I never laid claim to such an honor."

"Then perhaps," Johnson said, "there's a slim chance— however inscrutable to you—that Dr. Fletcher *is* part of God's plan and you are just too bullheaded to see it." He rose to leave.

Decker spoke to Johnson's departing back. "If the plaintiff doesn't accept my offer to appear on their behalf, I'll be making our position clearer in the *amicus* we'll be filing."

"Thanks for nothing" was the sharpest retort Johnson could summon. He slammed the door with unprofessional force and strode angrily to his car. As a pair of Huey Cobras whined a few thousand feet away, his brain burned with fury and incomprehension.

What was going wrong? Everything had seemed so clear and logical to him just that morning. Pro-lifers say abortion is murder; pro-choicers say forced motherhood is slavery. A doctor finds a way to end pregnancies without killing the fetus. Why weren't both sides of the issue rushing to her aid? Where was the united front he'd hoped to present? Why wasn't *either* side burning with rage at the persecution of a maverick scientist?

He sat in the car amid the noise and doubted his own ability to present his case cogently. *Maybe I just wasn't making myself clear enough. Maybe I'm just going to submarine the entire case by . . .*

He took a deep breath. He wasn't going to let such juvenile fears force him to give up the case. He knew what another more experienced lawyer would do: demur to the complaint, delay, argue trivial points of law, find loopholes, delay and attempt a settlement. That wasn't what he wanted.

Johnson wondered what it was he *did* want. In his fury at the dual snubbings, he realized what it was. He wanted to blow the whole abortion issue to pieces. *Decker and Burke. They're both petrified that transoption would put an end to their crusades. And they're both too lazy to find new evils to battle or just give up and get along, so they continue to fight each other and gang up on anyone who threatens to wage peace.*

He gazed up at the warbirds circling overhead. He felt that he had a tenuous grasp on some deeper wisdom. Something that could apply to more than just a custody trial.

The trial.

He keyed the ignition and floored the accelerator. He had thirty days to answer or demur. The game, though, had to be won *right now*, in the blaze of publicity.

He grinned with feral glee as tires squealed. He'd confuse Czernek by answering the complaint *today* and pushing for the earliest trial date possible, based on urgency.

XIII

Karen insisted on watching the transplant. "I don't care what any lawsuit says." She spoke through the mask of her isolation garb. "She's my daughter, and I want to be there for her."

Dr. Fletcher nodded, laying two sacks of pulpy red material on the cart. "Marrow transplants are no big thing. It'll be just like receiving an injection."

David stood by his wife to place a protective arm around her. "Will it hurt?"

"Oh, no," the doctor said in an easygoing tone. "We'll be injecting right into that IV tube."

Karen's eyes goggled when she saw the two huge 60 cc syringes Fletcher had prepared. She quavered slightly upon seeing the thick, soupy fluid withdrawn from the sacks. The doctor calmly and efficiently unfastened the tubing from the bag of IV fluid, connected the syringe, and bore down on the plunger.

Renata was awake now and stared at her parents with the blank, noncommittal stare of a newborn. Karen knew in her heart that the little girl was taking all of this in without any idea of what was going on. Being fed by tubes and diapered regularly, she was physically content. She must assume, Karen thought, that everything else must also be the normal way of life: electrodes, lights, beeps, plastic cribs, heat lamps, people in white robes wandering in and out.

She wondered what effect all this would have on her daughter's later perceptions of life. She wanted so much just to hold and cuddle the pale little child. Renata looked up at her, jerked her arms suddenly, and grinned a wide, toothless grin. The tubes shook.

"Hi, sweetie," Karen said, her voice catching despite her brave smile. She waved with broad motions. "We love you, little honey."

Evelyn met with the expected resistance. Bone-marrow stem cells were much thicker than blood. She put her shoulder into play, pressing firmly against the plunger with the palm of her hand. Slowly, a red strand of color mixed in with the IV fluid at the top of the tube. The entire length of clear plastic took on a red hue, then grew cloudy. The line of crimson life entered the isolation box, disappeared under cloth tape on Renata's chest, and began its short but vital journey along her veins to hidden chambers in her young bones.

After a minute of steady pushing, the first syringe was empty. Fletcher quickly inserted the second and continued the transplant.

David coughed into his mask. "Will we see some change?"

"Not immediately." Fletcher pushed the remaining few milliliters of Valerie Dalton's bone marrow into Renata's bloodstream. "It will take a couple weeks or even a month before we know if all three cell lines recover. Until then, it'll be touch and go, with ordinary blood transfusions as needed. There are a few new things we're doing to make it easier for her. We've found that the drug thalidomide can prevent graft versus host disease."

David immediately grew worried. "Doesn't that cause birth defects?"

Fletcher shook her head, nodding toward Renata. "She's already born. It's use is only contraindicated for women during pregnancy, something she is a bit young for. What I wish we could get is a lymphokine called GM-CSF. It could speed her recovery dramatically. It's only just been developed, though, and it's still hard to come by."

Karen put an arm around her husband for support. "I guess I did expect something dramatic. You think of transplants, you think of teams of doctors and hours of surgery and an instant improvement as the new parts replace the old."

Fletcher shrugged. "On the other hand, she wasn't put in such a dangerous situation as surgery. The wait will be tougher on you than on her. She has no idea what's going on." She waggled her fingers at the baby. "Do you, you little huggly wuggly?" She looked up at the parents. "I received a message from my lawyer, Terry Johnson. He wants us to know that everything is going according to plan. He's pushing for an early trial date so that we can get this cleared up as soon as possible. I don't think we have anything to worry about."

"What about the—" Karen's voice caught on a word. "What about Valerie Dalton? What does she think of all this?" She waved an arm at the syringes.

"She was very cooperative. I think we can avoid quite a bit of enmity if we remember one thing." The doctor covered the stained syringes on the tray with a Tyvek cloth, then turned to check the monitors recording Renata's heart rate and temperature. "Whatever the trial decides, the more important outcome is that the baby regains her health, right?"

The Chandlers nodded in urgent agreement.

"Then we're all on the same side." She looked at the young pair and spoke in soft tones. "We've all made choices that will have consequences for the rest of our lives. If we can come to a civilized decision about what to do next, our lives—and especially Renata's—will be made easier. We musn't see Valerie and Ron as strangers who are trying to steal your baby. I will do my best in court to convince them that *we* aren't, either. The blame for all of this will fall on me, and I'll gladly handle it. You should just concentrate on letting Renata see how much you love her. That will help her recover as much as anything I can do. Babies need smiles." She waved at the little one. "I wish you could give her hugs, too. Real ones, not glove-box caresses." She fell silent, staring at the protective cage that kept out both germs and affection.

"How's Valerie?" Karen asked. Her voice was subdued.

"She was very cooperative. We tranqued her out so that she could sleep without pain. But with ninety-three holes in her sternum, she's going to feel it tomorrow morning."

Karen turned white.

A burning pain in Valerie's chest awakened her from a dreamless sleep. Somehow she had rolled over onto her stomach. Now the aching forced her eyes open. In groggy semiconsciousness, she pushed up on an elbow and rolled over again.

That's when it hit.

In a surge of intense fire, the agony seared every nerve in her body. It caught her by surprise, rendered her unable to take a breath. Every drop of adrenaline in her body seemed to jet into her bloodstream at once.

"Ron!" she cried out breathlessly. Fingers clenched around the low bars of the hospital bed, eyes tried to shut out the red haze within them, teeth ground together for a hellishly long instant.

She forced herself not to move. Lowering ever so slowly back to the sheets, she rediscovered the ability to inhale. The events of the previous day came back to her in an overpowering rush of memory.

"Ron?"

"He's in court," said an unfamiliar voice, "arranging the trial."

Valerie rolled her head over toward the speaker. The dark-haired woman standing near the bed watched Valerie with undisguised curiosity and apprehension.

"You're Mrs. Chandler."

Karen nodded. After a moment of hesitation, she extended her hand. "I want to thank you for what you did."

Just staring at the proffered hand caused her chest to ache. "I didn't do it for you. I did it for my baby."

"Please." Karen lowered her hand, fighting hard to suppress her conflicting emotions. Here, after all, was the real mother of the child she gave birth to, ready to use the might of the state to force her return. Even so, she had endured a torturous operation for that same child. "We both love Renata. What you did yesterday may very well save her life. I just want to thank you . . . for her."

When Karen gently grasped her hand, Valerie did not pull away. She returned the clasp, tears coming to her eyes. The small sobs hurt deep in her chest. It didn't matter. So much more pain was being released by the tears.

"Hey!"

Both women looked up to see Ron standing in the doorway. With a dozen white roses in one arm and a box of Godiva chocolates in the other, he looked like a suitor coming to call. But he looked none too pleased.

"I won't have you in here disturbing Valerie."

"It's all right, Ron." Valerie reached for a tissue, but the pain stopped her arm. Karen pulled one out of the wall box and handed it to her. "She's here to tell me how Renata's doing."

Ron's lips curled inward meditatively until beard and mustache met. "Okay," he said with a sigh. "But I don't think it's a good idea for plaintiff and defendant to fraternize." He smiled with a reflexive sort of mock-friendliness. "I guess I mean sororize." He extended his hand. "I'm Ron Czernek."

"Yes," Karen said, taking his hand for a minimal duration. "I've seen you on the news."

"Well," he said cheerily, "you'll see a lot more of both of us real soon. Jury selection begins on Monday."

"What?" Valerie cringed at the pain associated with speaking.

"I asked the court to exercise its inherent power to set the earliest possible date. Much to my surprise"—he stared at Karen—"the other side agreed not to demur. I pointed out that the immediate health risks to the baby required that we determine custody as soon as possible."

A wave of illness permeated Karen.

"Fletcher's lawyer got the judge to spike my application for our taking temporary custody. The judge said that it was moot, since the child was in the hospital for the time being. And Shawn Deyo—the hospital's lawyer—he got the judge to sever the case against Bayside from the rest of the suit because they'd turned Fletcher in the moment they found out about it. We lost a deep pocket, but on the other hand, we'll get this over with in no time. Don't worry." He stood over Valerie and stroked her golden hair.

Karen stepped back from the bed. "I'll go, now. I hope you'll feel better soon."

"Thank you," Valerie said.

Ron muttered something under his breath.

When Karen's footsteps receded down the corridor, Valerie asked him what he had said.

"Nothing." He continued to stroke her head. "I'm sorry I couldn't show up earlier. It's just been a bitch of a morning. Want to hear it?"

Valerie closed her eyes for a moment. "Not really." She opened them. Her voice was soft but strained. "Could you call the nurse? I really need something to handle this pain."

Mark Landry would have preferred not to run into Dr. Fletcher, but by the time he saw her, there was no graceful means of escape.

"Morning, Doctor," he mumbled. He tried to keep walking, but Fletcher took him by the arm.

"Don't worry," she said in an even voice. "I'm not going to break your neck." Her hand released him. "It was all bound

144

to come out sooner or later. I just objected to your sneaking around instead of confronting me directly."

"You evaded my questions."

"You didn't ask what was on your mind." She folded her arms and looked at him with that weary expression doctors reserve for when they are particularly professionally frustrated. "Look, let's just ignore all that. I've got to concentrate on Renata *and* all my other patients *and* a lawsuit. You saw that line of pickets out there this morning. And the cops. And the reporters. Anyone in white coming and going here is going to be considered fair game. I admit I brought this down on all of us, but—"

"You certainly did," growled the voice of Dr. Lawrence. He strode up to the pair, dark anger across his brow. "I wish the board would get off its duff and agree to file a cross-suit against you. We had to admit one of our own residents with a gash on his head from one of the protesters. Damned pro-lifer tried to beat the kid to death with her picket sign." He narrowed his gaze to Fletcher. "I hear the trial begins next week."

"Actually, just jury sel—"

"I'd advise for everyone's safety that you attend all the proceedings and come here only under the most urgent necessity."

"I can't do that," she replied.

"Try." He turned to the young man. "And you, Landry. Back to the lab." He continued on his way.

"Pompous jerk," Landry muttered after the administrator turned a corner. He looked at Dr. Fletcher. "I always wondered why you seemed so unconcerned to be running both the baby factory and the abortion mill. I think I understand why you had to do things the way you did. Maybe after the trial I'll find out why you bothered at all. It doesn't seem to pay to rock the boat either way."

Fletcher's voice was grim. "Sometimes a boat has to be rocked hard to steer a new course."

XIV

Terry smiled with satisfaction. Using every peremptory challenge in his possession, he had managed to put three women on the six-person jury. Czernek had engineered three men. Now the battle for their souls could proceed.

He gazed at the six. He had wanted the full twelve, but Judge Lyang had pressured him to settle for six in order to save court time. He agreed—it was only fair, since Lyang had been kind enough to arrange for a speedy trial. Two of the women were in their thirties, both housewives. The third was in her fifties, a real estate professional. He figured he could get the young ones to side with Karen, the older one to identify with Dr. Fletcher. His task was to convince the men to see his side of it.

Piece of cake.

Ron smiled with satisfaction. Having exhausted his peremptory challenges, he wound up with three men to counter Johnson's women. He wanted men who would side with his own interests as the genetic father in this case. While he worried that his unmarried status might put them off, he hoped that he had tap-danced around the problem by making Valerie the sole plaintiff. The three men were all fathers, in their forties, from working-class backgrounds that most likely did not cotton to newfangled medical shenanigans. He pondered the women with amusement. If Johnson thought they would save him, he was wrong.

Rhetoric Ron will have you weeping for Valerie by summation time.

L.A. Superior Court Judge Madeline Lyang watched the court clerk swear in the jury. *They had to demand a jury,* she thought. Since the odd, hybrid suit dealt with issues of fact, though, and not just equitable relief, they had a right to it. A small sigh escaped her. Juries always meant greater histrionics on the part of the lawyers. In her fifteen years on the bench, she had developed a fair instinct for determining how a case would proceed.

This one will be a killer.

She was a woman of moderate height. Sitting at the bench, though, she looked impressive and forbidding. At fifty, she still retained the smooth, sculpted features of her Chinese ancestry. Open and expansive in private life, she capitalized upon the myth of oriental inscrutability in the courtroom setting, maintaining an impassive, unreadable expression when she wanted or needed to. Custody cases usually demanded that. Such trials involved few villains and fewer heroes—just two people trying to do what they saw as best for the children.

While this was not strictly a simple custody battle, it had wound up in her docket by those most powerful of judicial forces, expediency and mere chance. She knew on first sight, though, that this case would be a publicity H-bomb.

She used the gavel she'd received in high school, where she had served as chief (and only) justice of the student court.

"Court will come to order. In the case of Valerie Dalton versus Evelyn Fletcher and David and Karen Chandler, jointly, I'd like first to address the question of televised proceedings." *Here we go,* she thought, expecting the first of many tugs of war. "Counsels will please approach the bench."

"The plaintiff," Ron whispered to the judge, "favors allowing the presence of the press."

Terry chimed in immediately. "The defendants welcome the opportunity to let the truth be heard."

Judge Lyang permitted a smile to cross her face. *Publicity hounds.* "Fine." She addressed the courtroom. "Permission is gran—"

The sound of plastic and metal scraping and sliding emanated from the back of the courtroom. Photographers and video crews lined the back wall, eagerly setting up their equipment.

Lyang rapped once. "Granted, but on condition that courtroom decorum is maintained back there. Quiet down." She gazed at the plaintiff. Valerie Dalton sat beside Czernek. She wore a stereotypically middle-American house dress in light blue. It made her eyes take on a sapphire hue and went flatteringly well with her blond hair and very light makeup. Perfect, the judge decided, for someone playing the part of betrayed innocent. She admired Czernek for stopping at a solid color and not going all the way to gingham and bows. His own outfit was a solid navy business suit with a light blue oxford cloth shirt under a midnight-blue tie with the smallest, most tasteful maroon-dot pattern.

The defendants seemed to be using much the same tactic. David Chandler wore an unimpressive gray business suit, not expensive enough to seem like a spendthrift, yet just well fitting enough to imply fitness for fatherhood status. His wife wore a simple beige Victorian-collared blouse and matching skirt. Neither woman wore any extra jewelry, though—in addition to her wedding ring—Mrs. Chandler sported a nice little cameo on the collar of her blouse.

Darling, thought Lyang. Their lawyer, she mused, must have been brought up watching reruns of *The Paper Chase*—he wore appropriately rumpled brown tweed slacks and jacket over a sky-blue shirt with thin white vertical and horizontal lines. His tie was tan and narrow. He indeed looked the part of an energetic, young defense lawyer working sleepless nights to prepare his valiant case.

148

Dr. Fletcher was the only one who failed to fit in. Dressed in a dramatically white business suit that Lyang had seen the week before at Nordstrom's, she sat between Johnson and Mrs. Chandler with a notebook and pen at the ready. Her black hair, peppered with gray, was in place but for one strand that curled toward her right eye despite occasional efforts to brush it back.

She was the magnet that drew the gaze of the jurors and the spectators. Who, they must wonder, was this doctor who had performed such bizarre surgery? Judge Lyang took a deep breath and prepared to find out.

"Counsel for the plaintiff, you may present your opening statement."

Ron Czernek stepped from behind his table to address the jury. He made a point of stepping around the overhead projector that Johnson had asked to have available.

"Ladies and gentlemen," he said in a conversational, undramatic voice. "We're here today to decide something that's never been decided before. There have been countless trials in the past between husband and wife over the custody of their children. There have been battles between unmarried persons for children born out of wedlock. There have even been highly publicized cases of surrogate mothers demanding custody of the children they gave birth to under contract to others.

"But no one, ever before, has been asked to decide the fate of a child," he turned to gaze at Dr. Fletcher, *"kidnapped before it was even born,* and secretly planted in the womb of another woman."

Johnson rose to object to the prejudicial remark but hesitated. Maybe he would want equal latitude with his own opening statement. Letting the lawyer get away with it, however, was no guarantee that Czernek would reciprocate. He quietly sat down. It was worth the gambit.

Czernek pointed to Karen. "The evidence will show that this woman—Karen Chandler—paid a surgeon several thousand dollars to 'get pregnant.' " Ron made little quote marks with his fingers as he turned back to face the jury. "She got pregnant, all right. With a fetus ripped out of Valerie Dalton's womb and stitched into Karen Chandler's in a clandestine medical experiment carried out in the dead of night last March."

Valerie lowered her head, a vortex of conflicting emotions seeking to pull her down into despair. She looked to her side to see that everyone—*everyone*—was staring at her, including the unwavering glass eyes of video cameras. She thought her heart would seize up and never start again. And Ron, the only one there who could sit beside her to put an arm around her, paced around telling his tale, unable to comfort her. Watched by all, she had never felt more alone.

"A medical experiment," Czernek continued, "that the facts will reveal had been performed on human beings without the approval of the hospital in which it took place. Without any basis in animal research or medical theory. In short"—he leaned over Dr. Fletcher—"an experiment that used Valerie Dalton as an unknowing guinea pig in a conspiracy to sell her stolen embryo to a woman willing and able to buy it!"

Johnson sat quietly, gazing at his opponent with an unreadable expression. Inwardly, he burned with the desire to interject his own statements. *Just keep talking,* he thought as he took notes without even glancing down at the paper. *I'll tear you apart in* my *opener.*

Ron took a deep, emotional breath and let out a sigh. The courtroom smelled of air-conditioned humanity and stale autumn air. His face became a mask of hurt. "I can't pretend to maintain objectivity in this case. As Valerie Dalton's fiancé and the father of her child, I am as much an injured party as she." He leaned on the jury box rail to gaze at each person there as he spoke. "Did Karen and David Chandler want a child to raise and love as their own? Then why didn't they adopt one? We shall show that this baby is as far removed from them genetically as an adopted child. And Lord knows there are plenty of children rotting in orphanages who could use a little love and tenderness. No, their interests were not with the child itself."

He stared coldly over at the Chandlers. Karen buried her face into David's chest. He comforted her and stared back at Czernek, wishing looks could not only kill but maim as well.

"No," Ron said. "To them, the fetus they bought was simply an amusement. A way to play at being pregnant, at giving birth to a child. No matter to them that a woman had been invaded—raped, more accurately—to tear the living child from within. No matter that the true father and mother would never know their daughter, never even know that they *had* a daughter. No matter that the child could have died at any point in this outrageous procedure. No, pregnancy at any price was the Chandlers' goal, and they got it."

He took a moment to calm his anger, flamed by his own well-rehearsed words. He faced the couple. "But what happens when the novelty fades? They've had the fun part. The baby showers, the expectation, the approval of relatives, and the excitement of anticipation. They've shared the ecstatic joy of seeing a life come into this world—a joy denied to the true father and mother—and now what? Now begins the drudgery of child rearing. Will they maintain an interest in the little gadget they've bought? Or will they lose interest, shunt Renata off somewhere while they pursue other amusements? Will they regret their purchase?"

David tried to suppress his anger, gazing up at Czernek. His head, held stiffly by his rage-clenched neck, began to tremble in an effort to remain still. Karen lowered her gaze to hide from the lawyer's eyes, convinced she had entered hell.

Ron turned back toward the jury. "The evidence will show that as we speak the baby they call Renata lies in the infant intensive care unit of Bayside University Medical Center. She is deathly ill. Can Karen and David Chandler do anything to save her? No. She needed bone marrow from her nearest relative. Is her nearest relative the woman who gave birth to her?" He pointed at Karen. "It is not. Her bone marrow would at best do nothing to save the baby's life. At worst it could kill her." Turning to Valerie, he said, "The only person in the entire world who can save that little baby is right here in this room. Valerie Dalton, the *real* mother of Renata Chandler."

Dead silence in the courtroom, the absence of any muttering, let Czernek know that he had everyone caught up in the web he spun.

"You are here," he said to the jurors, "to make a simple choice. You are here to declare that a baby should not be cut away from its mother without her knowledge or consent. That brutal, unauthorized medical experiments have no place in civilized society." He stared at Fletcher. "And that Dr. Evelyn Fletcher should pay for the misdeeds she performed in full knowledge of their danger and impropriety."

He gazed at each member of the jury, silent for a long moment. Every one of them, he was certain, had listened to and appreciated his statement. No sleepers or blockheads on this jury.

"Thank you." He walked sedately to his table to sit beside Valerie, who—having waited for him alone in the crowded courtroom—clasped his shoulders and placed her head against him.

The cameras zoomed in.

Judge Lyang avoided any show of emotion, though Czernek's arguments made sense to her. She wondered if Johnson had anything that might sound equally compelling. It was not often that a judge usually stuck with family law cases had an opportunity to preside over a landmark suit. Yet this, she realized with a warm glow of satisfaction, was what she had entered the judiciary for.

"Thank you, counselor," she said. "Counsel for the defense may make his opening statement."

Johnson stepped in front of his table. "Thank you, Your Honor." He paused for a moment, seeming to gather his thoughts.

God, that was good, he marveled in panic. *How can I top that?* He turned to face the jury and looked up at their inquisitive faces. He had watched their reactions at listening to Czernek. *Hit them on the same points, I guess.*

"Ladies and gentlemen of the jury," he said. "This is not a custody battle. This lawsuit is not the result of righteous indignation at discovery of some sort of evil crime. We are all here because of a nuisance suit brought by a money-hungry couple who are more interested in the thirty-million-dollar so-called 'damages' than they are in the welfare of Renata Chandler."

He looked down at the plaintiff. Czernek took notes, while Valerie stared at Terry in disbelief.

He turned back to the jury box. "Mr. Czernek may indeed view himself and his live-in lover as the injured parties, but the tale he spins is one of purest fantasy. What he skillfully neglects to mention—and what the evidence will show—is that we are here today because Renata Chandler was rescued from death nearly eight months ago."

Johnson's hands began to move as he spoke, weaving their own spell. "Think back to a day in early March when Valerie Dalton discovers that she is pregnant. It's unplanned, a surprise. Well, Valerie's a modern woman. She has a job of her own, and she's just gotten a promotion. She's living pretty well in a Palos Verdes home overlooking the ocean. She has no need for the commitment of marriage to enjoy life with the moderately successful lawyer Ron Czernek, her lover of several years."

Valerie, despite her best efforts, turned red with anger and embarrassment. She knew she had no reason to react to what everyone who mattered already knew. But *strangers* were hearing about it, here and on TV all around the country. People who had no way to judge her life except for the selective words uttered by a hostile attorney.

"What's a modern woman to do?" Terry paced slowly about, looking as if he were thinking on his feet. "Giving birth to a baby would just be an intrusion on her life. How could she work effectively at her job? How could she take pleasant vacations in Hawaii and Europe?"

That bastard, Czernek thought, *has done his homework.*

"How indeed?" Johnson gazed from juror to juror. "Some of you have children. You know what they can do to your lives. A baby changes you forever. Some of you are unmarried. I know a couple of you are career women. You know what I mean. You know what Valerie feared. Being tied down. Having to care for a defenseless, demanding infant. She wasn't ready for it. Wasn't ready to commit the rest of her life to supporting and nurturing the child she and Ron Czernek had begotten." He smiled at the word, paused to scratch at his chin.

"So what's a modern woman to do? Well, she sought the venerable solution of abortion, a convenience women have turned to for thousands of years." He paused to let them mull that over.

"What is abortion? The word comes from Latin. *Oriri* means to rise, appear, be born. *Ab*, meaning off or away; it's a prefix that means 'badly,' as in abnormal or abuse. So an abortion is a bad birth. The dictionary describes abortion as 'the *fatally* premature expulsion of a fetus, whether natural or induced.' " He stopped in front of the plaintiff's table. "We're here today because Valerie Dalton and Ron Czernek sought to abort their child. Attempted to kill it. And it survived."

This time, he managed to coax a murmur out of the spectators.

Valerie tried to look straight ahead without emotion, but tears leaked from her eyes. As she dabbed at them with a tissue, Ron stopped taking notes to put his arm around her.

Terry wandered over to the jury box. "You'll probably hear a lot of talk during this trial about a wicked medical experiment conducted in secrecy by a mad doctor." He waved a hand in Fletcher's general direction; she smiled imperceptibly at the description. "You'll hear a lot about a woman so desperate for a child that she paid for her pregnancy. I intend to demonstrate, however, that this was a far nobler act than that of the plaintiff, who paid to have a living being torn from the womb of its mother and disposed of like so much garbage. A living

154

being actually *rescued* by Dr. Fletcher and Karen Chandler. If they had not done what they did, Renata Chandler would not be alive today to be reclaimed by the very people who eight months ago paid for her *death.*" He looked at each member of the jury. "A killing that, I assure you, Dr. Evelyn Fletcher was fully certified to perform by the laws of the United States and the codes of the American Medical Association."

He walked back to his table. "Had Dr. Fletcher not had a rare and amazing conscience coupled with an astounding medical insight, Renata Chandler would have been just one of millions of aborted fetuses tossed away every year. Instead, she is a beautiful, living baby girl who is the center of a controversy that is shocking to behold: her attempted killers demanding custody on the specious argument that *they* would be better parents!"

Terry Johnson shook his head and stepped to his seat between Evelyn and Karen. "That's all I've got to say for now. Let's see what happens." With that, he sat down.

The murmuring behind the bar grew louder. The judge rapped gently a couple of times to bring silence. "Mr. Czernek, you may call your first witness."

Valerie looked at Ron with apprehension. He clasped her shoulders, looked her in the eyes, and whispered, "Just be brave and tell it the way it happened. Make eye contact with the jurors. Answer my questions and nothing more." He stood.

"Your honor, I'd like to call the plaintiff, Valerie Dalton, to the stand."

Valerie approached the stand and was sworn in by a tall, aging Latino court clerk who spoke with a deep, solemn voice. She sat in the wooden chair, adjusted the drape of her dress, and tried to be calm.

Czernek's first few questions were standard. She stated her name, her address, her age, her educational and business background. The recitation of such simple facts soothed her. The sense of panic subsided.

"Now tell us what happened on March third of this year."

"Well, I had discovered that I was pregnant, so I made an appointment with Dr. Fletcher for an . . . an abortion."

"Something," Czernek said, "that millions of Americans do every year with no complications."

Valerie nodded. "You drove me out there and helped me fill out what I thought was an ordinary consent form for the operation."

"What time was this?" he asked.

"About seven in the evening."

"Basically," he said, "after hours."

"Yes."

"Did the hospital appear fully staffed at that hour?"

"I don't know. It seemed pretty empty there."

"Go on."

Valerie looked at the jurors. They appeared to be listening with interest and without prejudice. "I was led into an operating room and got undressed."

"Was this a big operating room?" Ron asked. "With several surgeons and lots of equipment and lights?"

"No," she replied, events of the evening unfolding in her memory. "It was small, more like an examination room. Just the table and stirrups and some cabinets and a sink. The only equipment was the thing the nurse wheeled in." At Czernek's request, she described as much as she remembered of its white exterior, the video monitor and switches.

"Did you know what this device was for?"

Valerie looked at Evelyn. "Dr. Fletcher told me that it was for a suction abortion."

"Objection!" Johnson stood forcefully and walked to the bench. "Your Honor," he whispered, "use of the word abortion to refer to transoption will be prejudicial to my clients' case."

Judge Lyang looked down at the man. "Does this really have any bearing?"

"Immense bearing, Your Honor."

She shrugged. "Sustained."

156

Czernek asked his question again. Valerie answered uneasily. "She told me that it was a suction device. I was given a local anesthetic, which didn't do much good. Then she turned the machine on, and it started to make these hissing and sucking sounds."

Ron turned around as if in thought. "At any time," he asked, "were you aware that anything was out of the ordinary?"

"Well . . ." She frowned. "I had never seen an abortion before, so I had nothing to compare it to. High school sex education classes and college women's studies both seemed to ignore the actual medical procedure—"

"Please, just answer my question."

She frowned again, this time at Ron. "I'd never seen an abortion, so, no, I didn't think anything was wrong. I figured I knew it might hurt, so when she inserted the tube, the pain was no real surprise, I guess."

"Was there any talk between Dr. Fletcher and her nurse that might have aroused your suspicions?"

"I can't remember any."

"So as far as you were concerned," he said, facing the jury, "Dr. Fletcher had performed an abortion by medically approved means."

"Yes."

"Did you later find out that this was not the case?"

"Yes," she said, rage at the memory of the day growing in her.

"When?"

"Twelve days ago when Dr. Fletcher called me to ask for a blood test. She said a sick baby needed a transfusion."

Czernek nodded and stroked at his beard. "Did she tell you at this time that the baby was yours?"

"No."

Dr. Fletcher gazed steadily at Valerie, though she noted through peripheral vision that the jurors stared at her now, not the witness. She labored to avoid looking guilty at hearing her deception revealed.

"Did you later discover this fact?"

"Yes."

He asked her when she found out.

She replied with obvious bitterness. "The next day in the hospital. A lab technologist was interested in why my blood would be more useful to a baby than the blood of its own supposed mother. He left the room while I was donating the pint, and when he came back, he started asking me what I thought were crazy questions about whether I'd regretted having my abortion and what if my baby had lived."

"What did you say?"

"Nothing. Before he could finish, Dr. Fletcher walked in, and he stopped talking."

"Did Dr. Fletcher tell you then that Renata was your child?"

"No. First she asked if I would agree to a bone-marrow transplant. I said I wanted to see the baby. When I did, I had the feeling that she was mine. Then the technologist—"

"Do you remember his name?" Ron asked.

"Yes. Mark Landry. He told me his theory that Dr. Fletcher had invented some way to implant aborted fetuses into other women and that the child born to Karen and David Chandler was actually mine."

"What happened then?"

"I fainted. Mr. Landry brought me about with smelling salts. Then Dr. Fletcher walked in."

"Did she tell you then?"

"No. Only when I confronted her did she bother to tell me that my child had been given to someone else."

Throughout the morning, Czernek questioned her on every minute detail with repetitive precision and through her answers painted a portrait of irresponsible medical experiments performed on an unsuspecting woman without benefit of informed consent. All the while, Dr. Fletcher watched with intense concentration.

"Valerie," Czernek finally asked softly, "would you be a good mother for Renata?"

158

"Yes," she said, barely audible.

"Could you tell the court why?"

Valerie thought about the question for a moment, though the time was mostly spent remembering what she and Ron had decided the night before. She turned to the jury. "My baby was born to another woman, who claims that makes her the child's mother. Yet when the baby fell ill, *I* was the only one who could save her. Dr. Fletcher would not have been forced to bring everything out in the open if there were anyone else who could help. That baby needs me. She needs her real mother in order to survive." Her voice was level, unemotional. "She needs her true parents to love her, not two strangers. Strangers who considered her a commodity to be purchased. And I hope that along with returning my little girl to me, this court decides that no one else should ever have to suffer this deception again."

Ron waited for her words to sink in, then asked, "Did you bring this lawsuit just to get money?"

"No! What Dr. Fletcher did to me was wrong. She should be stopped. That's why I brought this lawsuit. To get my baby back and to prevent future abuses."

He paused again. "Thank you, Ms. Dalton. No further questions."

Judge Lyang looked over to Johnson. "Would the defense care to cross-examine?"

Terry rose. "Yes, Your Honor." He sidled out from behind the table to approach the witness stand. He put his hands in his pockets as if in deep thought. He looked up at the ceiling. "Ms. Dalton, when you discovered you were pregnant, what did you see as your options?"

"Objection," Ron said. "Counsel must restrict himself to areas covered in direct examination."

Johnson snorted and looked at Lyang. "Counsel for the plaintiff is trying to restrict me a bit too much. He *did* cover her choice to get an abortion."

"Overruled," the judge said flatly.

"What options did you consider, Ms. Dalton?"

Valerie sat admirably still. Inside, she wanted to shake free. "I had no option besides abortion."

"Did you consider giving birth? Raising the child?"

"We weren't ready for that. I wasn't ready."

"That's fine," Johnson said in a calm, accepting tone. "Lots of people have abortions. It's legal. It's relatively safe. Were you aware at that time that abortion was the only *known* method of pregnancy termination?"

"I certainly didn't know about transoption, if that's what you mean."

"It is indeed." Johnson put his hands back in his pockets and strolled around with a meditative air. "Did you know that abortion entailed the killing of the fetus?"

"Objection," Czernek said. "To use the term 'killing' in regard to abortion implies that a first-trimester fetus is a living human being, something denied by every major court decision of the past thir—"

"Sustained, Mr. Czernek. I am familiar with the law."

Johnson smiled. *Right where I wanted you, you litigious bastard.* "Allow me to rephrase the question. Did you know when you went in for an abortion that the individual cells in the tissue removed from you during the abortion would, one by one, cease to function after said removal?"

Valerie shook her head. "I don't understand the que—"

"Surely, Ms. Dalton," Johnson's voice rose, "you can comprehend that when a piece of living tissue is deprived of its source of nutrients, it won't survive long. Did you know that extraordinary measures are taken during organ transplants to keep a heart or a liver viable—'alive'—while being transported to its new host?"

"Yes. I guess I—"

"Did you know that once aborted, your fetus would soon cease to be a fetus and become a mass of nonfunctioning tissue?"

"Well, yes. Of course."

He turned to her. "So you didn't really consider it alive to begin with?"

"No. I mean, not in the sense of it being a person. That's the way I learned it." She sounded more confident.

"And if you had lived in the South a century ago and had 'learned it' that blacks weren't human, you'd believe that, too, right?"

"Objection!" Czernek shouted, Johnson mouthing the word in perfect synchrony.

"Sustained." Judge Lyang leaned slightly forward to address Johnson. "Your analogy is totally prejudicial. The difference between a fetus and a human is far greater than that of mere skin color. And may I remind you that the Supreme Court has long ago recognized the humanity of all races."

"At one time it had not," Johnson replied. "Just as at one time it had not considered children to have human rights." He stared at Lyang. "Or women." Before the judge could react, he immediately said, "I'll retract the question, of course, and ask Ms. Dalton if she did not in fact sign a waiver of claim to the non-living bit of tissue she wanted removed. Did you?"

"I signed something."

Johnson reached into his briefcase. With a flourish, he placed a transparency on the overhead projector and threw the switch. On the screen opposite the jury box glowed several pages of typescript. "Would this be the contract?"

She looked at it. "Yes," she said, "it is."

"Am I correct that it says nowhere on that contract that you were to receive an abortion?"

She looked at Ron, then at the jury. "Yes. I thought the wording was a bit strange, but the way people use euphemisms for everything these days—"

"What term do you see that you *thought* meant 'abortion'?"

"The term was 'pregnancy termination.' "

"And you thought that the only way to terminate a pregnancy was through an abortion?"

"Of course."

Johnson pointed at the screen. "It says right here that the undersigned—that's you, Ms. Dalton—'relinquishes any and all claim to tissues removed during said pregnancy termination.' Did you agree to that?"

"I don't remember," she said. She took a deep breath to calm herself.

"Are you in the habit of forgetting what you sign?"

"No, I remember it."

"Did Ron Czernek read it?"

"Yes."

"I see." Johnson began walking about again. He handed a copy of the contract to Czernek, then to the clerk, saying, "Please make this contract Exhibit A." He put his hands in his pockets. "So you knew that the abortion you wanted would result in the—Well, I want to say 'death,' but how about the 'cessation of viability' of the fetus?"

"Yes," Valerie said.

"Since you didn't consider it a living human being, though, you contracted with Dr. Fletcher to have it vacuumed out of you and disposed of. Is that a clear statement of the facts?"

Valerie paused, looking to Ron for guidance. The lawyer's jaw tightened. He could object to the argumentative nature of the question, but the issue would remain. His head nodded ever so slightly.

"Yes," Valerie said without emotion.

"And you meant to sign away any claim to this non-living bit of tissue?"

"Yes."

Johnson walked over to the witness stand, placed both hands on the rail, and looked her fiercely in the eye. "Why, then, are you now laying claim to this bit of garbage you threw out?"

Czernek shouted a loud objection. Johnson shouted even louder over the other lawyer's protest. "Why do you suddenly care about this child that a few short months ago you paid to have killed?"

"*Objection!* I want that stricken from the record! Harassing the wit—"

"I am capable," the judge said loudly, "of discerning harassment, Mr. Czernek."

Ron sat down, fuming. Lyang laid down her gavel and folded her hands. "Approach the bench." The lawyers stepped toward the judge.

"Mr. Johnson," she whispered, "the entire subject of abortion and the rights of the unborn is frightfully emotion laden, as the two groups of protesters outside this courtroom demonstrate. You do your clients' case no good by harassing the plaintiff." She glanced down at the court reporter, a young man fingering the keys of a battered old Stenotype. "The last two questions shall be stricken from the record, and"—she turned to the jury box—"the jury is to disregard the nature of the question and any inferences they may draw having heard it. You may continue, Mr. Johnson."

"No further questions, Your Honor." *I've never heard of a jury yet that could erase its own memory.*

"Then I suggest we recess for lunch," Lyang said, knocking once with her gavel.

XV

"If his tactic is to act self-righteous and abusive," Ron said, "it can only help our case."

He faced Valerie across a small blue table in the courthouse cafeteria. A few yards away sat Johnson, the Chandlers, and Dr. Fletcher. Johnson spoke quietly, but with intense emphasis about something. Czernek glanced over at them, then turned his attention back to Valerie.

"I'm not going to redirect you, so I don't think you'll have to worry about any more testimony." He bit down into the club sandwich, chewed on it while thinking. "I'm going to call Mrs. Chandler next. If I can establish that she was a knowing accessory to the transoption, that'll draw a pretty bad picture of her for the jury. Then I'll follow up with the expert witnesses—"

"Is it okay if I talk to Dr. Fletcher now? There aren't any reporters around."

"Legally you can, but I don't think you should," he said.

She stood. "I just want to find out about Renata."

Ron grunted and took another bite of the sandwich. Mentally, he rehearsed his line of questioning, knowing that if he kept it narrow enough, Johnson would have practically nothing to seize on in the cross-examination. Calling a hostile witness was risky, but he calculated that he could turn that hostility to his advantage.

164

"How's Renata?" Valerie asked, sitting in an available chair next to Dr. Fletcher.

Fletcher gave her a comforting smile. "She's still in guarded condition. We just won't know for a while. She's hanging in there, so *we've* got to, too."

"Valerie?" Terry looked at her.

"What?" Her voice was as cool as the air in a glacial cavern.

"I'm sorry I put you through that. You know why I had to, don't you?"

"Lawyers will be lawyers," she said, rising.

"Mr. Czernek will be just as rough on Karen," he said. His tone was matter-of-fact, but his eyes revealed an apprehension about something, the nature of which Valerie was unaware.

She chalked it up to the trial jitters she assumed everyone else also felt and returned to Ron. He hovered over his coffee, searching his notes to prepare for the afternoon.

"How is she?" he asked without looking up.

"They don't know yet."

It was strange reporting to him in such a way. His attitude seemed almost that of a man in some gothic romance. Dark and brooding, he pondered his own thoughts while expressing only a cursory interest in their child. He flipped over a sheet of the yellow legal pad, continuing to read his hasty shorthand.

Suddenly, a repetitive beep erupted from his jacket. For a moment, he was unsure what it meant. Then he remembered that in his haste to bring the case to trial, he had rented a pager to keep in contact with his office. He pulled it from his pocket, noted the phone number on the LCD display, and switched it off.

"That's my callback from the doctor I asked to be an expert witness." He headed for the phone booths. "I hope he agrees to testify—it's cutting things close to do this so far into the trial."

Valerie watched him go, then turned to observe the defendants. It was her first opportunity to view them together in a relaxed climate.

David Chandler doted on his wife so sweetly, she thought. Always an arm around her or a hand touching hers. She knew it couldn't be an affectation. Ron sometimes did that: a pat on the hand or an obligatory hug. The impression she received, though, was one of distraction, as if her lover had more on his mind than pleasing or soothing her.

Karen had that troubled look of a mother concerned about her child. Valerie could tell that the woman was unable to concentrate on the courtroom proceedings; her mind was miles away in a hospital room at Bayside. Renata created a bond between the two of them that was even stronger than the one between Ron and her. It was a bond, though, with built-in stress, one that could never be acknowledged as long as they vied for possession of Renata.

It was Dr. Fletcher's fault. Valerie glared at the woman, at her black and silver hair, at her starched white demeanor. She acted as if she cared about Renata, about Valerie—indeed, about everyone. Was it a sham? Just so much bedside manner repeated rote? What really lurked behind that doctorly exterior? Was she trying to help all women and unborn children, as Johnson implied? Or was Ron more correct that she had used her and Karen as a means to test her theories?

She knew Ron's reasons for being here. What were Johnson's? He seemed sincere to the point of a stroke, yet he used every nasty rhetorical technique available. Stuff she'd seen Ron use in other trials. He knew how to play the jury, just as Ron did. Was that the key? Would the best player win regardless of who was right or wrong?

"He's in!" Ron returned to the table, scraping the chair across the linoleum to sit. "He'll be available tomorrow to give expert testimony on embryo transfer. And here's something I didn't know: he's on the ethics committee of his own hospital, so he *really* knows the implications of Fletcher's actions."

"Tomorrow." Valerie finished her coffee in one swallow. It

166

went down bitter despite the two packets of Equal. "What about today?"

Ron grinned and looked across the room at Karen. "Leave that to me."

Karen sat in the witness stand, determined to answer the questions without overreaction.

"We had exhausted all other—"

"Just a yes or no answer," Czernek said coolly. "Did you enter the Bayside University Medical Center fertility program to become pregnant by any means possible?"

"Yes."

Rather than stroll around before the bench in Johnson's manner, Czernek stayed close to Karen, facing her to ask his barrage of questions in a clipped, businesslike manner.

"Were you aware that your problem could have been solved by the medically accepted method of nonsurgical ovum transfer?"

"We'd tr—"

"Yes or no?"

"Yes, but—"

"So you knew about nonsurgical ovum transfer?"

"Yes. We tried—"

"Just yes or no, Mrs. Chandler. Did you know that clinics performing the procedure regularly contract with women as conscious, informed ovum donors?"

"Yes."

"And you knew that the Bayside clinic had a frozen supply of fertilized and unfertilized eggs available for you to pick and choose the traits you want in a child?"

"Yes." Karen burned to tell the jury about her failures with the procedure.

"Yet you instead allowed Dr. Fletcher to implant an embryo in you by surgical means?"

"Yes."

"And you allowed this even though you knew that such an embryo must have been torn from the womb of another woman?"

Johnson popped up. "Objection! The question is argumentative and establishes nothing new."

Judge Lyang nodded. "Sustained."

"Were you aware that the embryo must have come from an abortion?" Czernek asked.

"Yes," she answered firmly.

"And yet you allowed Dr. Fletcher to perform this procedure?"

"Yes."

"And you carried this child to term and gave birth to it?"

"Yes."

"And you filled out a birth certificate naming you and David Chandler as the mother and father even though the child bore no genetic relation to either of you?"

"Dr. Fletcher told—" She stopped just as Czernek opened his mouth. "Yes, I did."

"And you had no compunctions about that? You didn't think that perhaps there was something dishonest or perhaps even illegal about it all?"

"I object!" Johnson said. "Mrs. Chandler is not a legal expert."

"Sustained."

Czernek rubbed the bridge of his nose. "It's a simple question, Mrs. Chandler. Did you suspect that you were involved in something that was wrong?"

"No, I did not."

"I see. And now that you have been caught, do you feel any remorse?"

Johnson shot to his feet again. "Objection, Your Honor! The question of remorse is totally irrelevant."

Judge Lyang sustained.

Czernek shrugged and turned to face Karen. "I have no more questions."

On his way to the witness stand, Johnson glared at the more experienced lawyer, turning his head so that his expression was hidden from the jurors' view. Czernek smiled cordially and returned to his seat.

"Mrs. Chandler," Johnson began, his hands in his pants pockets, jacket bottoms draped over his wrists. "Please tell the court why you had to seek out the services of a fertility clinic."

She looked at the women in the jury, speaking softly. "David and I had always wanted to have children, and we tried right from our wedding night. But nothing ever seemed to happen. We went to doctors, and they determined that it was sort of both our faults." She lowered her head for a moment, then looked up, this time at the men. "I had very poorly developed ovaries, and David had an industrial accident when he was twenty and had a very low sperm count."

"And what options did you consider?"

"Nonsurgical ovum transfer was one method," she said, glancing over at Czernek in pleasure that the truth could now get out. "Of course, since David couldn't contribute the sperm, we used eggs that had already been fertilized."

"Did you actually undergo such an operation?"

"Yes. Four times."

The spectators began to trade whispered sounds of astonishment. Johnson stepped close to Karen.

"What was the outcome of each?"

"I miscarried all four."

The murmuring in the courtroom increased an increment. The judge gaveled for quiet. The sounds abated momentarily.

"At what point did these pregnancies spontaneously abort?"

"All of them within the first three weeks."

"And were these your first attempts?"

"No. We had tried *in vitro* fertilization with donor ova and sperm."

"How many tries there?"

"Three."

"Any other methods?"

"Yes," she said in an almost ashamed tone. "Three attempts at artificial insemination before my problem was properly diagnosed. But that was long before I found Dr. Fletcher."

"So altogether, how many times had you tried orthodox methods of artificial impregnation?"

"Ten times."

"And the outcome each time?"

She looked straight at the jury. "They all miscarried."

"How soon after each procedure?"

"All within the first three weeks, when they took at all."

Johnson gazed at the members of the jury as if to drive his point home. Actually, he scanned their faces for some sense of their reaction. He read sympathy on most, but the two young women seemed a bit put off by the idea of such colossal efforts. One of the older men, too, appeared embarrassed by the clinical details.

"Did Dr. Fletcher," he asked, "say why she suggested surgical embryo transfer? Transoption, as she calls it."

"She said she suspected that a more fully developed embryo might have a better chance of thriving. We were at our wits' end. We'd tried everything else under the sun." Tears welled in her eyes. She pressed at them with a tissue. "We just wanted a baby."

Terry held up his hand and nodded in sympathy. He ran the hand through his curly mop of hair and said, "Did Dr. Fletcher ever speak to you about abortion?"

"Yes."

"What did she say?"

Karen put her hand in her lap and crumpled the tissue in its grasp. "She said that transoption was something that she hoped would make abortion obsolete."

"I object," Czernek said loudly. "This line of questioning is not germane—"

"On the contrary, Your Honor." Johnson stepped over to face the judge. "Counsel for the plaintiff has raised the question of the defendant's awareness of abortion. I am merely probing the question further."

Lyang mulled the problem for a moment. "Overruled," she said.

Johnson strolled around the witness stand. "Mrs. Chandler," he said, "were you aware of the identity of the embryo donor?"

"No. Dr. Fletcher insisted that we have no contact with the donor."

"Did you know that the donor was unaware of the use to which her aborted—I'm sorry." He nodded at Dr. Fletcher. "I mean her *transopted* fetus. That she was unaware of the use to which it would be put?"

"No. She never really discussed the source with us. Just that embryos were available."

"Where did you think the embryo must have come from?"

"An abortion," Karen replied. "I mean, that was pretty obvious, don't you think?"

Several spectators laughed in a nervous sort of way and almost immediately shut up.

"Was it your intent to become pregnant simply to enjoy being pregnant?"

Karen shook her head, an inadvertent smile crossing her face. "Pregnancy isn't something you do for fun. David and I wanted to bring a child into the world. To raise it with love."

"Did it make any difference to you that the donor was totally unaware that her child would be transopted?"

"No."

The muttering increased. People nodded to themselves and one another.

Karen continued, staring squarely at the jurors. "I had *no* uncertainties. I knew that I wasn't taking a child from someone who would miss it. It's not as if the donor had an abortion just to provide me with a fetus. I knew that I was saving a child from absolutely certain death."

Looking out at the spectators, she saw and heard dozens of

people arguing with one another. Some expressed astonishment at her blatant statement; others spread their hands in reluctant agreement with her logic. She glanced down at Valerie.

The plaintiff lowered her head in an attempt to hide her tears. Unsuccessful, she grasped Ron's shoulders and clung to him.

"Please, Val," he said. "I've got to stand up to object." He stood, letting her arms slide down him. "Objection!" he shouted. "The defendant's personal opinions are of no consequence here."

"Sustained," Lyang said. She looked down at the court reporter. "Strike the last question and answer from the record. And counsels will please approach the bench."

Czernek and Johnson stepped over to the base of Judge Lyang's dark wooden tower. She looked down at both of them and whispered.

"What is going on here? This is a custody lawsuit we're hearing, and neither of you has addressed the issue of the best interests of the child." She pointed a dismissive hand at Czernek. "Well, maybe *you* have, perfunctorily. Neither of you, however, has bothered to raise questions of financial resources, parental fitness, personal habits, or any issues of fact that I would normally hear in this court."

"Your Honor—" Johnson glanced hesitantly at Czernek. "This case is not one of divorced parents deciding on custody. That is why we all agreed to forego the discovery phase. This is a case of two sets of parents, both well-off, who dispute the—I don't know how to put it—the *parentship* of a child, who dispute its *maternity*. *That* is an issue of fact. I am of the opinion that the standard criteria for determining the best interests of the child are superfluous here and that once we determine whether or not transoption is a legitimate medical procedure, the answer to the question of Renata's custody will follow *ipso facto.*"

Czernek frowned at his adversary. "I'm afraid I have to agree," he whispered to Lyang. "The entire question of custody hinges on whether or not Dr. Fletcher kidnapped my daughter. If she did so by performing an illegal operation—"

"If the question is one of legality," Lyang said, "I can end this trial right now by taking judicial notice of transoption one way or the other. Transoption is not on trial here."

"The contract is," Johnson said. "Whether Ms. Dalton's contract is legally enforceable—"

"Or fraudulently induced," Czernek muttered.

"—determines what claim Dr. Fletcher had to the fetus after its removal. That's the impasse we encountered at the mandatory settlement—"

"All right," Lyang said in a harsh whisper. "So both of you think we'll be creating big precedents here. Fine. Just remember that the law is what the judge says it is, and don't either of you be so eager for headlines that you abuse these women." She nodded at Johnson. "You may resume."

"I have no further questions, Your Honor," he said to the court at large.

"Does counsel for the plaintiff wish to redirect?"

"No, Your Honor," Czernek said, "I would now like to call on expert testimony. Will Pastor Avery Decker please step forward."

The minister hefted himself out of his seat next to his assistant, James Rosen, in the first row of the spectator's area. Karen looked at the large man in his fine dark brown business suit, light blue shirt, and silk rep tie. She stepped out of the witness box, passing him as she returned to her seat.

"Is that the man you interviewed?" she asked Johnson.

The lawyer nodded in annoyance. "You're about to hear the self-proclaimed pro-life stance on saving Renata's life." He poised his pen over his legal pad, ready for anything.

"Do you swear," the clerk said, "that the testimony you are about to give shall be the truth, the whole truth, and nothing but the truth?"

Decker pressed his palm lovingly on the Bible. "So help me *God,*" he said with pride, "I do."

Czernek strode over to the witness stand. "Please state your name for the record."

"Avery Hamilton Decker."

"What are your qualifications as an expert witness in ethics?"

Decker eased back in the wooden chair, which creaked under the load. Looking at Dr. Fletcher, then at the jury, he said, "I'm a minister in the Universal World Christian Church and president of the Committee for Preborn Rights. I have a Doctorate of Div—"

Johnson stood quickly to interrupt the recitation of credentials. "The defense stipulates that Pastor Decker is qualified."

Czernek smiled. He stepped closer to the witness. "What, Pastor Decker, are the ethical problems with transoption?"

Evelyn looked over to Johnson, waited, then scrawled a hasty note and slid it under him. He read it.

No objection?

He wrote at the bottom and handed it back.

Let Decker braid his rope. I want to hang the SOB on X-exam.

Fletcher read it and smiled. Karen tapped her arm to see. When the younger woman read it, she frowned.

"The problem," Decker said, "simply stated, is that transoption is an unwarranted intrusion into the bodies of two separate women and a threat to the life of the preborn. There can be no justification for such interference with God's plan." He smiled cordially at the spectators, recognizing Jane Burke in their midst. "Or, to those who refuse to acknowledge God, interference with the functioning of nature."

"Isn't it ethically proper," Czernek asked, "to bring more children into the world?"

"Outlawing abortion outright would be a far greater step in that direction," Decker replied. "If even one preborn died as a result of transoption, it's reason enough to forbid the entire procedure. At the very least, it is an unnecessarily risky procedure, since the real mother could always have given the child up for adoption *after* birth. At the worst, transoption is nothing more than kidnapping, child abuse, rape, and murder. It is an offense against God and the dignity of man."

"For the purpose of such an ethical position, where would you say human life begins?" Czernek realized that he was on shaky ground. Anything Decker might accidentally say attacking abortion could redound to the detriment of Valerie's character. He had discussed the problem with Decker, who had agreed to stick to lambasting transoption. Ron, though, remained alert and ready for anything.

Decker smiled. "Life begins at conception. Most people assume that because a preborn grows inside the mother, it must be part of the mother. Not true." He settled in, folding hefty arms across a stout belly. He nodded toward Dr. Fletcher and smiled sardonically. "I'm no medical expert, but I believe it has been confirmed that the preborn actually creates a barrier against the mother, which is called the placenta, out of its own genetic material. The placenta filters the mother's blood and only permits certain nutrients through into the preborn's own bloodstream. The placenta is Checkpoint Charlie for the fetus."

"So what is your conclusion?"

"A fetus is a human being with full human rights." Decker made an expansive gesture with his hands. "And a doctor has no more right to relocate a fetus—by force—on an adult's whim than a government has to relocate its citizens by force. No surgeon should be allowed to play pharaoh."

"Who then, has the ethical right to claim motherhood of the baby named Renata?"

"Without a doubt, in the name of God and morality, she is the daughter of Valerie Dalton, though stolen even before infancy."

"Thank you, Pastor Decker." Ron returned to Valerie's side. "No more questions."

"Well," Johnson said, rising to his feet, "I have a few." With controlled eagerness, he walked over to the witness box and leaned forward.

"You told the court little about your organization. Does it not in fact advocate the right to life of preborns?"

"Indeed it does, sir."

"And you take a rather zealous approach to opposing abortion, do you not?"

"What do you mean?"

"I mean," Johnson said, striding to the jury box, "that you picket abortion clinics, lobby for legislation banning abortions, and counsel pregnant women against having abortions, correct?"

"All true."

"Has your rage against abortion ever led you to engage in illegal activities?"

"Objection!" Czernek shouted. "Counsel is asking the witness to incriminate himself."

Judge Lyang sustained, but Decker raised a hand.

"I'd like to answer that at length, if I may."

"As you wish," Lyang said, her dark eyes observing the man with curiosity. She held up a finger of caution. "However, bear in mind that what you say becomes part of the public record and you are *not* under a grant of immunity."

"My life," he replied, "is part of the public record." He shifted about to lean against the wooden rail before him.

"Your Honor, members of the jury—I understand what Mr. Johnson's question attempts to wrest from me. If the defense can show that I have ever broken the law in my opposition to abortion, then Dr. Fletcher and the Chandlers could jump on the coattails of my moral position to prove that they were acting in the best interests of the child. I have never broken any law in my quest to outlaw what I and God consider to be murder in the first degree. Some supporters of the cause *have* bombed abortuaries and physically assaulted abortionists. If you encountered a man or woman who freely admitted to having murdered thousands of defenseless babies and merely shrugged their deaths off as the removal of unwanted tissue, you'd be shocked and moved to violent outrage, too. I mean, how did the Jews feel when confronted with doctors who treated them as little more than experimental animals? Imagine our rage and understand our reactions."

He sat up straight, hands on his knees. "But none of us has ever assaulted a pregnant woman. None of us has ever wrenched a living baby from inside a woman and claimed that we were *saving* it. And *that* is what separates the sometimes illegal actions of a pro-life activist from the unconscionably evil actions of this mercenary doctor and her child buyers."

Decker stopped, leaning back. Johnson said nothing for a moment, merely looking the minister in the eye. *Now what?* he thought.

"An interesting point of view, in that it reveals a good deal of bias on your part."

"Is it biased," Decker asked with an astonished tone, "to reach an ethical opinion and then act upon it?"

Johnson smiled. "No. The evidence is clearly demonstrating that Dr. Fletcher did just that." He resumed his stroll around the courtroom, hands in pockets. "So, your group seeks to preserve the life of the preborn?"

"Yes. And its right to be born according to God's plan."

"And you seek to outlaw abortion. At least until people come to their senses and never choose it as an option."

"Correct," Decker agreed.

"And do you acknowledge that simply by outlawing abortion, you will not put an end to the practice?" He stopped to stare at Decker.

"You'd certainly cut down on—"

"Just yes or no, Pastor."

"Yes."

"So even with laws forbidding it, women will still seek abortion, and preborns will still be murdered—at *far greater* risk to the mother from botched, illicit abortions. Correct?"

"They'd get what they des—"

"*Yes or no?*"

"Yes. Women will break the laws of the state *and* the laws of God." He shook his head. "The curse of Eve."

"Curse or no, Pastor, if you so highly value the lives of these preborn babies, why are you opposed to the only technique that gives them a fighting chance for life?"

Decker jabbed a finger into his palm with emphatic force. "Leaving the preborn *alone* gives it an even better chance for life."

"Does it?" Johnson stepped over to the jury box without looking toward the jurors. "Are you aware of how many pregnancies end in spontaneous abortions and stillbirths?"

"No." A small laugh erupted from his depths. "It must be small or we wouldn't have overpopulation problems."

"The answer is about fifty percent."

"Objection," Czernek said.

"Sustained." Lyang gazed down at the defense counsel. "A lawyer's statements are not evidence, Mr. Johnson."

Johnson paused to rephrase his question. He was surprised at how he considered each objection to be a personal affront. It hadn't seemed that way in law school. After a moment, he asked Decker, "If you knew it was fifty percent, would transoption be less ethically objectionable?"

"No."

"You mentioned that the preborn builds a barrier against the mother. Did you know that from the point of conception onward, the mother's immune system wages an unrelenting war against the embryo?"

"I've read about it." Decker smiled wryly. "The curse of Eve again."

"You didn't know, however, that most pregnancies abort spontaneously—miscarry—within the first month?"

"No." Decker shifted restlessly in the chair.

Johnson turned toward the jury. "All those actual human beings with rights to life, all dying without the mothers even knowing they're pregnant." He turned back toward the pastor, raising his voice. "Where, Mr. Decker, did *you* receive the godlike ability to determine who shall live and who shall die? Or do you simply resent the idea that a woman can have her freedom of choice without any moral complications?"

"Objection, Your Honor." Czernek's voice boomed with stern force. "The witness's personal opinions do not affect his expert testimony."

"On the contrary," Johnson countered. "It bears heavily on the issue of bias."

"Overruled."

The younger lawyer nodded thanks toward the judge. "Is it not ethically superior for a woman to terminate an unwanted pregnancy *without* becoming a murderess?"

"Not," Decker said angrily, "if she becomes a party to kidnapping."

"Do you feel that you have lost a little of your moral high ground to Dr. Fletcher, who labored for years to find a way to protect the rights of the preborn while you just pushed for laws to make pregnant women a new criminal class?"

"Not at all."

Johnson shrugged. "You said that if just one preborn were lost in a transoption, that was reason enough to forbid the procedure entirely. Would you say the same for prenatal heart surgery? I submit that if transoption *saves* even one preborn that might otherwise be lost to abortion—*as it has*—then Dr. Evelyn Fletcher is closer to the spirit of God than you or anyone in this room!"

Turning his back on the minister, Johnson looked triumphantly at Czernek and said, over his shoulder, "No further questions."

Czernek, annoyed at being upstaged by his opponent, glowered at the tangled-haired young man. Looking up at the judge, he said, "I wish to call Ms. Jane Burke to the stand."

Burke arose, catching the attention of the courtroom cameras not simply because she was the next witness. Years ago, Jane had realized that it did her movement no good for their proponents to look and dress like frumps. Men *and* women, it turned out, rejected the feminist message from women who looked as if they spoke through a mouthful of sour grapes. She had lost weight, toned up, and dressed for the public eye. Looking more like someone from the cover of a fashion magazine than someone from a politically active organization, she wore a white-and-mauve business suit with broad shoulders, narrow waist, and a skirt that ended a few inches above the knee. She clasped a thin, matching mauve notebook in her hand. Striding gracefully past the bar, she nodded cordially to the departing sour-faced minister.

"Do you swear," the court clerk said in sonorous tones, "that the testimony you are about to give shall be the truth, the whole truth, and nothing but the truth?"

"I do," she said simply, and sat in the witness chair.

She inadvertently cringed at the warmth left by Decker's corpulent flesh, as if both his girth and his philosophy might be contagious. She suppressed it almost instantly, though, sitting up with composure and elegance. Her walnut-hued hair possessed a fashionable wave, and she left her glasses in her purse.

"Please state your name for the record," Czernek said, approaching her casually.

"Jane Harrison Burke."

"And what are your qualifications as an expert in reproductive ethics?"

She touched her Sisters Network pin unconsciously and said, "I am the president of Women for Reproductive Freedom. I have a Ph.D. in—"

"Defense stipulates she's qualified." Johnson knew the breadth of her education and did not want the jury to hear it.

"Ms. Burke, as an expert in reproductive ethics, tell the court your observations concerning transoption."

She sat back, straight in the chair, like a queen on a throne. "Ethically, transoption is a dehumanizing abomination."

Czernek nodded toward the jurors. "Could you tell the court why?"

She turned toward the jury. They watched her and listened, some with admiration, some with cautious distrust. "Over the past decade, advances in reproductive science have been made in an absolute moral vacuum. Purely in the interest of male genetic narcissism, doctors have labored mightily to devise ways that a man can have a child—usually a male child—in spite of a woman's inability to conceive. Transoption is just another part of the mosaic."

She used her long, graceful hands to explain, emphasize, illustrate. "New treatments for infertility, whose basic tenet is that an infertile woman is 'sick' and must be 'healed' at any cost, really do nothing more than reduce women to depersonalized breeding machines. Billions of dollars are being poured into research that tells a woman, 'Look—all that you have done with your life is meaningless if you can't make babies. We'll find a way to make them in spite of your shortcomings. You are superfluous.'

"*In vitro* fertilization meant that a woman who once could not conceive normally could now be forced to bear an heir for her husband. Surrogate motherhood went one step further by cutting the woman out of the man's plans for fatherhood entirely. Now he could hire a woman—usually someone who had no choice but to accept the thousands of dollars offered—to undergo a pregnancy that would shove his chromosomes forward one more generation. Thank goodness laws are being made to ban *that* bit of mercenary bondage." She looked at the women in the jury. "Transoption goes totally beyond anything yet encountered. It allows a man to seize a fetus from one woman and force it into another woman so that he can claim an heir even if that heir has absolutely no relation to him whatsoever! It is the ultimate cruelty for the ultimate in hollow victories. For the maintenance of the sham of fatherhood, women are now to become completely interchangeable wombs, totally robbed of any say in the use and disposition of their bodily tissues.

"Mr. Decker made a big point about the fetus being genetically different from the woman simply because it contains a little genetic matter from a man. May I point out that it receives *everything else* from the woman? It wouldn't be able to convert nutrients into its own genetic matter if there weren't a woman eating, breathing, and living to surround and protect it.

"Or does Dr. Fletcher intend to cut out the woman entirely? Why should a man even marry? Is Dr. Fletcher working on ways to remove the entire uterus from a woman, connect it to a machine, and churn out babies on male demand? All for a price?" She stared hatefully at Fletcher. "A price not calculated just in dollars but also in the immeasurable suffering and oppression of the entire female species."

Applause erupted in scattered portions of the courtroom. Cameras swung about for reactions. Judge Lyang gaveled for silence.

Czernek let out a breath he had been holding, spellbound. "Thank you, Ms. Burke. Thank you for your insight on this. I have no further questions. You've covered it all." He returned to his seat.

Johnson stood, running a hand through his hair. "Ms. Burke," he said with a touch of confusion, "you leave me at a loss for words. I can't understand how someone who battles so valiantly for women's rights can support something as brutally murderous as abortion. Doesn't abortion deprive an unborn woman of her right to life?"

Burke smiled at the obvious baiting. "There is no such thing as an unborn woman," she said with a touch of condescension. "A fetus is a piece of tissue inside a woman, just as much a part of her as an appendix. It cannot reason, it cannot survive outside her body. It only has the *potential* of someday being a human being. And that point comes at birth, when it becomes a separate and distinct human being."

"Maybe I'm a little thickheaded," Johnson said. "Doesn't the fact that we are here today arguing over the custody of Baby Renata *prove* that a fetus can survive outside its mother's body?"

"By planting it in another woman's body, certainly. But that's the same as saying a parasite can survive without its host if one can move it around from host to host."

Terry raised a surprised eyebrow. "Fetuses are now parasites?"

"In a sense, yes. It is an invading organism that takes nourishment from its host."

"So now you admit that it is a distinct organism."

"No," she said. "Well, yes, inasmuch as it is a tumorlike growth that swells at a fantastic rate."

"Tumor, parasite." He stared at her for a moment, then back at the jury. "Don't these words describe unnatural invasions of the human body that can happen to both men and women?"

"Of course."

"Isn't pregnancy, though, something that is not only natural but *vital* to the human race, which can occur *only* in women?"

"Put that way, yes. But—"

"Parasites stay with their hosts until the host dies. A fetus stays with a woman for nine months *max*, correct?"

"Yes," Burke replied in a tight voice. She knew where he was leading her.

Mild laughter mixed with whispered comments from the spectators.

"It's common knowledge," he continued, "that a tumor can either remain one size indefinitely or grow until it kills the victim but a fetus grows at a specific rate to a specific point at which it signals the woman's body to expel it. Why do you support a woman's right to expel a fetus and let it die but not another woman's right to rescue an expelled fetus and implant it in her own body? Shouldn't that *also* be a reproductive freedom?"

"The fetus is not another woman's property."

"True. And I'd question whether it is the first woman's property. Let's assume, though, that it is. If I abandon my property, can't someone come along and claim it?"

"This is the problem, don't you see?" Burke pounded her fist on the chair arm. "Treating human beings like property whose title can be—"

"Excuse me?" Johnson nearly shouted. "What is *that* conclusion based on? When did fetuses become human beings to you? How can you object to the buying and selling of tumors and parasites?"

"That's not what I mean. A fetus is like a houseguest of the woman. The uterus is the home, and the woman is the landlord. She has a perfect right as landlord to evict the tenant at any point. To demand that she care for the tenant against her will is slavery. But that doesn't mean a landlord can *sell* the tenant to another landlord."

Johnson waved his hand dismissively. "Once again, only human beings can be considered tenants. But let's get back to body tissue. I presume you have your hair and nails done at a salon?"

"Objection!" Czernek said loudly. "What possible bearing does the witness's groom—"

"I am trying to establish a line of questioning, Your Honor."

Judge Lyang, intrigued by the left-field nature of the question, said, "Overruled. Be aware, though, that I may interrupt at any time if I think you are harassing the witness."

"Thanks, Your Honor," Johnson said. Turning back to Burke, he lowered his voice "Well?"

"Yes," she said. "I do."

"And when your hair and nails are trimmed, do you demand that the trimmings be burned in your presence?"

"Hair and nails are composed of already dead cells."

"Just yes or no, Ms. Burke."

"No, of course not."

"Have you had your appendix removed?"

"Yes."

"Do you have any idea what the surgeon did with it afterward?"

Burke smiled wryly. "No."

"I see." He paced around for a moment. "Have you ever had an abortion?"

Some spectators frowned at hearing such an intrusive question.

Burke sat up straight. "Yes, I have," she announced with pride.

"Oh? And what did the surgeon do with the abortus?"

"I don't know. I presume she disposed of it properly."

Johnson slammed his fist on the rail. "You *presume?* Did you know that aborted fetuses are the major source of liver cells for transplant research?"

"No."

"Did you know that their pancreatic islets are cut out and used for insulin experiments?"

"No." She shifted uncomfortably in her chair.

She wasn't alone. Spectators and members of the jury found images coming to mind that generated a queasy discomfort.

Johnson pressed on. "Did you know that some brands of hair spray contain human placental extract?"

"Yes." She laughed nervously without realizing it.

"Did you know that fetal brain tissue is being used to treat Parkinson's disease? That fetal nerve fibers and astrocytes can be used to treat spinal injuries?"

"I've read something about it."

"And none of this disturbs you?"

"Why should it?"

Johnson turned toward the jury to make a helpless gesture with his hands. "You attack the mercenary nature of surrogate mothering and of doctors who charge fees for their services, but you seem unconcerned that there exists an entrenched financial interest involved in the practice of abortion. Researchers, after all, are getting valuable fetal material for free from women—in fact, charging women for having the material removed after the dubious privilege of being incubators. Do you find no ethical conflict in that?"

Burke tried to formulate a reply to the lawyer's question.

"At first glance," she said, "there might seem to be . . ." Her voice trailed off, her confidence slipping like a worn stocking.

"Why do you support abortion and not transoption? Is it because abortion allows a woman to ensure that her mistakes don't live to haunt her?"

Czernek shot to his feet. "Objection, Your Honor. Badgering the witness won't—"

"Sustained."

"—make up for his dearth of—"

"*Sustained*, Mr. Czernek."

Ron sat down. Terry slipped his hands into his pants pockets.

"What, Ms. Burke, makes you think that Valerie Dalton was deprived of control over her body by transoption but that *you* were not deprived by abortion? Neither of you knew what became of your fetal tissue. Would it have been better if Renata had been sent to a lab to have her liver, pancreas, and brain removed? Would it really have been better?"

Burke stammered for a moment, her composure faltering. "I . . ." She stiffened. "Valerie Dalton expected an abortion, not an embryo transfer."

"What she expected," Johnson said, "is what she *contracted for*. To be free of her pregnancy." He pointed to the screen. "Exhibit *A* once again. Does the word 'abortion' appear anywhere on it?"

"A legalistic, semantic trick," Burke replied.

"Is it? Valerie Dalton went into Bayside Medical pregnant. She came out not pregnant. She contracted for a pregnancy termination, and that's what she received. She explicitly signed away any claim to the tissue removed. She took full responsibility for her body, Ms. Burke, when she signed this paper. Her pregnancy was terminated just as surely as *your* pregnancy was, Ms. Burke. Now what's the difference? Why didn't *you* sue *your* abortionist?"

"Because *I* received an abortion. *Her* fetus *lived*!"

"So it's not the right to a terminated pregnancy that you defend. It is the right to a dead fetus. Your ethical concern is with the life or death of the child. Is that correct?"

"A fetus is not a child, God damn you!"

Johnson slammed both hands on the rail and stood inches away from her. Sweat beaded on his face. An anger that was not feigned burned in his expression. In a voice that thundered, he said, "Everything you say and support *screams* that a fetus is a child. You have no objection to individual fetal cells living on inside another person's liver or pancreas or brain. The only thing you object to is letting those cells remain intact to become a living, breathing human being!"

"Mr. Johnson!" Lyang slammed her gavel. "You—"

"No more questions, Your Honor."

He turned away from Burke and returned to his seat. Karen Chandler hugged him, tears flowing down her face. Dr. Fletcher patted his arm with approval.

The whispering from the spectators threatened to erupt into loud arguments. Everywhere, opinions polarized. Judge Lyang pounded away to no avail.

"Court is recessed until"—she glanced down at her calendar—"November tenth. Jurors are instructed not to discuss this case with anyone. Bailiff, clear everyone out!"

XVI

Czernek made a note to call the doctor to reschedule his testimony. "Let's go," he said to Valerie, standing to extend his arm toward her. "Be prepared for a mob."

Ron became a flying wedge through the crowd of spectators. When they reached the double doors at the rear of the courtroom, many of the spectators transmogrified into reporters, shouting questions and producing microphones from nowhere. Lights blazed suddenly, and the black glassy eyes of camera lenses dilated to view the pair.

"Do you think you can win the trial against such a brash young lawyer?" a woman hollered.

"Do you think the expert witnesses harmed your case?" shouted a spectacled man.

Ron led with one elbow jutting forward like a ship's prow, cutting through the sea of faces. His other arm twined with one of Valerie's to keep her close.

"I won't comment on the trial," he said loudly. "I have a worthy opponent, but we shall win nonetheless. Valerie is the true mother of Renata, and nothing can change that." He barged through the swirl of reporters that seemed to move with them toward the exit.

"How painful was your bone-marrow transplant?" another woman shouted, jabbing a microphone at Valerie.

"It hurt," she said. "It still hurts."

"Why did you want an abortion?"

"Did you ask your boyfriend's opinion?"

"Do you plan to have other—"

"Hey!" one of them shouted. "There they are!"

The tide suddenly went out on the ocean of newshounds. Lights and equipment bobbed hastily back toward the courtroom to surround the defendants. Ron lowered his arm and walked briskly with Valerie toward the exit. He glanced back at the crowd and smiled. *Let* him *get grilled for a while.*

Johnson welcomed the barrage. With Evelyn on his left arm and Karen on his right—protected on her other side by David— the young man forced a winning grin onto his face. Inwardly, though, being the center of such a crowd made him nervous.

"Of course we can't read the minds of the jurors," he said loudly to the microphones, "but we're certainly putting our point across."

"What point?" shouted a voice from somewhere in the knot of questions.

"That Dr. Fletcher helped Karen and David Chandler rescue a defenseless baby from the jaws of death and that they would be better parents than the plaintiffs."

"Mrs. Chandler," a blond woman called out. "Do you feel that carrying Renata to term makes you more of a mother than the woman who conceived her?"

"How did you feel when you found out your blood couldn't save her?"

"Dr. Fletcher! Will Renata survive all this?"

"Will she need more transplants?"

Terry increased his pace in an effort to move toward the exit. It was like moving through the tar pits.

"Please," he said. "Let my clients through. Contact me and we'll set up interviews."

His clients stared at him in shock. "I'll explain over dinner," he said in low tones.

The promise did nothing to abate the storm of interrogation. Sighing, he raised his elbow and began his charge.

Czernek thought he and Valerie would be safe once past the reporters. Then he saw the crowds outside.

Two lines of picketers, separated by a double line of blue uniforms, shouted at each other and the police. Pro-life to the left, pro-choice to the right. And the police opening a corridor right down the middle.

He was unsure which group would give them worse treatment. He read the pro-lifers' signs.

IF SHE HADN'T ABORTED, THIS WOULDN'T HAVE HAPPENED
TRANSOPTION IS BABY STEALING
ABORTION AND TRANSOPTION: HIGH-TECH CHILD ABUSE
STOP NAZI EXPERIMENTS! FLETCHER = MENGELE!

He couldn't tell if they were on his side or not. He scanned the pro-choice side.

TRANSOPTION IS NOT AN OPTION!
FLETCHER STEALS OUR RIGHT TO CHOOSE
WOMEN ARE NOT CATTLE
END REPRODUCTIVE SLAVERY
STOP NAZI EXPERIMENTS! FLETCHER = MENGELE!

Ron stared at the last sign, then back at the pro-life group. *Great minds think alike*, he mused.

Fear rushed through Valerie as she and Ron walked slowly down the courthouse steps toward the crowd. It was a bright, sunny afternoon. A fresh sea breeze blew over the shouting, turbulent crowd. It should have been a beautiful day, but the rival factions turned its loveliness into a mocking counterpoint. She could make out individual voices.

"Hey, hey, AMA—How many babies d'you kill today?"

"Our bodies—our choice!"

"God said thou shalt not kill!"

"Gods and governments enslave women!"

190

"Sez you!"

Then the picketers saw Dalton and Czernek enter the blue-bordered no-man's land.

Valerie didn't know what to expect. The pro-lifers probably hated her for having the abortion in the first place. The pro-choicers probably hated her for wanting the baby back.

Both sides merely grew quiet. They watched the pair pass between their warring camps. It was an uneasy truce, with scattered troops on both sides clapping here and there, booing there and here. The ranks were divided, cohesive action impossible.

Valerie and Ron passed unchallenged. Then the rival protesters' collective attention shifted to the four people at the top of the steps.

The cries and epithets from both sides erupted with such forceful outrage that no intelligible word or phrase escaped the crowds. Raised fists shook. Angry hands waved signs. The police locked arms and stared over their shoulders in red-faced, strained frustration at the opposite blue shore.

Johnson led the quartet into the narrowing chute. The thin lines of police were no match. The people, united, could not be defeated. They overcame from the right. Onward marched the Christian soldiers from the left. They converged on the mutual enemy.

The police closed ranks around the four, the outer shell of officers raising their batons to threaten. The circle moved toward the parking lot as if it were a single cell.

"Get back on the sidewalk!" shouted an officious voice on a bullhorn. "Get back or face arrest."

The threat worked. The picketers quieted down one by one and returned to a more orderly arrangement on the sidewalk. The police drifted back between them.

"Thanks, Officer," Evelyn said to the last man to leave.

He looked at the doctor with a hateful gaze on his gnarled, tanned face. "Don't thank *me*. I'd have to protect you if you were Satan's stepdaughter. And I think you are." He turned away and returned to the crowd, stopping for a moment to spit in the gutter.

Johnson shook his head. "I've always wondered why public servants treat their employers so poorly." He put an arm around Dr. Fletcher's shoulder and said, "Let's all go eat and plot our strategy."

They sat in a booth at Doolittle's Raiders, a restaurant hidden from the Pacific Coast Highway by the Torrance Municipal Airport's landing strip. Small planes lifted off and touched down outside the tinted windows. The faint sound of engines augmented the World War II music and decor. Among the Halloween decorations and costumed waitresses, Terry laid out his plan.

"We have ten days. I think we're winning the fight in the court, but the biggest battle is going to be in the press. That's why I want us to do as many interviews as we can."

Karen shook her head in a near tremble. "I don't think I could do—"

"Not you," he said. "Just me. And Dr. Fletcher. We're going to skip the question of custody entirely to concentrate on the moral question of transoption." He turned to Evelyn. "Did you go through all this just for the money they paid you? Of course not. You did it because you thought it was *right*. If we can seize the moral high ground, public sentiment will slip right into our pocket."

"The way Burke and Decker did?" Fletcher asked.

Johnson frowned sourly.

Valerie said little on the trip home. Ron did most of the talking.

"There's an old saying 'If the law is against you, argue the facts. If the facts are against you, argue the law. If the law *and* the facts are against you, pound on the table.' That's what Johnson's doing. A lot of pounding. It may look great on the evening news, but it's not going to win the case for him." He pulled into another lane to go around a slow car. He watched the road with a detached intensity that revealed his thoughts to be far removed from the act of driving.

"He thinks he can make a big production number with fireworks to dazzle the jury into believing that Fletcher's a champion of the oppressed." He turned to look at Valerie, then back at the road. "He's an amateur, raised on too many episodes of "Perry Mason". Amateurs always get slaughtered in a real court."

"You're losing, aren't you?" Valerie asked softly.

Ron replied with instantaneous anger. "I am *not* losing! Nobody knows what's going to happen. He's out there dancing about, harassing my witnesses, trying to score debating points. You want hostile cross-examination? Wait till I get *his* witnesses under my thumb. This isn't even half over."

"I wish it were," she said. "I wish we could just settle this quickly and be done." She gazed out the window at the blur of light and darkness, wondering about Renata. Karen and David had a room next to her ICU where they slept every night. She, the baby's true mother, had to live on TV news and the occasional terse report from Dr. Fletcher. Fletcher tried to be cordial, but the strain of the trial and the ethics hearings showed in her voice and demeanor.

"I set the evening news to tape," Ron said, pulling into their driveway. There were no news vans present at the moment, just a handful of reporters staking out the place. He parked and helped Valerie out of the car.

The reporters switched on recorders and videocams in a practiced, routine manner. Ron, taking a calming breath, decided to grant them an audience. He stepped into their circle of light. Valerie watched from the safety of the porch.

"Do you think you'll win custody?" asked an older man armed only with a hand-held recorder.

"That's up to the judge and jury, but the facts and the law are on our side. Nobody can steal a baby from an unsuspecting woman and seriously call it the moral equivalent of adoption."

"What is your opinion about the BMQA?"

"What about it?" Ron asked.

"They're meeting to decide whether to pull Dr. Fletcher's license."

"Well," he said, facing the cameras, "I can certainly understand why, can't you?"

With that, he thanked the reporters and joined Valerie at the front door. She had already unlocked it, so he put an arm around her and crossed the threshold with her.

"Fire up the VCR," he said, closing and locking the door.

"Do we have to?"

He was already at the living-room machine, punching buttons and rewinding. "We've got to know what the press thinks of all this. It's a good indication of public opinion." The television screen glowed with a high-speed backward view of the evening report.

Valerie stepped into the kitchen to prepare some herbal tea. She watched the screen from the warm environs of the other room.

"There!" he said. "Looks like a good one." The tape stopped rewinding, the picture dancing about as the playback attempted to locate and lock onto the control track. Suddenly, the image and sound united. Jill Knudsen, the young, brunette anchor for the station, spoke with an intense, serious expression. Behind her hung the superimposed artwork of the scales of justice balancing a fetus lying in one pan and a scalpel stabbed into the other.

". . . continued today. Attorney and plaintiff Ronald Czernek produced testimony from pro-life *and* pro-choice groups. Both sides denounced transoption as an invasion of a woman's body."

The image switched to a courtroom camera scene of Avery Decker saying, ". . . transoption is an unwarranted intrusion into the bodies of two separate women and a threat to the life of the preborn."

194

An instant later, Jane Burke's testimony received its sound bite: "It is the ultimate cruelty for the ultimate in hollow victories. For the maintenance of the sham of fatherhood—"

"Val—come and watch!" Ron craned his neck to look into the kitchen.

"Coming."

Silent shots of both Valerie and Mrs. Chandler in tears alternated as Knudsen's voice-over said, "Emotions ran high at the trial, with tears and harsh words from both sides." The scene shifted back to the studio set. "The trial recesses until November tenth, at which time an as yet unidentified surgical expert will testify about the medical implications of transoption."

"I hope," Ron muttered, putting the tape on hold and reaching for the phone. He punched the autodialer code for the surgeon's answering service and left a message about the date change, apologizing for the fickle nature of court calendars.

He hung up and punched the pause button on the VCR. Jill Knudsen continued her story without offense at the interruption.

"In a related story," she said, "Dr. Evelyn Fletcher, the surgeon who performed the unauthorized embryo transfer, faces an inquiry into her actions by the State of California Board of Medical Quality Assurance. The BMQA has the authority to strip her of her license to practice medicine in the state. More on that as it develops. Jerry?"

"That was great!" Ron said, switching off the machine. "They totally downplayed Johnson's side. We've got it in the bag from a PR standpoint."

Valerie gazed at the teapot atop the blue gas flames, thinking of Renata's isolation tank, where she was safe from reporters, lawyers, judges, and juries. Yet they surrounded her from afar, deciding her fate. She had done what no other child before her had ever done—survived an abortion to find shelter inside another woman. Now the publicity would mean that she could never again find shelter no matter which mother won her.

The pain in Valerie's chest once again began to gnaw at her. From without and within.

Evelyn sat on the stage set, trying to collect her thoughts while a young man fiddled with her bodice in an attempt to hide a small condenser microphone. He gave up after a moment and clipped it to the maroon piping of her gray lapel, trailing the wire beneath the jacket and across the floor. She sighed with relief at his departure.

Terry had arranged this interview on the "Gerry Rivers Show," one of the hottest new talk shows in syndication. He had spent half the night convincing her to go. It wasn't that she doubted the need for publicity; she doubted Gerry Rivers' willingness to give her the right kind.

"You're a fine speaker," Johnson told her. "You'll captivate them all."

She wasn't so sure.

Rivers was a young man, mid-twenties at most, who had made his name as a deep-digging investigative newspaper reporter. It had won him this talk show, which he had promised would be just as incisive. Fletcher doubted it, having watched him for the first time the day before. He had built the entire hour around the beauty secrets of celebrity call girls.

The floor director waggled his digits for attention as the set fell silent. Dark-haired and sturdily handsome, Gerry Rivers stood in the studio audience to await the countdown. He was not as tall as Evelyn had expected, which seemed strange to her when she considered how small her TV set was.

The floor director folded all but his index finger, which he pointed at Rivers. A weak, filtered version of the show's theme song came over a monitor, and Rivers switched on a winning smile.

"Gerry Rivers here with the controversial surgeon Evelyn Fletcher, woman of the hour, and the question of the hour:

Transoption—kidnapping or salvation? What do you think of this whole thing?" He stuck his microphone in the face of a woman in the audience.

She looked up at him as if she had been waiting to be called. "I think it's really wrong," she said in a soft voice. "I don't think doctors should go around experimenting on babies."

"Dr. Fletcher?" Rivers looked toward her. A red light suddenly glowed on the camera covering her portion of the set.

She frowned. Though she welcomed a format that required her to think on her feet, she objected to such obvious setups. "Doctors already perform experiments on aborted fetuses," she said. "Experiments that require the fetuses to be freshly dead. Why is *that* permitted to occur thousands of times a year while I am being persecuted for a single experiment that allowed one fetus to *live?*"

Rivers laughed and held up his hand. "Whoa, Doctor. I can't interview you if you ask the questions." He looked down at a man in the audience. "How about you? Any questions?"

"Yes," the balding man said. "I'd like to know how Dr. Fletcher developed transoption."

"Good question." Rivers looked over to her. "Dr. Fletcher?"

That's more like it, she thought. "I first became interested in alternatives to abortion about twenty years ago, when I saw what psychological devastation such a life-or-death decision imposed on women. When the processes of laser microsurgery and fiberoptics became widely available, I realized that a fetus could probably be removed intact from one woman and implanted into another with only a moderate amount of difficulty. Even though I hadn't done any animal experiments, I was certain that a method could—"

"I'm sorry to interrupt," Rivers said as the audience camera zoomed in on him. "We've got to cut away for a moment and take a break. We'll be right back."

"Clear for commercial," a tinny voice called over the studio speakers.

Rivers flashed Evelyn the okay sign. "Doing great!" he said, barely looking at her as he bent over to speak to one earnest woman.

"Ten seconds," the lo-fi voice announced. "Nine . . . eight . . ." At three seconds, the speaker fell silent, and the floor director took over with his own fingers, then pointed at Rivers.

"Welcome back. We're talking to Dr. Evelyn Fletcher, currently on trial in the Baby Renata case. We're—"

"I'm not on trial as such," she interjected. "The plaintiffs are seeking an injunction against me for—"

"You could lose your license to practice medicine, couldn't you?"

"Yes," she said irritably. "But that's a BMQA hearing, not a trial."

"BMQA," he said, turning to the audience, "is the California Board of Medical Quality Assurance, am I right?"

"Yes," Fletcher said. He was asking questions, she realized, in the same tone and manner he had asked the celebrity hookers about their opinions of liposuction and tanning booths. This would not be a productive exercise unless she could seize the cameras.

"You've got an urgent question, don't you?" Rivers asked the woman he had spoken to at the break.

"Yes," she said, standing. "Would you perform animal experiments if you could?"

Fletcher knew a trap when she saw one. Not wanting to go off on that particular tangent, she said, "Most medical scientists would prefer that there be a strong basis in animal research before a medical technique is tested on human subjects. Because of what I was forced to do with transoption, we now know it works and animal research would seem to be unnecessary."

Scattered applause arose from the audience. Rivers patted his hands against the air.

"Now wait. That's fine that you don't need to test it on

Lassie and Bonzo. But you performed your first experiment on an uninformed human female. How—"

"Karen Chandler knew exactly what sort of surgery she would be getting."

"I didn't mean Karen; I meant Valerie Dalton."

Fletcher's voice grew stern. "Valerie Dalton was not 'experimented' upon. She came in for a pregnancy termination and received just that. I could have used a coat hanger and gotten less outrage than I have for using a device that removed the fetus alive. Why doesn't anyone focus on that? I was legally and professionally entitled to suck out and cut up that fetus to free Valerie from her pregnancy. I did it in a nondestructive manner that—"

"We've got to—"

"Let me finish!"

"I'd love to, but we've got to break away for just a moment."

The audience muttered and jabbered among themselves during the pause. Fletcher merely sat in her chair and fumed. She could not simply storm off the set, though that was her initial instinct. Instead, she sat furiously still, arms gripping the chair, awaiting the next brief opportunity.

"Ready to sum up?" Rivers asked, joining her on the set.

"Sum up?"

"I've got two other guests after you. We've got to give transoption a balanced viewpoint."

"I thought I'd be the only one."

Rivers looked shocked. "There must have been a screwup in communication. No, I've got two others scheduled."

"Anyone I know?" she asked slowly.

"Jane Burke and Pastor Avery Decker."

Get me off this show, she pleaded to an unhearing deity. "Then let me have my say right now."

"Fair enough."

When the director cued him, Rivers looked deep into the camera with his dark eyes and said, "Dr. Evelyn Fletcher—

pioneer or mad scientist? Here she is in her own words." He nodded over to her.

"Thanks, Gerry." She gazed into the camera as if she could pinion the viewers to their couches. "What no one is willing to acknowledge in this entire affair is that I managed to save a baby from certain death. And even so, I gave Valerie Dalton the way out of pregnancy that she wanted. I satisfied her minimum requirement—that her pregnancy end. As a bonus, though, I also gave another woman a chance to bring a baby into the world. They both got what they wanted. And I'm certain that if you interview Renata in a few years, she'll be happy with the outcome, too."

"So you feel," Rivers cut in quickly, "that Valerie Dalton has an obligation to keep Renata alive? After all, it's her bone marrow that is vital to Renata's health."

Fletcher thought for a short moment. "That," she said, "is actually a very good question. No, I don't think Valerie has any more obligation to keep Renata alive now than she did when she came to me last March. All she has is the obligation *not to kill* Renata."

Rivers seemed genuinely puzzled. "What's the difference?"

"It's the difference between acceding to transoption and demanding abortion. It's the difference between expelling a fetus and killing it. It's the difference . . ." she searched for the concept, "between abandonment and infanticide. One allows the possibility of rescue. The other takes an active hand in making rescue impossible. That is the difference between transoption and abortion." Fletcher shook her head. "No. If I believed that Valerie was under some sort of obligation to care for Renata, I would never have performed the transoption. There are some rights that you must recognize whether you approve of them or not. A woman has a right at any point to abandon her child. Anything less would be slavery. She has no right, though, to kill that child. And I have every right to take in an abandoned child of any age."

"We'll be right back," Rivers said to the camera. When the

red light flicked off, he turned to Fletcher and smiled. "Well done. If I could have you move down one seat, we'll get into a discussion with Ms. Burke—"

"Sorry." Evelyn stood, removing her microphone to lay it on the chair. "I made my point. I'm not going to endure their abuse."

"Why not? I mean, they aren't here to abuse you. They just want their points of view aired, too."

"Then air them. You don't need me for that. Theirs are the same viewpoints that have been aired for centuries: slavery for women or death for infants. Have fun." She stepped off the risers. A voice over the loudspeaker demanded to know what was going on.

Rivers sat back in his chair. "People might draw the wrong inference if you're not here after the commercials."

She turned to face him. "If my words didn't convince them of anything, neither would my forbearance."

Rivers raised a hand in defeat. "Have a nice day."

The door to Terry Johnson's office swung open. Dr. Fletcher stood there, staring at the cramped enclosure. Her eyes narrowed, focusing in on Terry behind the small gray military-surplus desk.

"Don't you ever put me on one of those things again," she said.

He looked at her with a merry expression. "You were great," he said. "A few more of those and you'll have the press in your pocket."

"I'm a doctor. I have to keep my pockets clean."

"It's the doctor part we've got to worry about." He pulled a small sheaf of papers from under a coffee cup. "BMQA." He pronounced it *Bumqua*.

She took the pages from him and looked them over. Her eyes revealed the pain the words caused.

"It's only a temporary suspension," he said.

Fletcher reached inside her jacket for her pack of Defiants. "Effectively permanent if they sit on their duffs and do nothing else. I could have been convicted of malpractice and manslaughter, and they'd take years to suspend me. Get a little publicity, though, and *pow*."

Terry moved quickly with the table lighter to strike up a flame for her. She took a long drag on the cigarette without even a thanks for the light. Her gaze fixed upon some distant vista outside his window, even though the view stopped four feet across at the masonry of another drab Long Beach building.

Johnson filled the silent void. "Nurse Dyer was flat out fired as well as having her credentials pulled."

"She told me she's moving back to San Francisco." The cigarette glowed orange at her fingertips. "I guess I'm available for lecture tours."

"Don't let it get you down. If we can win the trial, we can file—"

"I can't bother thinking that far ahead. I've got to arrange something for Renata." She blew a cloud of smoke off to the side. "Can I use your phone?"

"Sure."

She called the hospital and paged their best pediatrician, who, though he was not a favorite of Dr. Lawrence's, carried considerable clout. He agreed to take over Renata's case, even giving Fletcher a brief rundown on her current condition.

"Look, Lon," she said. "All I have left is my personal pager. I'm sure Lawrence's shut my hospital one down. If her stem cells kick in or if her condition declines, let me know right away."

"In the same breath I'm telling the Chandlers," said a resonant voice on the other end.

"A breath sooner," she said.

"Sure, Ev. Sure. I'm sorry about Bum—"

"Forget it," she said. "Just take care of Renata. So long."

She gently replaced the receiver in its tray. "DuQuette's a good doctor," she muttered. "She'll be all right."

"How about you?" Johnson stared at her as she flipped idly through the BMQA decision.

"It's less than thirty years of my life. I figure I've got thirty more." She stubbed the half-smoked cigarette until it disintegrated into a crumbled pile of burst paper and dark shreds of tobacco. "Let's finish off this trial so I can decide on my career change."

XVII

The next few days consisted of a numbing series of interviews with newspaper and magazine reporters, television talk-show hosts, and radio call-in shows. Fletcher discussed transoption with a growing fervor nurtured by her sudden fall from medical respectability.

"I'm free," she told one interviewer in her living room, "to discuss transoption without fear of losing my medical credentials. They're gone. I can step on all the toes I want."

The reporter—a science correspondent for a midwestern newspaper—behaved differently from most of the people who had interviewed Fletcher. The majority were either openly hostile, surreptitiously hostile, or confused about just what she was trying to prove. The rest performed their jobs with a straightforward, emotionless technique that caused her to wonder whether they held any personal beliefs whatsoever.

This one, though—Lester Joseph Neilson from the Iowa *New Dealer*—was a small, tough-looking man in his forties. He appeared to have been built more for welterweight wrestling than for pounding a word processor. He watched her with iron-gray eyes under graying close-cropped hair, chewing on the end of his pencil between scrawls on a dog-eared notepad.

"You dealt with death continuously," he asked her with a voice like gravel in a gearbox. "Why should one more abortion have bothered you?"

He probed too deeply, she thought, reached too closely to truths she could not yet reveal. "I realized that abortion had to come to an end," she said. "That somebody had to be the first to find another way. No one else had taken the risk to use the new surgical advances available, so I did. It could have been anyone."

"Anyone with a conscience," Neilson muttered, making notes. "Do you feel morally superior to the doctors who didn't?"

"The first person to jump into a fire would be petty to chide others for not going ahead of her."

"And if they don't follow?"

"Only the hindsight allowed by history will determine whether they behaved with cowardly sloth or wise restraint."

Neilson flipped through his notes. "Good stuff, Dr. Fletcher."

"There's no need for the 'Doctor' part anymore."

He smiled. "Let's keep it there just in case." He mused silently for a moment, then asked, "What if the medical establishment finds it wise to restrain themselves permanently? What if research into transoption is banned outright?"

She smiled as she took a sip of coffee from her pale blue cup. "This isn't the only country in the world. And only natural laws last forever. Somewhere, sometime, someone else will pick up the scalpel and decide to save a life rather than end one."

"How do you feel," he asked gingerly, "about all the babies you aborted up till Renata?"

The cup paused halfway to her lips. Her mind raced furiously, then, calmly, she said, "Catholics once believed that the souls of unbaptized babies dwelt in limbo, awaiting Judgment Day. That's how they exist . . . in my mind. In limbo, waiting for the atonement of sins. Others', not theirs."

Neilson tapped the pencil against his teeth. "Pretty mystical stuff. Let's talk about your personal Judgment Day. Your opponents have a medical expert going on the stand tomorrow. What do you feel about such testimony?"

Setting the coffee cup down, she said, "Without making any comments on the course of the trial, I can only say that I will be very interested in this person's opinions. I'll value his or her insight. A doctor's viewpoint has yet to be heard."

Evelyn stared in shock at the man called to testify.

Dr. Ian Brunner, sworn in, sat in the witness box. Evelyn marveled at the way he had changed. He was still a tall man, with long-fingered, strong hands. The rebel in him, though, was gone. With a receding line of dark brown hair and glasses through which cool eyes gazed, he seemed every bit the image of the dedicated man of science. He wore a somber gray suit with a small gold lapel pin in the shape of a caduceus. When he spoke, his voice filled the courtroom with a Los Angeles–softened version of crisp New England diction. An affectation, she realized, that he must have cultivated over the years.

He gazed at her without emotion. It was another man who sat in the witness stand. Not the Ian she had hurt with her choice so many years ago. Had she done this to him? His face revealed nothing. *Would he wait this long for his revenge?*

Ron Czernek stepped forward, flashing a feral grin at Johnson. *Just try badgering this one*, he thought. "Please state your name."

"Ian Wilson Brunner, the Third." His hands, fingers intertwined, rested comfortably in front of him.

Terry stood to say, "The defense stipulates that Dr. Brunner is qualified as an expert in medical ethics."

Czernek smiled, then asked Dr. Brunner, "Are you familiar with the work of Ms. Evelyn Fletcher, formerly a doctor at Bayside University Medical Center?"

"I am familiar with Dr. Fletcher's work through what I have read in the newspapers, from speaking to colleagues, and from reviewing her proposals as an outside consultant, yes."

"Are you sure you should call her 'doctor'?"

"Objection!" Johnson said loudly. "Permission to approach the bench."

Judge Lyang motioned him forward. Czernek followed.

"I move for a mistrial," Johnson whispered. "Informing the jury that BMQA pulled her credentials is incredibly prejudi—"

"I said no such thing," Czernek countered swiftly.

"You were lucky," Lyang said softly to Czernek, "that he cut you off when he did, or I would have had grounds to declare a mistrial. Keep calling her 'doctor.' They've suspended her privileges, they can't revoke her degree."

Czernek nodded silently, turning back to the witness stand. Johnson smiled at Fletcher as he sat between her and Karen.

"Strike the last question from the record," Lyang said. "And proceed."

"Speaking as an expert in medical ethics," Czernek resumed, "did *Doctor* Fletcher behave ethically in transferring a fetus from the uterus of Valerie Dalton to the uterus of Karen Chandler?"

"I would have to say no."

Evelyn gazed at him with barely veiled misery. His words were those of an objective expert, but she knew that after so many years he still had not forgiven her.

"Why is that?" Czernek asked.

"What Dr. Fletcher has done is to move into a new medical realm that is so controversial, so loaded with emotion on both sides of the issue, that anyone working legitimately in the field—people with reputations to protect—would never risk their professional lives in something so dangerous not only to the fetus but to both women as well."

"Both women?" Czernek said, turning toward the jury. "The defense has maintained that Valerie Dalton received an ordinary abortion and suffered no additional risk."

"Well . . ." Dr. Brunner unclasped his hands and began using them for emphasis. He spoke at a slow, professorial pace.

"As I understand her technique, the suction device she used had been modified to remove the fetus intact, chorionic membrane and all. To do that without damaging the tissues would require a tube nearly an inch and a half in diameter." He looked at the female jurors. "Imagine inserting that past the cervix and you can see the added opportunity for trauma the procedure entails. To me, that qualifies as battery."

The doctor shook his head. "And the risk to Karen Chandler is unconscionable. She may have volunteered, even pleaded, for such an operation to get pregnant, but she had no idea that a transoption had never been performed before, that there was no basis in animal research, no peer review, no approval by any committee of ethics. Nothing. Just one doctor saying, 'What the hell, let's give it a try.'"

Karen watched the jury during Dr. Brunner's interrogation. They all listened with rapt attention, many taking notes. They would give his testimony great weight. She glanced over at Terry, who took notes at a furious pace, his head hunched over the yellow pad. Dr. Fletcher seemed calm, almost detached. *Her part*, Karen thought, *is over. But we still have to fight for Renata.* She clasped David's hand tightly and gazed up at Dr. Brunner.

Czernek stroked at his beard. "Dr. Brunner, your work in nonsurgical ovum transfer has given you a great deal of insight into alternative forms of pregnancy. Can you tell the court what ethical or medical value transoption has?"

"It has very little, I'm afraid. As a novelty, it has some value regarding microsurgical technique, but that is no reason to risk the health and reproductive potential of two women for the sake of doing something new simply because it is new." The spectacled man gestured as he spoke to the jury. "It would be like taking two people with healthy hearts and switching them in transplant operations. Well, you might say, they both got what they wanted—a healthy heart—but the surgical risk is incredible compared to the alternative of just leaving them alone." He was pleased with the analogy.

A few of the jurors smiled, won over by the man's quiet charm. Czernek felt the tide turning in his favor again.

"And what is the ethical status," he said, "of novelty operations performed on human subjects?"

Brunner spoke with emphatic sincerity. "Completely immoral. What Dr. Fletcher did was outrageous. She ignored every procedure designed to safeguard patients and protect the integrity of the hospital—"

"I object!" Johnson shot to his feet, missile-like. "Dr. Fletcher endlessly requested peer review from a slothful bureaucracy more concerned with avoiding litigation than with saving human li—"

A gavel bang silenced him.

"You'll have your chance to grandstand, Mr. Johnson." Lyang turned to Dr. Brunner. "Please explain to the jury how she ignored procedures."

Brunner nodded. "Certainly. I understand that though she requested an ethics committee to approve the concept of such an operation years before and then again months before, she proceeded before any final decision had been made, thereby effectively evading the extremely important medical process of review and approval."

Evelyn glared at him from her seat, fuming. She grasped a pencil with both hands, flexing at it. Terry patted her hand gently. "I'll take care of him on the cross," he whispered. He looked over his shoulder at the spectators to see Jane Burke and Avery Decker sitting nearly side by side. They both seemed to be having a good time. *They should sell popcorn at these things,* he thought.

"Dr. Brunner . . ." Ron looked his quizzical best as he framed his question. "Does transoption totally solve the problem of abortion, as Dr. Fletcher implies? Is it the moral solution to abortion that the world has been searching for?"

Brunner mulled over the question for a moment. The jurors leaned forward as if to hear the answer a few microseconds sooner.

"In some very few, rare cases, it might be an answer. It is not the answer to infertility, because virtually any problem a woman has in that department can be handled by nonsurgical ovum transfer, a highly advanced, medically approved, and *ethical* treatment. There you have professional ovum donors inseminated by the husband's own sperm. We can take that ovum and determine its sex, examine its chromosomes for genetic flaws, use a library of what we call probes to check it for proclivities toward over *two thousand* different diseases, and implant it into the recipient mother without any complicated, dangerous surgical techniques. It fastens itself to the uterine wall naturally, and grows there naturally. And if the recipient wants a few extra eggs set aside just in case, the fertilized ova can be frozen cryogenically and stored. They'll be viable for up to ten thousand years."

Fletcher's fingers snapped the pencil in two. She looked around her as if awakening from a dream.

"With transoption," Brunner continued, "a woman whose, shall we say, *significant other* you know nothing about gives you an embryo she doesn't want. It's too far along in its development to use a lot of the probes and hence is an unknown quantity. Why use it when women today demand quality pregnancies?" He looked at Fletcher as if he had been delivering a lecture to her. His earnest desire that she understand him showed in the eyes that dwelt behind his glasses.

"And," Czernek asked quietly, "would transoption help the woman who seeks to terminate her pregnancy?"

The doctor shifted about in his seat as if wrestling with the question. "Most women," he said, "do not think about the consequences of an abortion. Most women who get abortions are young, late teens, early twenties. They want to end their pregnancies and get on with their lives. Many abortions are the result of a liaison the woman would prefer to expunge completely, right down to the product of that relationship. To insist that such a woman undergo an operation that has just as much—if not more—risk as an abortion does of damaging her reproductive potential, simply to save an eight-week-old embryo that lacks a full bundle of human rights, is asking too much of most women and of the medical profession."

"So," Czernek said, "transoption is no real cure for the problem of abortion."

"No, it is not."

"Thank you, Dr. Brunner. I believe I have no further questions." Czernek turned to send a challenging glance at Johnson.

Terry looked down at his notes, thinking. There wasn't much he could nail the doctor on, but he decided to try. "The defense wishes to cross-examine, Your Honor."

Judge Lyang made a gesture to proceed.

He approached the witness stand slowly, assembling his thoughts and developing a tactic for handling the doctor. It was obvious that the jury was impressed with the man, so an outright assault would be useless.

"Dr. Brunner, you are a gynecologist and an obstetrician, the same as Dr. Fletcher, correct?"

"Yes."

"So you see a lot of pregnant women every day. And women who want to be pregnant, and women who *don't* want to be. Correct?"

"That is correct." Dr. Brunner, half expecting theatrics, grew calmer at Johnson's mellow pace. He sat back in the chair, adjusted his glasses, and set his arms on the rests.

"Have you ever encountered a woman who wanted an abortion but wished she could do something other than kill her unborn child? I use the word 'kill' as a concerned, uninformed pregnant person might."

Brunner nodded. "I have had several women come to me with such a request. One sees it in women in their late twenties or so. Something happens to them around the age of twenty-seven that makes an abortion a very traumatic experience. Eighteen-year-olds barely notice; they use abortion almost as a form of contraception. In fact, when the abortifacient RU 486 becomes more readily available, morning-after contraception will put the whole question of surgical abortions to rest once—"

"Please just answer my question, Dr. Brunner. Are there women who would prefer to have their pregnancies terminated in such a way as to avoid harming the fetus?"

"Yes, there are. Generally older women who sense their biological clocks ticking away and fear they're missing what might be their last chance at motherhood."

"And," Johnson asked, pacing between the witness stand and the jury box, "have you seen women who are not able to become pregnant by any means, including ovum transfers?"

"Yes, even though such a woman is rare. We can take a woman who has no ovaries at all, implant a donor egg, and bring her to term using supplemental hormones until the fetus takes over producing them."

"So there are women who might benefit from a transopted fetus?"

Brunner sighed, shifting in the chair. "I don't dispute that there might be someone, *somewhere*, who would benefit from transoption. It is clear, *in retrospect*, that Mrs. Chandler benefited from the procedure. But this is an extremely rare case that does not justify such a risky, unresearched, unapproved operation."

"Could it be," Terry said evenly, "that it is unresearched and unapproved because the medical establishment finds abortion to be easy and lucrative compared to making any effort to save the life of a tiny human being?"

The surgeon hesitated for a moment, frustrated that the whole question of fetus rights kept bubbling up like gas in a swamp. "When you say 'tiny human being,' you're packing a lot of emotion into three simple words. Deciding when a fetus becomes a human being with full human rights is one of the hard questions of medicine. Is a full-term baby human at birth? Only a cynic would deny that. What about five minutes before birth? If birth confers humanity, abortion should be legal all the way up to that point. It is not, of course, and the standard is that abortion is inadvisable after the second trimester. But where in the second trimester? Is a fetus human at twenty-six weeks but not at twenty-five? Is it human at one thousand grams' weight but not at nine hundred ninety-nine?"

"Thank you, Doctor, for—"

"May I finish? I think this illustrates Dr. Fletcher's fallacy."

Johnson began to speak, glanced at Judge Lyang and the jury, and then nodded. "Be my guest," he said, trying to mask his trepidation.

"These line-drawing arguments are used with astounding effectiveness by the pro-life groups. Some people, such as Mr. Decker—and I presume, Dr. Fletcher—reach back as far as the point of conception to declare that *that* is when a human being with full human rights is created. I thought so, too, at one time. But the more you discover about fertility, the more trouble you have finding a distinct point of change. Conception takes place over several hours. Do an egg and a sperm become a human being at the point that the sperm fuses to the outer membrane of the egg? When the egg finally admits the sperm that has survived its immunological attack? When their respective DNA intermingle? When mitosis begins? When the blastocyst nestles in the uterine lining? When?

"Life is a continuum, stretching ever backward and forward through time. You can't take a certain arbitrary point and say, 'Humanity begins here,' as if it hadn't been present before." Brunner pinched thumb and forefinger together. "To say, though, that a blastocyst smaller than the human eye can see is a human being with as many rights as an adult is like saying a one-year-old should be able to vote. Rights accrue in increments over time, and the prevailing consensus is that the right to life begins at some point when *most* fetuses could *generally* be expected to survive outside the womb."

He turned from the jurors to gaze directly at Fletcher with sympathy growing in his eyes. "Dr. Fletcher's concern for unviable fetuses is touching but not worth the risk to the adult women involved. It certainly merits no serious effort to research. If she values human life so, she should have worked exclusively in the fields of fertility and contraception—as I have—instead of trying to find loopholes and rationales for abortion. She was wrong even to pursue such a goal."

Evelyn felt the crush of his words as she did three decades ago. His hurt had not diminished. He had sublimated his pain into his work as she had buried her regrets in hers.

Salvage what you can, Johnson mused during the brief silence, then said, "You admit, though, that transoption *did* help Karen Chandler in this instance—a woman who was unable to become pregnant by any current means."

"She seemed to have exhausted all the legitimate methods. Was pregnancy so important to her, though, that she overlooked adoption agencies?"

"That is not at issue here."

"Isn't it?" Brunner looked around the courtroom. "There are tens of thousands of unwanted children languishing in orphanages and state facilities—"

"At least," Johnson said, "they are alive to languish. Or would it have been better for *them* to have died before birth?" Before Brunner could reply, he sharply said, "No further questions, Your Honor."

XVIII

The trial became an official media circus with the establishment of a reporters' outpost in a room at the Torrance courthouse. Permanently staffed every day with gofers and assistants, well provided with food and every imaginable soft drink, it served as the central gathering point for newspaper, magazine, and TV reporters. It was also on the same floor of the building as the cafeteria.

"Your tax dollars at play," Fletcher muttered as she and the others pressed past the crowded doorway, surrounded by strobes, floodlights, microphone-wielding hands, and strained faces. They listened intently to Dr. Brunner's answer to a question.

Brunner gestured toward the rear doors. "Protesters on both sides aren't squabbling over human rights. They're arguing over questions of funding. Should the *government* fund abortions or not? A lot of your so-called pro-life people are more concerned with the fact that tax dollars are being used to fund large numbers of abortions than they are with the question of human rights *per se.* Conversely, many pro-choice people are more concerned with sustaining abortion subsidies than they are with the rights of women. If transoption were available, it wouldn't end the controversy. You'd see a very different landscape of debate if federal money were *not* involved, but it *is.* Abortion in and of itself does not affect enough people long enough to produce the social outcry that would lead to"—his hands made motions as if he were trying to fashion a planet in his palms—"to *harnessing* the financial resources necessary to research this properly."

"Doesn't public outcry lead to reforms?" asked one reporter in the rear.

Brunner looked over the crowd at her. "It's a lot easier," he said, "to fire bomb a building or take a day off from your job to march in protest of this or that than it is to work for months or years to shake loose enough money to fund a solution. The former makes for flashier news coverage. The latter can actually improve the human condition."

Terry held the floor among another clot of newshounds, his hair glistening under the lights.

"We're very confident," he said. "Dr. Brunner was an excellent expert witness, and I think his testimony can only help our case. And now we'd like to eat."

Members of the press were considerate enough to leave the cafeteria as a haven for the litigants. To ensure such consideration, a pair of sheriff's deputies stood at the doorway. The newshawk cluster disintegrated like a cell membrane to allow its nucleus to push through the entrance.

Karen and David shared a tray. Neither bought much. Just half sandwiches and half-pints of milk. Evelyn picked up two cups of coffee, a bearclaw, an RC cola, and a turkey sandwich.

Terry eyed her tray as he arrived with his. "Caffeine and sugar. That would completely unhinge my brain."

"The protein and tryptophan in the turkey make up for it," she said deadpan. "Besides"—she scanned his tray—"I don't think I'd last long on tomato soup and crackers."

He smiled, setting the tray down next to hers. "Force of habit from law school. I was one of three who worked our way through without scholarships or loans."

"It must have been hard work," Karen said.

Johnson shrugged. "It wasn't that prestigious a school." He unconsciously added some catsup to the tomato soup, then crumbled in the crackers. "I was able to graduate before malnutrition set in." After a few sips, he pointed his spoon at Fletcher.

"You. When Czernek's through with his side, I'm—"

The sharp, insistent sound of Fletcher's Metagram receiver chirped through the cafeteria. Her hand jammed into her jacket pocket to silence it, withdrawing it in the same motion. She had it clipped to her pack of cigarettes. The LCD display on the pager held a message from Dr. DuQuette.

STILL NO STEM CELL ACTIVITY.

She pressed the advance button to display the next line.

NEARING ABSOLUTE NEUTROPENIA.

Evelyn took in the news without emotion. It meant that Renata was nearing the total loss of any ability whatsoever to fight off infection. Anything could attack her now—even the sort of usually benign bacteria that floated around on dust motes and lurked on nearly every common surface. Were it not for the isolation chamber she lived in continuously, even the most ordinary and unlikely minor infection could invade and overrun her, bringing death within hours or minutes. She depressed the key one more time.

CALL ME ASAP. LON.—

"Would you excuse me?" she asked the group. "I've got to return this call."

"How is she?" David asked.

"Dr. DuQuette just has some questions," Fletcher replied in a casual tone. She pushed the chair out to rise. "Be right back."

She found a booth and called DuQuette's office. His tenor voice—normally cheerful, currently tight with concern—answered. "DuQuette."

217

"Evelyn," she said. "What's her white?" DuQuette read her the figures on Renata's white blood cell count. It was close enough to zero to be inconsequential. "All right," she said in a clipped tone. "Give her a few more hours with a count every hour. If you see any activity at all, call me. If you don't, call me."

"Right." He rang off hurriedly.

She returned the receiver to its cradle. Walking back to the table, she announced that she was stepping out for a smoke.

"How's Renata?" This time Karen asked. Her eyes held a fatal concern.

"She's steady. Babies have a will to survive." Fletcher laid a gentle hand on Karen's shoulder. "It's only grown-ups that can choose to give up. Hang in there." She clasped David's shoulder for good measure. Her gaze met Johnson's. She signaled him to follow and turned away.

Johnson finished his soup in a few easy spoons and stood. "I want to review some testimony with Dr. Fletcher. You two take it easy."

The courtyard was blissfully free of reporters. A cool sea breeze wafted through the building while patches of high clouds scudded overhead. He saw Fletcher lighting up and joined her.

"How is she really?" he asked.

"In trouble." She took a short, nervous drag. "I should be there."

"DuQuette's good, you said."

She threw the cigarette to the ground half-smoked. Her shoe rammed down to crush out its flame. "Sure. But if she dies, I'll never know if I'd have been able to save her. I might have known one extra protocol, seen one additional symptom, recognized some obscure infection." Her eyes turned toward the clouds.

Johnson's watch chimed. He reached over to silence it. "Time to head back."

She put an arm across his shoulders with weary friendliness.

"When Czernek rests his case, what have you got in store for Karen?"

"I've decided not to put Karen on. I got the most I could out of her during my cross-exam. I want you to go up."

Her arm dropped. "What?"

Johnson grinned.

XIX

Judge Lyang entered the courtroom and took her place behind the bench. She rapped the gavel lightly once.

"Court will come to order. I have been notified by counsel for the plaintiff that they have rested their case." She looked at Czernek and Dalton as if in confirmation. She nodded to them with a slight turn of her head, then shifted her attention to Johnson, Fletcher, and the Chandlers.

"The defense may now present its case. Mr. Johnson?"

Johnson rose. "The defense has only one witness," he said. "Dr. Evelyn Fletcher."

The Chandlers turned toward each other in shock and surprise, then stared back at Johnson. Cameras swiveled about for reactions. The spectators murmured among themselves or into pocket recorders.

Before she could comment, Johnson faced the judge to say, "Your Honor, I could present the Chandlers to argue that theirs would be the preferred home for Renata." He turned toward the jurors. "They are already paying for her medical care and are in all other ways serving as her parents. I think, though"—he approached the jury box slowly, somberly— "that the question of custody in this case does not rest so much with the fitness of the parents as it does with the nature of the operation and the explicit agreements involved. Dr. Fletcher, as a co-defendant in this case, is as much an interested party as the parents. And it is my contention that transoption is implicitly on trial here today via the question of the status of Exhibit A—the contract Valerie Dalton signed. If the contract is found to be fradulently induced, then Renata is rightfully the daughter of Valerie Dalton and Ron Czernek." He leaned on the bar separating him from the six jurors. "If, however, the contract is determined to be legitimate, then transoption will be recognized as a moral, life-saving alternative to abortion, and Karen and David Chandler would be the rightful parents of Baby Renata."

He turned to look up at Lyang. She raised one eyebrow as if to say it was his case and he could blow it however he wanted. "Counsel is free to proceed," she said, sitting back in her black vinyl chair.

Dr. Fletcher ascended to the witness stand and was sworn in. Valerie Dalton stared impassively into the woman's eyes as they chanced to gaze down at her. She saw no anger, even though her actions had cost Dr. Fletcher her career. Valerie lowered her gaze to the papers on her part of the table. Her fingers twined in a tight, anxious double fist.

"Dr. Fletcher," Johnson asked after she had been sworn in, "what are your qualifications to be an expert witness in medical ethics?"

The spectators watched in silent amazement.

Czernek jumped to his feet. "While we stipulate that she is qualified, we object to her testimony as utterly biased!"

Johnson turned toward the judge. "Your Honor, Dr. Fletcher's testimony as an expert in medical ethics is crucial to determining her intent."

"On that point you may question," Lyang said in a cautioning tone. "Proceed."

"Thank you, Your Honor." Johnson focused his attention on Fletcher, who sat in the witness box as straight and unwavering as a statue. "Dr. Fletcher, this court has heard a lot about transoption but very little about how it actually works. Could you explain to the jury just what this medical procedure is?"

Fletcher turned to the jurors. Her voice was even, her delivery flat and pedagogical. "The first half of a transoption is similar to a suction abortion. The abortion would be accomplished by dilating the cervix of the pregnant woman, inserting a tube into the uterus, and suctioning the fetus out. The big difference in transoption is that I used a fiberoptic scope to locate the fetus and a tube large enough to capture the entire fetus without damage to the chorionic membrane."

"What happens to the fetus in a normal suction abortion?" Johnson asked.

"Generally, the chorionic membrane is ruptured; delicate parts such as arms and legs sometimes tear away. In the rare cases where the fetus is suctioned out intact, it doesn't survive long in the holding tank."

"What happens in the holding tank of your transoption machine?"

"The low power suction delivers the fetus to a holding tank consisting of Ham's F-10 and buminate in a solution of. . . ."

Valerie listened to Fletcher's description of the operation. Vivid memories of that evening churned within her. She remembered the eerie glow from the machine, the cryptic dialogue between Fletcher and her nurse, the spot on the ceiling that held her attention.

Most of all, though, she remembered the searing pain. The cramps for days afterward. The bright red blood on the tube, the gloves, the sheets. Blood everywhere, her baby gone. For months she fought to suppress the feeling that what she did was wrong. She eventually succeeded. Then to discover that her baby still lived—that brought a pain greater than any physical agony imaginable.

She reached out to touch Ron's hand. She almost recoiled at the feverish heat. It held down a pad while his other hand wrote out extensive notes. She wondered if he was remembering that night or if his mind was racing over possible tactics and scenarios.

"And why," she heard Johnson ask, "did you choose that

moment in time and these two women to attempt such an operation?"

Fletcher sighed. "I'd been arguing for the opportunity for years. To me, the ethical separation between donor and recipient was clear. The donor was *not* having the pregnancy terminated simply to provide the fetus; she wanted an abortion. It was certainly not my intention to deprive Ms. Dalton of her child. She made that choice. And the precedent of using aborted fetuses in experiments was already established." Her speech quickened as the anger and frustration of years surfaced. She looked around the room, her gaze slowly fixing on Dr. Brunner. "Sure, researchers could find ways to use the parts of a fetus—pancreas, liver, brain tissue, and probably a lot more I haven't read about—but to try to *save* the fetus, try to give it another chance at survival, I—" She stopped to look at Johnson. "What did you ask?" Her eyes glistened, wet.

"Why did you pick Ms. Dalton and Mrs. Chandler for—"

Fletcher nodded. "Because there was Karen, unable to conceive in any normal way, blowing thousands of dollars with each try and her body going crazy with hormones to match cycles, and in walked Valerie, who wanted to destroy a perfectly healthy baby and—"

She paused, realizing that an anger had arisen. She took a calming breath, then looked at the jurors. The men stared at her with poorly disguised curiosity. The women watched her with an understanding that may or may not have been sympathetic.

Johnson stepped over to her. "Let me ask you this," he said gently. "Why didn't you announce this attempt to the hospital administration?"

"Because by then I had realized that every step forward in human rights is always opposed by those who gain privileges from the status quo."

Czernek shot to his feet. "Objection! This case is not a civil rights battle; it is a custody dispute, and such pronouncements from Dr. Fletcher are irrelevant to the issues raised here."

Johnson approached the bench. "Your Honor, this is clearly a case of rights. Both Ms. Dalton and Mrs. Chandler are claiming a right to be Renata's mother. Dr. Fletcher is defending her right to perform transoptions. I suggest that human rights are quite germane to the question of custody rights."

Judge Lyang mulled over the problem. "Overruled," she said quietly, leaning back in her chair to listen.

Johnson smiled at her, then turned to Fletcher. "Please elaborate on your remark."

"I mean that just as the abolition of slavery was opposed by slave owners and the rights of women were opposed by men in power, so the rights of unborn children are opposed—even by those who claim to defend them. And their opposition—which seems so logical to them right now—will be viewed by history as the outrageous ravings of vested interests."

She sat up straighter in the wooden chair, looking from the jurors to Jane Burke, seated in the second row of the spectator area. "I suggest, for instance, that Jane Burke overcome her hostility toward sex in order to examine history a bit more carefully. Contraception—invented, as she said, by men for their beasts of burden—was used *secretly* by women *in defiance* of their male oppressors. It was woman's first major victory in reproductive rights."

Burke shook her head pitifully, smiling the sort of disappointed smile that told everyone watching that the poor doctor was obviously gravely in error. She looked down at her notepad to jot down another idea for an article.

"Adoption," Fletcher continued, "also began as a sexist male tool. It allowed a nobleman to acquire a male heir to inherit his land and fortune. It permitted a man to pretend that he had a son when in fact the boy bore no genetic relation to him. Girls weren't adopted. Infanticide was acceptable for eliminating them and still is in parts of the world. Yet because of the sexist invention of adoption, a few young boys were spared from early death or lives of poverty. Over the years, the origins of adoption were forgotten by most, until today people adopt children of both sexes and all races for reasons of love, not primogeniture. And because of that, infanticide is now considered a foul crime in societies that revere human life and human rights. The invention of adoption did nothing to erode *women's* rights; it extended the concept of human rights to children. I am extending it to embryos."

A few seats down from Burke, Avery Decker and James Rosen sat together. Decker watched the feminist out of the corner of his eye, a half-victorious smirk curling at his lips.

Rosen, though, focused all his attention on Fletcher. The younger man had never heard such an argument before. He concentrated on her words to the point of waving away a poke in the ribs from Decker.

Johnson put his hands in his pockets to stroll around the floor in a meditative posture. "Why draw the analogy between transoption and adoption? One is a surgical technique, the other a legal procedure."

Fletcher's hands gripped the ends of the armrests. "Transoption is *prenatal adoption*, pure and simple. A woman adopts an unwanted fetus and takes from another woman the burden of bringing it to term. There can be no moral objection to its use. It protects a woman's right to terminate a pregnancy while protecting a defenseless human's right to life." She turned in the chair to stare straight at the women in the jury. "Jane Burke drew the analogy between a fetus and a houseguest. Whether initially invited in, as in the case of a woman who chooses to have sex without using contraceptives, or whether a trespasser, as in the case of failed contraception or rape, the woman has the ultimate say in whether the guest may stay or must go."

She raised a finger in emphasis. "It's immoral to forbid that. Everyone has the right to expel or evict an unwanted guest from her home. But some neglect to take the argument to its reasonable conclusion—that nobody has the right to evict a houseguest by resorting to *murder*. A woman has a right to expel a fetus, not to kill it."

She glanced at Burke for a moment. The woman shook her

head again. She clearly rejected the implication. Fletcher pounded her fist on the chair arm. "I could have just refused to perform abortions and fought to keep women enslaved. Instead, I searched for years to find a way to protect our rights. Transoption is the method you should welcome, not reject!"

Judge Lyang tapped her gavel lightly. "Counsel will instruct the witness to avoid addressing the spectators."

"Sorry, Your Honor," Fletcher said quickly. "I thought I was addressing Jane Burke's testimony."

Lyang smiled in a pleasantly sardonic manner. "Continue."

Johnson nodded thanks toward the judge. *Doing great, Doc. Just keep the logic and the passion going together.* "In his testimony," he said, "Pastor Decker made it sound as if transoption were a crime against man, woman, *and* God. Did your decision to perform the transoption take account of religious considerations?"

Fletcher addressed the jury, this time concentrating on the older men. "Mr. Decker claims to have personal knowledge of what God does or doesn't want. I don't buy that. If God exists at all, he wouldn't work through such scatterbrained, fuzzy thinkers. Decker and others have declared that transoption is an offense to God because it puts fetuses in jeopardy. I will grant that it is a dangerous operation. There *is* a high risk of morbidity."

Decker nodded in triumph, poking Rosen lightly in the ribs. Rosen shifted over to the far side of his seat, leaning on the armrest to listen intently.

"But remember our source," she continued. "Victims of abortion." She looked from one juror to another. "Suppose you found a baby that had been abandoned, thrown out of its home. It has no way to take care of itself. It will die; the homeowner knew that when she evicted it. Yet you know of a home where the child would be welcome. Wouldn't you take the child there? Is that not in fact a most Christian thing to do?" She glared at Decker. "Would the infant Moses not have died if Pharaoh's daughter hadn't taken him in?" She faced the jury once more, her voice rising. "Isn't such a rescue in fact a most *humane* act? Let's go further and ask, what if the homeowner had asked *you* to take that child out of the house and abandon it to die? Or even ordered you to kill it? What would *you* do?"

Fletcher took a deep, trembling breath.

"I'll tell you what *I* did. I found a new home for Renata. Because I knew that if I didn't save that baby, no one else would. And that is what Mr. Decker and his cronies conveniently overlook: That despite transoption's risk, it *saved a child's life.* It can save the lives of millions more." She threw the pastor a killing glare. "If he is so concerned with saving lives and souls, he should be transoption's most fervent supporter. He should be rescuing all the abortuses he can. I wonder if he really wants to help women or simply control them."

Decker glowered at her with cold anger. James Rosen stared at her in loose-jawed shock, a new vista of possibilities opening up before him. He had read many times of epiphany but had never felt the surge of emotion that accompanied such a clarity of revelation. His heart raced as he saw not just an isolated operation but a world transformed. Where once the scattered bodies of infants lay, there rose adoption centers. Where clinics now filled their trash bins with dead preborns, there could arise a new choice for women, a new chance for the preborn.

A poke from Decker shattered his vision.

"Sure," the pastor whispered with acid sarcasm. "I can just see us with our hands up feminist cunt—"

"*Shut up.*" Rosen stood without looking at Decker and moved to a seat five rows back. He sat, visibly shaken, and backhanded the tears from his cheeks.

Fletcher saw the exchange. She looked Rosen in the eye.

"Why," Johnson asked, "did you take Valerie Dalton's fetus? Was it your intent to harm her in any way?"

"She didn't want her fetus. I removed it. She didn't ask that anything special be done with it after its removal. At that point, her contract waived any claim to what became of the fetus. I determined that it was immoral and unethical to kill that fetus or merely let it die, so I transopted it into a willing recipient. What I have done is neither criminal nor immoral. The AMA and the state of California had granted me the power to commit murder and call it abortion. I refused to exercise that power. Like the woodsman in the tale of Snow White, I pretended to commit the act for the queen while secretly permitting the child to live. I found a way to eliminate the moral dilemma of pregnancy termination.

"For you cannot make people behave morally by passing a law or blowing up a building. But you *can* make a moral choice technologically possible. You can make it fashionable, acceptable. You can make it as cost-effective as the immoral choice. You can make it marketable, easily available. And then I guarantee that people will make the right choice *if you just leave them alone.*

"All that I have done with my life is on trial here, so my life itself is on trial. Why? Because a bit of tissue was legally abandoned by Valerie Dalton. I saw in it a human quality that she and the state chose not to acknowledge. I gave that tissue to someone who saw in it the same quality I did and wished to nurture it. Within her body, it grew into the baby named Renata. She is a distinct, individual human being, not chattel over which we can squabble about ownership. She is a human being in her own right. And Karen Chandler—by contract, by birth, and by choice—is her mother."

Rosen and several others applauded. More joined in just as Judge Lyang slammed the gavel for attention.

"Quiet down, please."

Johnson smiled, spreading his arms expansively. "I have no more questions for the witness."

"I do."

Czernek stood. Valerie grasped his sleeve, looking up at him. "What?" he whispered.

She almost spoke, then shook her head and said nothing. Her fingers released him.

"I'd like to ask you," he said, "*Doctor*, whether you think society has any say in what is or is not right or wrong."

"Who *are* society?" Fletcher looked around the room. "Everyone except me? Society is composed of individuals. The sum total of their separate choices is their 'say.'" She leaned forward to gaze at Czernek with just the barest smile on her lips. "If fifty-one percent of society approved of infanticide or slavery, should I approve of it? Would you?"

"Just answer the question."

"No, 'society' has no say distinct from the choices of individuals." She settled back in her chair. "Immoral laws and primitive opinions should be ignored with impunity, even if society has to be dragged kicking and screaming toward a new respect for life and rights. Those in the pro-life or pro-choice camps who refuse to embrace transoption are enemies of both life and choice and will alienate themselves from the mainstream consensus that *will* form around transoption as it did around adoption."

Czernek's voice boomed out at its most theatrical level. "Oh, you're a fine one to defend life and rights. You've been performing abortions for years, but you save one fetus, and that gives you the high moral ground."

Fletcher's face was a grim mask. "No one knows the truth. I never—"

Czernek cut her off. "I haven't finished yet. You deceived Valerie Dalton into giving you her child, you risked the life of Karen Chandler in an untested operation, you let the baby get sick—"

Fletcher coolly interrupted him. "I've stated before that Valerie was not deceived. She received the pregnancy termination she wanted. Karen agreed to the operation and has not expressed any displeasure with the degree of risk. Renata had no say in the matter, but I suggest that we wait twenty years and ask her if she would have preferred to have been aborted."

Valerie wept silently, her head down on the table.

"As for your rights as the father, as I see it, you have none. You have no say in whether the woman should keep or expel the fetus; it is her body, her right. You do, however, have the right to rescue that fetus and find a new womb for it, something you chose not to do."

She looked out at the spectators to stare at Ian, searching his eyes for something, anything. He gazed back at her, dispassionately cool. Their past was a closed book; she could no longer read him.

She paused, her mind suddenly focusing on a new thought. "In fact," she said slowly, still looking at Brunner, "there are places inside the male body where a fetus could be attached, brought to term and delivered by Caes—"

Her Metagram receiver beeped inside her jacket pocket. She reached in to silence it.

"I'm not interested in your scientific fantasies," Czernek said sternly.

Fletcher withdrew the receiver and read the LCD display.

Czernek continued, not noticing the doctor's action. "The evidence has shown that she's suffered incredible pain, both mental and physical, to keep Renata alive—"

Fletcher stared at the words. Her worst fears had come to pass.

NO STEM CELL ACT. TEMP. SPIKES 101 +

"Dr. Fletcher, are you listening to me?"

"To hell with you," she said, holding up the receiver. "Renata's dying, and you're bickering over who'll get the corpse." She bounded from the witness stand toward Valerie.

"Bailiff—" Lyang pointed at Fletcher. The tall, husky man stepped toward her as she leaned over Valerie.

"Renata needs marrow. Right now. Let's go."

"Stay right here, please," the bailiff said, firmly gripping Evelyn's arm.

"Motion to recess!" Johnson shouted.

"Move to declare a mistrial!" Czernek said even louder. "She's clearly seeking to prejudice the jury—"

A single nerve-stunning blow from Lyang's gavel silenced everyone except Fletcher.

"—got to do it now before the temperature spikes get too—"

"Dr. Fletcher." The judge's voice ran cold. "Is this mere histrionics, or is the child's life really in danger?"

"She's running temperature spikes. That means some infection's taken advantage of her depressed immune system. She'll be put on antibiotics and antifungals, but she needs more marrow. Now. We've got to try to kick start her stem—"

"Very well, Doctor. Court is recessed until Monday." The gavel fell. Its sound was lost in the chaos that erupted.

Valerie stood. The bailiff released Fletcher's right arm. Her left was seized by Czernek.

"Val—you're not going through with this, are you? The jury's watching."

Valerie stared at him with an arctic gaze. "Let go of her."

The two women strode from the courtroom into a sea of reporters, lights, and shouted questions. Fletcher said nothing, using one arm to blaze a trail while holding Valerie's hand tightly in the other. They made it to the steps of the courthouse in record time.

The crowd outside must have been watching Fletcher's testimony. Shouts emanated from both sides, accompanied by thrusting signs and waving fists. Toward the center, though, stood a tiny knot of people with signs lettered in bright Day-Glo colors. They stood silently. Then, as the pair approached, they pressed backward with all their might to create a narrow path for Evelyn and Valerie.

Valerie read the signs. Each one said the same thing.

TRANSOPTION:
A WOMAN'S *choice*
A BABY'S *right!*

They guided Valerie and Dr. Fletcher through the crowd. The faces on the men and women—nearly all of them in their early twenties—possessed the serious intensity of people who had just found a new battle to fight, a new precept to defend. Or perhaps an old one to attack.

Several of the young people laid their hands on Fletcher's shoulders and back as they propelled the pair toward the car. Sympathetic arms gently embraced Valerie.

A woman not more than twenty wedged her way up to the pair to announce, "If I'd only known transoption existed, I wouldn't have had an abortion." Her pretty face was set in a grave expression. The jostling of the crowd around them forced her to bob and weave like a boxer. Her piercing blue eyes, though, remained fixed on Evelyn's.

"Please don't give up. There are thousands of us out there. We'll help you save—"

The swirl of bodies moved her away from Fletcher, back into the crowd. They had broken free of the two clusters of demonstrators and rushed toward the parking lot. Scores of members from the rival groups followed quietly, observing Fletcher with undisguised curiosity. Newspeople closed in with more questions.

"We're going to the hospital," Fletcher shouted, unlocking the passenger side of the Saab to admit Valerie. "Medical emergency. Clear a path or you'll be wearing tread marks."

She jumped around to her side, fired up the engine and punched it. Reporters and onlookers leaped away from the squealing machine. The sparse pro-transoption forces cheered, waving their signs with visceral enthusiasm.

Valerie looked behind her to see Ron's BMW in hot pursuit. They raced down Crenshaw toward the Pacific Coast Highway.

"What kind of car do the Chandlers drive?" Valerie asked.

"I'm not sure." Evelyn pumped the brakes every few seconds to avoid rear-ending cars. She swerved smoothly into another lane and then slammed the accelerator. Traffic signals seemed to turn from amber to red every time they entered an intersection.

"Someone's following Ron." She turned to watch the road ahead. "Can we save her?"

Fletcher nodded. "I hope so. It just worries me that none of the three cell lines have recovered." She hit the brakes and turned the wheel hard. "I want to cover all bases, so I'm going to administer more marrow." She glanced quickly at Valerie. "Are you up for it?"

Valerie nodded. "I'll do anything to save her." She fell silent for a long moment, then said, "If Renata needs me this much, doesn't that prove I'd be the better mother?"

"I don't know, Valerie." Though she drove with sharp concentration, her voice sounded weary. "Motherhood isn't a tug-of-war with a human being as the prize."

"I saw a play once," Valerie said. "In high school. Two women both claimed to be the mother of a baby, so the judge drew a chalk circle and put the baby in the middle and said that he would determine who the mother was by who pulled it out. They both grabbed the baby and started to pull. It cried in pain. One woman couldn't stand the cries, so she let go, and the other woman pulled it out of the circle."

Evelyn nodded, jerking the wheel to the right. "And the judge knew that the woman who wouldn't hurt the baby was the real mother."

"You've seen the play, too?"

Fletcher smiled. "I know the story of Solomon. But I've also seen enough child-abuse cases to know that it's just a story, not a reliable human trait."

Valerie sat in silence for the rest of the trip.

Fletcher parked in the emergency lot and ushered Valerie past the handful of reporters staking out the area. The pair rushed up to the infant ICU before anyone had time to react.

Valerie stared through the glass at the plastic box around which two nurses and a doctor hovered, gowned and masked.

"How is she?" Evelyn shouted when she saw Dr. DuQuette down the hall.

DuQuette, a large, gray-bearded, pleasant-looking man, gazed at his former peer. "Platelets at twenty thousand, but only because of transfusions. Almost no white. Red being sustained—"

"I want another transplant. I'll get her prepped."

"I can't let you do that," DuQuette said. "Lawrence would yank me out of here, and then where would we be?"

"To hell with Lawrence," Fletcher snapped. "That baby—"

"I can handle a marrow job. You'll just have to watch out here." He gave Valerie the once-over. "Ready?"

"Yes," Valerie said, preparing to unbutton her blouse.

"No!" Czernek's footsteps resounded in the hallway. Behind him ran Johnson and the Chandlers, catching up at the observation window. Karen and David immediately looked inside, trying to get some glimpse of Renata.

Ron's eyes flashed with fierce inspiration. "We're all here. I've decided that we can come to an agreement. Out of court."

The Chandlers turned to listen, stunned apprehension growing within them.

Johnson spoke with caution. "Let's hear it."

Czernek took a deep breath. The sprint had been more than he had anticipated. "Either the Chandlers agree that Valerie is the legal mother and they grant us permanent, uncontested custody, or we refuse to provide the transplant. If you really want to play hardball, I called my office from the car, and they're preparing an application for a restraining order until the suit is settled. Take your pick." He smiled triumphantly at Valerie and reached out to draw her near.

Shock and agony raced through her. His words slashed at her with a blade that carved into her soul. Squirming to break free of his embrace, she stared at him in horror.

"*No!*" she cried. Pain and revulsion contorted her face.

"That's my *baby* in there! She's not a hostage. I can't threaten her life that way."

"Val, I only—"

She slapped his arm away with stinging force, then turned to Dr. Fletcher.

"I paid you to kill her once and you saved her. I won't endanger her again."

Ron took another deep breath, this time to calm his own rage. "Then let me get—"

"*No!*" She turned her back on Ron to grasp Fletcher's arms. "When I went to you for an abortion, I signed my child's life away. You and Karen saved her. I should have given you nothing but thanks, and instead I tried to ruin your lives. I'm sorry." She turned to Karen and David.

"There is no lawsuit. Renata is your daughter."

"*You can't do that!*"

All eyes turned toward Czernek. He was not the source of the outburst, though. He was staring in silent bafflement at Johnson.

Black eyes flashing with anger, his hair disheveled, Terry looked like a madman.

"You can't give up the lawsuit," he cried, desperation searing a violent edge into his voice.

Fletcher and the Chandlers exchanged puzzled glances. Dr. DuQuette spoke firmly. "We've got to get her prepped."

Johnson followed Valerie and Fletcher down the hallway, the others behind him.

"If you drop this suit," he said, "there'll be no judicial decision. No precedent to use in subsequent cases. We've got the chance to *set* that precedent. Both sides agree on what the outcome of this suit should be. Can we hope that a future landmark case would be settled as easily?"

"Just a minute," Czernek said loudly. "Do you expect—"

"You mean you want them to continue with the lawsuit?" Fletcher asked. "What if we lose?"

"We can't." Johnson nodded at Valerie. She stopped in the

doorway to the dressing room, staring back at him. "Not if the plaintiff is on our side."

Ron reached out to turn Valerie toward him. Her cold eyes were no longer fathomable to him. He released her.

"I guess you won't be needing counsel for the rest of this." He turned to leave, then stopped. Over his shoulder, he said, "I'll wait to drive you home."

"Don't bother." Her voice held no emotion, just the flat statement of a fact.

XX

Evelyn watched through the observation window. Dr. Du-Quette hovered over Valerie while an intent young resident transferred syringes back and forth. A small team of four nurses and technologists kept their attention on the bank of monitors.

She was lucky even to be watching. Dr. Lawrence had only grudgingly allowed Fletcher into the ICU as a personal courtesy to DuQuette. Lon mentioned to her, *sotto voce*, that he outranked Lawrence "at the lodge." It apparently had some utility at the hospital, too.

So she sat watching DuQuette aspirate the marrow from Valerie while the resident gently shoved the viscous fluid into Renata's IV tubing. Fletcher's hands unconsciously moved now and then, as if her motions could assist in the operation. She saw nothing wrong in their coordinated movements, but she felt she had the right and obligation to be in there doing it herself.

Beside her sat Karen and David, their arms, hands, and fingers intertwined in a clutch of fear and support. Karen flinched the first few times the thick needle rammed into Valerie's chest. After the tenth time or so, she grew accustomed to the way the doctor would raise his arm, press the aspirator against her flesh, and shove hard with a quick, powerful motion.

David observed the others at their stations in front of the

monitors. He watched for some evidence in their eyes that everything was all right or getting better. What he feared most was to see a look of alarm on one of them, followed by a flurry of activity. The vignette would play over and over in his mind until he knew for certain what it would look like and what it would portend.

They stood there, though, gazing at their equipment with steady eyes. Occasionally, one's lips would move, or another would turn to call out information. DuQuette and the resident nodded, muttered back instructions. Whenever the doctor had accumulated enough marrow, the resident transferred the syringe to Renata's IV tube and pushed firmly. The tubing blushed pink and then deep red.

Fletcher whispered to the Chandlers, "They were finally able to get hold of some GM-CSF. That ought to speed her recovery this time around."

"How long will this take?" David asked.

"Another ten minutes or so. Renata doesn't have room for much marrow. But she can use as much as we can give her."

Karen tried to catch a glimpse of Renata. "When will we know if it works?"

"It might be another two to four weeks for the new cells to start up. Or the cells already in her may get a boost and start producing right away. We won't know." She put an arm around Karen. "It's a waiting process more than anything else. We were able to stabilize her temperature for the transplant. I mean, *they* were."

Renata was not her patient anymore. Sitting there behind a glass wall, unable to participate or even to hear, she could only use her knowledge of medicine to determine that all was going well. She used that knowledge to keep Karen and David informed. It was the best that she could do. It was something.

Valerie dreamt. Images raced past her. Or was she running past images of children? A lost legion of children staring mutely, captured in some halfway state between life and death. Crystallized, frozen in time.

The lines and ranks of them spread forever, their weight threatening to crush the earth. At the same time, Valerie felt that their tiny shoulders could support the world, their young arms could lift it to new heights. She couldn't decide which it was to be. She only knew that they could not stand immobile forever. And she couldn't run forever.

The crystals shattered with a multicolored electrical spiral of light.

She awoke with a start, then closed her eyes groggily, trying to grasp the remains of the dream that had been wrenched from her by the opening of the door.

"Valerie?"

She opened her eyes again to see Dr. Fletcher standing over her. Behind her stood Dr. DuQuette.

"How's Renata?" Valerie asked. The effort caused her chest to ache with familiar pain. She withstood it, even welcomed it. If it helped Renata . . .

"She's stable," Dr. DuQuette said. "We won't know for a while."

Fletcher nodded, gazing into Valerie's eyes with warm affection.

"I've got to know she'll be all right," Valerie said. "I had such a strange dream."

Evelyn stroked her forehead with a gentle hand. "You've done everything a mother could do for her daughter. Just rest."

"Where's Ron?"

Fletcher's smile faded. She simply shrugged.

DuQuette's pager cricketed in the depths of his coat pocket. He shut it off and excused himself.

Alone, the two women gazed at each other. Outside, the sound of birds and street noise drifted through closed windows.

"Is it Saturday?" Valerie asked.

Fletcher nodded.

"I can go to court on Monday?"

"Yes. If that's what you want to do."

"I want to help you. I want to help Renata. I want to help the women who can't keep their babies but don't want to kill them."

"It might not help. One lower-court decision won't shift centuries of outdated opinion."

Valerie smiled in spite of the ache in her chest. "It's a first step."

The hospital became, over the weekend, a refuge for Valerie and for the Chandlers. Stern, granite-faced nurses, muscular Johnny Mason and other grim orderlies, borrowed from the neuropsychiatric wing, guarded Renata and the trio from reporters and miscellaneous gawkers with an intransigent glee that bordered on feral savagery. When Karen Chandler's mother and father arrived for a visit, the receptionist sent her a Xerox of their driver's licenses for confirmation of their status. They passed. Few others did.

Dr. Lawrence showed up once to "check on the baby's progress." He gazed for a moment through the ICU window, nodded, then glared at Evelyn. She smiled wearily.

He walked away in silence.

XXI

The steps to the courthouse swarmed with reporters, protesters, police, the curious, and the unfortunate. People with business that had nothing to do with *Dalton* v. *Chandler et al.* had to wade through the swamp of humanity, cursing their luck. Some granted interviews solely on the basis of being in the right place just as an opinion-hungry newshound decided to grab a few sound bites for local color.

"And what's your outlook on the Baby Renata case?"

"I dunno, lady. I'm here about my landlord."

The word was out that something big would happen today. The betting was that the defendants would either continue presenting their side of the case or the judge would dismiss the suit. Or something. Rumors flew like pigeons around the courthouse steps.

A Bayside General employee van pulled up to the sidewalk. Audio and video electronics vied with eyes and ears for position around the blue-and-gray vehicle. The side door slid noisily aft, and out stepped Johnson, dressed in a gray suit, crisp white shirt, and navy tie. He grinned in triumph, shouted, "No questions, please!" and urged the crowd to make room. The Chandlers followed him, smiling and waving at the cameras.

This was new. The photographers fired vollies of shots. The videocams captured every motion. Karen looked as if she had just stepped out of the beauty parlor. Every strand of her dark hair was in place, her makeup subtle and perfect. She wore a deep emerald dress with a matching knit sweater, the cowl draped over her shoulders. Her matching handbag and pumps were just a shade darker. If green meant go, the reporters had their signal.

David dressed in beige slacks and yellow polo shirt under a tan cardigan sweater. He looked like a young version of the classic American father figure. It might not have suited him very well, but the way he beamed with joy told everyone that he sensed victory.

Dr. Fletcher was the next to step out. Her outfit was a simple, austere gray suit with a black cowl-neck blouse.

"How's the baby?" someone shouted.

"Renata is stable at the moment." Evelyn gazed around at the farrago of lenses and microphones. "We still don't know whether her stem cell activity will return, but for now her temperature is normal, and she's resting quietly."

She turned to extend a hand into the van. Valerie Dalton nervously made her way to the sidewalk, then looked up into the wall of noise and light. Her light blue skirt and vest over a taupe blouse gave her an authoritative air that contrasted sharply with her apprehension.

The questions erupted immediately.

"Is it true Ron Czernek walked off the case?"

"Are you in pain from the second transplant?"

"Will you drop the suit?"

"Will you continue the suit without him?"

"Why are you here with the defendants?"

The noise level threatened to overwhelm her. She gripped Evelyn's hand tightly. Evelyn squeezed back with even stronger pressure.

For a long moment, Valerie said nothing. Then she seemed to straighten under the onslaught. She shook her head, tossing her long hair back over her shoulders. Holding up a hand for silence, she waited.

242

The reporters quieted down. Most of them. When it was quiet enough, she spoke.

"I intend to see this case through to victory. And by that I mean I intend to lose. Thank you."

As if on cue, Johnson pressed forward through the crowd. The protesters had been split far asunder by the wedge of reporters. Patches of blue that were the police orbited around the periphery, powerless and unnecessary. The circle of demonstrators surrounding the center of activity carried signs in support of transoption.

James Rosen stood with them, arguing to an unlikely pair.

"Don't you see?" he said to the cadaverously thin woman carrying a small sign that read ABORTION IS MURDER—TRANSOPTION IS THEFT. "It's not theft. It's more like salvage. Rescue. During the Depression, people found babies on doorsteps and took them in. This just substitutes wombs for rooms."

The man wearing a button reading NOT WITH MY LIBERTY, YOU DON'T tried to get a word in edgewise. With the fervor of all new converts, though, Rosen turned to him and continued without interruption.

"Don't you see that the fetus creates a property sphere by enclosing itself in a sac made from its own genetic material? That it is saying, 'This is where your body stops and mine begins'? Its *actions* speak where it has no words. . . ."

None of them noticed the passage of the litigants.

Judge Lyang entered the courtroom, viewing everything within her domain. The defendants were all present, she noted. And, as the clerk had informed her, Ron Czernek was absent. In fact, Dalton sat at the defendants' table, calmly finishing a bit of conversation with Dr. Fletcher. In the spectator area, among reporters and the curious, sat the expert witness Dr. Brunner. Lyang noted that the other two, Decker and Burke, had not shown up today. *It seems that word of Valerie's defection spread quickly over the weekend,* she mused. *Well, let's get this over with.* She eyed Johnson. *You're not going to like this.* She took a deep breath.

"Court will come to order." The judge turned toward the jurors. "In my chambers a few moments ago, the litigants presented this court with a rare opportunity." Her voice was metered and assured. She leaned forward, folding her hands on the bench.

"The purported function of the judicial system is to provide peaceful solutions to profound disagreements between individuals. Right or wrong, we have that power. Well or poorly, we use it. The decisions we make, however pleasing they are *supposed* to be to both sides, are seldom viewed by the losing side as either fair or pleasant. While this may seem trivial in criminal cases, where one side has engaged in violence against the other, it can be disquieting in civil suits, in disagreements among ordinary people. In custody battles, either-or outcomes can be horribly tragic."

She looked at each member of the jury in turn. "You have spent several days listening to testimony from both sides pertaining to the question of who is the rightful mother of the baby, Renata. The natural mother has brought suit to reclaim her child, which she claims was taken from her by fraud and deception. The so-called transoptive mother and the doctor involved have built their defense on the fact that the natural mother had contractually surrendered claim to a fetus that is not legally considered to possess human rights. In so doing, they have raised a fascinating collection of legal and moral questions unsettling to our concepts of abortion, definitions of humanity, contracts, abandonment, Good Samaritanism, and even rights of salvage.

"It would seem that your task as jurors will be more difficult than that of a Solomon. Not only must you decide whose claim to Renata is valid, but—in order to make that decision—you must redefine human rights in regard to adults and the unborn. It is a task I would not wish to place upon myself."

She turned to gaze at the litigants. "I have, however, been asked by both the plaintiff and the counsel for the defense to grant a directed verdict. However—" She paused, gazing first at Dalton, then at Johnson, the Chandlers, and Dr. Fletcher. "However, a directed verdict has always seemed to me to carry a stigma of arbitrary unfairness. It is a judge's assertion that she doubts the ability of a jury to reach a verdict that serves the interests of justice. Therefore, in the interest of justice, and because I think there are issues to try, I will allow this trial to follow its natural course."

Johnson's jaw dropped. He stared as if he had been pole-axed.

Valerie turned in confusion to Fletcher, her composure evaporating. "What?"

Fletcher shook her head, smiling. "Well, Terry," she whispered, "here's your chance."

He stood, clearing his throat and glancing sourly at Lyang. She smiled warmly back at him.

"Ladies and gentlemen of the, uh, jury, the defense would like to call a final witness—Valerie Dalton."

Valerie looked from Johnson to Fletcher and back again. "Me?"

Johnson nodded.

"You can do it," David said quietly.

Karen nodded in agreement. "Just tell them what you told us in the van."

Hesitantly, Valerie arose to approach the stand. Noting that she had been sworn in previously, Judge Lyang merely reminded her that she was still under obligation to answer truthfully. Valerie moved as if in a dream.

"Ms. Dalton." Terry's voice snapped her back into reality. "You brought suit against Dr. Evelyn Fletcher, Karen Chandler, and David Chandler for custody of Baby Renata. Can you explain to the jury why you are here as a witness for the very people you are suing?"

With a quick glance at Judge Lyang, Valerie turned toward

the jury. Her stomach quavered. She took a deep breath. *I'm sorry, Ron. This is the right thing to do.*

"Judge Lyang spoke about the interests of justice. This lawsuit was never in the interest of justice. I'd forgotten what justice was."

She looked at Dr. Fletcher. "At first, I didn't want to be pregnant. Abortion was the easiest way out. I thought. Then, too late, I began to have my doubts. It was as if everything I had been told about abortion didn't matter. I had been told that a fetus wasn't human, that it only had the *potential* to be human. That made sense before, but then I thought about it. Isn't a baby only a potential teenager? A teenager a potential adult? Did I have the right to draw the line between potential and actual with the stroke of a knife? When I found out that my baby had survived the abortion, that there hadn't been any abortion at all, I felt tricked, robbed. It took me this long to realize that *I* was the one who was tricking and robbing. I tricked myself into thinking that having an abortion wouldn't be killing a real human being, and I almost robbed Renata of her chance to live." She turned to face Karen.

"I won't rob her a second time."

Looking back to the jury, she said, "I ask you to think about the life Evelyn Fletcher saved. I want you to consider what would have happened to Renata if Dr. Fletcher hadn't rescued the fetus *that I wanted killed* and implanted it in Karen Chandler. I want you to remember that Karen and David wanted this child and I didn't. They took her in when she could not speak for herself or provide for her own survival. I abandoned her to die, and they saved her.

"I had no duty to keep Renata alive. Neither did they. We all made our choices freely. But where I thought my only choice was my freedom or Renata's death, Dr. Fletcher knew there was a third path—freedom *and* life."

She paused, gazing for a moment at the empty chair at the plaintiff's table.

"I ask you to think of me as someone who abandoned her

child with full knowledge of the consequences. And I demand that you acknowledge both my ability to make *and my obligation to abide by* a simple contract. *Then* justice will be served."

She looked at Johnson for a sign. He nodded.

"Ms. Dalton, are you making this statement under duress?"

"No."

"Have the defendants or anyone else offered you any compensation for saying what you said?"

"Not at all."

Johnson looked at her carefully, gauging her emotional state.

"Valerie," he said, "do you love Renata?"

Tears welled. "I love her with all my heart. I've given her my blood. I've—" She fumbled with her vest and blouse, unbuttoning them, spreading the fabric wide to expose the scores of purple marks between her breasts. "This," she said, turning toward the jury, "this is how much I love her." She let the blouse fall back into place. "I'm begging you to think about *her* best interests. If Dr. Fletcher hadn't invented transoption and Karen Chandler hadn't volunteered, we wouldn't be here to argue about her best interests. Renata would be dead. Garbage long gone. Think about all the others that could be saved. They're waiting out there. They're dying *right now* while other women struggle desperately to become pregnant. You have the chance to tell the world that we can and should bring them together. We don't need laws to force them. We just have to let them know the technique exists and then stand back."

She looked around helplessly. "I guess that's all I have to say."

"Your Honor, the defense rests."

Lyang nodded at Johnson. "You may step down, Ms. Dalton."

Valerie glanced around the courtroom. Karen and David returned her gaze with tearful smiles. Their hands rested on the table, intertwined in a lover's knot. Fletcher, beside them, gave her an encouraging thumbs up. In her eyes glowed the approval of one who had fought long and hard for her values and had finally found one who suffered just as much to attain them.

The opinions of the jurors appeared to be easy to read. Two of the women dabbed at their eyes, while one of the older men wristed away some tears. The others observed her with a range of expressions from the impassive approval of the oldest woman to an emotional, smiling nod of agreement from the young man.

Valerie rejoined her friends at the defendants' table. Evelyn hugged her, whispering, "You were wonderful, Valerie." The Chandlers agreed, turning their attention to the judge when she spoke.

"Do the defendants or plaintiff have summations?"

"No, Your Honor," Johnson said.

"No, ma'am," Valerie said when Lyang looked her way.

"Then I shall request the jury to deliberate until such time as they come to a decision." Lyang took a moment to look over some notes. "It shall be your duty to decide whether the baby named Renata shall be placed in the custody of Valerie Dalton or remain in the custody of Karen and David Chandler." She gazed at each of the jurors in turn. "Custody shall, in large part, be determined by the best interests of the child, based upon the evidence presented to you in court. In addition, there is the matter of the injunction against Dr. Evelyn Fletcher and the thirty million dollars in damages. Your decision in this matter must be based upon the question of fraud or criminal intent as answered by the evidence presented in this court."

She glanced at Valerie with a professional lack of emotion. "Please keep in mind the unusual nature of the final witness's testimony." She flipped open a book to read the jurors a lengthy set of instructions. Each of the six took extensive notes. These were their guidelines, the rules by which they would render their verdict.

When Lyang finished reading, the bailiff strode over to the jury box to open the railing. One by one, the six jurors solemnly stepped through the door in the rear of the courtroom.

When they were out of the room and the door closed with a heavy sound, Lyang took a deep breath and settled back in her chair.

"This should be quick," Johnson murmured happily to Fletcher. "She just about handed them a directed verdict."

"I'd pop out for a smoke," Evelyn whispered, "but I don't want to miss this."

After five minutes passed, Valerie leaned over to Johnson. "How long does this usually take?"

He shrugged. "I've observed trials where juries walk in and turn right around again."

"What's taking them so long?" Karen asked.

"They probably wanted some coffee." Johnson turned his attention to his notes. He sorted them, numbered pages, assigned sheets to various manilla folders. Karen and David whispered something between themselves while Fletcher leaned back along the bar.

"So what do you think, Ian?" she casually whispered to Dr. Brunner. Her heart raced at a pace fueled by her brash attempt to bridge a years-long gap in conversation.

"I think you're in a frightening amount of hot water outside this courtroom," he whispered back, folding his arms on the rail. "Even if they granted *you* custody of the kid, it won't mean a thing to Bumqua."

She nodded casually. "Yeah, I know I'm washed up here. Think there'll be any interest in transoption research outside the U.S.?"

Brunner's expression softened. "What floors me," he whispered, "is that my office has registered over one hundred calls this last week. All of them from women who want to get hooked up with a recipient for their embryos."

Fletcher jerked her head around to stare at him in utter shock. *"What?"*

Judge Lyang glowered down at them.

Brunner nodded. "I seriously think you've tapped into some sort of *zeitgeist.*" He circled his finger around to indicate the room. "The state may not be ready for transoption, and the Christians and the feminists may not be ready, but the pregnant women are."

Fletcher laid a hand on his sleeve. "Listen, if you need my notes or a working model of the suction—"

"Forget it," he said. His voice revealed a mixture of regret and fear. "Transoption is going to have the status illegal abortions had for the last century. And that's probably how they'll be performed for years to come. In the counter-economy. *I'm* a reputable researcher." He paused, then leaned closer, his voice dropping nearly to the limit of audibility. "I've submitted a carefully worded request for animal-research funds, though. I've got a protégé who's keen to start a legitimate, peer-reviewed project."

"That's *great,*" she whispered. An ancient wall between them had crumbled.

Brunner shook his head. "A lot will depend on what the jury has to say." He pointed to his Breitling watch. "Doesn't look good."

Fletcher leaned over to Johnson. "It's been fifteen minutes. What's going on?"

Damned if I know. "I think they may be dotting *i*'s and crossing *t*'s." He was unable, though, to hide the concern on his face.

"Are we sunk?" she asked.

Judge Lyang cleared her throat. "The jury seems to be taking their time, so court will recess until a verdict is delivered." The gavel rapped once.

Reporters assumed their positions outside the courtroom. Most of the questions Johnson fended off concerned the fate of the trial and any insight he might have into the minds of the jurors.

"I have no idea what they're thinking," he said. "There can be only one verdict for them to reach. All we have to do is wait."

After a long lunch in the cafeteria, Johnson left to spend a few minutes with the court clerk. He returned with a crest-fallen expression.

"He said the jury's informed Lyang that they won't have a verdict today. He's told the rest of us to go home and return tomorrow."

"That's bad, isn't it?" Valerie asked.

Johnson nodded. "All they had to do was grant the verdict for us. I'm afraid they've found some reason to grant you custody."

Valerie frowned. "Can't I say no?"

"Sure," Terry said. "But I was trying for the legal precedent. Future courts won't care what you decided on your own." He looked around at the others. "We might as well go."

Karen patted his back. "We're sorry," she said.

"Thanks," he replied, thinking, *But* sorry *doesn't change the law books.*

XXII

Valerie returned to an empty home. The lights on the Phone-Mate indicated thirty-four messages awaiting her attention. She ignored it. The only sound drifted in from outside, where TV vans camped and reporters hovered like gulls around a trawler.

She flopped down on the bed, which had not been made from the night before. A glowing red eye glared at her beneath the TV. The VCR. Ron had set it to record the local news at five every day. Picking up the remote, she flicked on the TV, ran the tape back until she found a story about the case, and played it.

The male newscaster made a somber face. Superimposed behind him was the familiar scale with a baby in one pan, scalpel in the other. "The saga of Baby Renata continues with a surprising turnabout." The image cut to a shot of Valerie on the witness stand.

"The plaintiff in the landmark custody battle, Valerie Dalton, today dismissed her attorney and took the stand as a witness for the people she was suing. Her testimony took a dramatic turn when she discussed the bone marrow she'd donated to the infant."

"This," she watched herself say as the woman on the screen opened her blouse, "this is how much I love her." There was a distinct break in the image to edit in a later shot. "Think about all the others that could be saved. They're waiting out there. They're dying *right now* while other women struggle desperately to become pregnant." Another splice. "We just have to let them know the technique exists and then stand back."

Valerie recalled very little of her testimony. It was as if she were hearing it for the first time. Something about hearing her words on television brought her out of her own constricted world. For nearly a month her focus had been upon Valerie Dalton and how others had wronged her. Eight months ago, her thoughts had centered around Valerie Dalton and how pregnancy would interfere with her life.

She lay atop the rumpled covers and stared at the TV. *There are millions of Valeries out there,* she thought. *How can I help them?*

She shook her head. *I'm only one person.* She gazed up at the ceiling. A paint chip there reminded her of the tiny stain on the ceiling of the operating room. All the events of the last few months came back to her in a sudden rush of awareness.

Dr. Fletcher was only one person, she realized. *She saved only one life and changed the lives of everyone forever.*

Valerie Dalton saw the rest of her own life spread before her like a broad, rich valley seen for the first time by an explorer who had just crossed the summit of a treacherous mountain.

She jumped out of bed, energy surging through her. She wanted sparks to fly.

"Do you have a verdict?"

Judge Lyang gazed expectantly at the foreman. So did Valerie, the defendants, and everyone else in the court. It was three o'clock in the afternoon. The jury had been at it since nine that morning. All eyes and ears turned toward the slender, graying man holding several sheets of yellow paper in his hands. Cameras focused in on him. He stood, visibly nervous about speaking in public, and addressed the judge.

"We do have a verdict, Your Honor." He paused, staring down at the paper to avoid looking anywhere else.

"Please read your verdict to this court," Lyang said with a bit of nudging impatience.

"Your Honor," he said slowly. "This verdict has been a very difficult one to make."

Karen grasped her husband's hand tightly. Valerie glanced at Fletcher, worry in her eyes. Fletcher watched the foreman intently, as did Johnson. As ever, the lawyer's pencil hovered over his notepad, ready for anything.

"Your Honor, the jury has asked that I preface our verdict by stating that the reasons for our decision undoubtedly exceed the scope of this trial." He looked down at the paper, taking his words from what was written there. "No one judicial decision is ever the final word. We only hope that the basis of our verdict can serve as a reasonable foundation for the controversy that will undoubtedly result."

He cleared his throat. "It is the decision of the jury that the baby named Renata is the natural daughter of *both* Valerie Dalton and Karen Chandler."

Voices whispered and muttered throughout the courtroom in confused surprise. Lyang gaveled for order, staring with incomprehension at the foreman.

"This is highly unusual," she said. After a moment of thought she added, "So's this whole case. Continue."

"There's more," the foreman said.

"I should be very interested to hear it," Lyang said quietly.

"While the jury determines that Valerie Dalton is the *genetic* mother of Baby Renata, this finding is only part of our verdict, but a necessary one. It is an undeniable fact that the fetus removed by Dr. Fletcher contains genetic material formed from that of Valerie Dalton and Ron Czernek. In this way, Valerie Dalton is the genetic mother of Renata. Yet after transoption the fetus received protection, sustenance, and life from the body of Karen Chandler. Karen Chandler is the *birth* mother of Renata. This is also a definition of motherhood. Therefore, faced with these conflicting definitions of motherhood, the jury has chosen to declare that the two women are both *co-mothers* of Baby Renata."

He turned to the next page. The ruffle of the paper sounded like the crackle of electricity in the hushed courtroom.

"That leaves us with the dilemma of custody. The precedent of adoption was raised by some members, but in such cases there is indeed only one natural mother—the genetic mother also gives birth to the child. She would seem to have the stronger claim in the absence of an explicit contract that spelled out what would happen in the event she wanted her child back. The case of a surrogate mother is similar. She donates her genetic material *and* gives sustenance and birth to the child. Her claim, too, seems valid—once again, in the absence of an explicit contract with clauses to address such conflicts."

Evelyn laid a hand over Valerie's and clasped firmly. Neither took their gaze from the man who held the future in his hands.

"The long legal tradition in such cases," he continued, "has been to ignore any contract and award custody to the natural mother, making a strange, implicit judgment that the natural mother is incompetent to make a contract and abide by its principles, yet is capable of caring for another human being. Whether this is right or wrong, it has been the tendency."

The foreman turned another page. He peered even more intently at the paper. "Here, though, *both* women have had a turn at creating the baby Renata. If Valerie Dalton had not conceived the child, the fetus would not have existed. If Karen Chandler had not taken the abandoned fetus into her womb, Renata would not have been born.

"It is in light of these conflicting claims that the jury has elected to declare the women co-mothers and to determine that Valerie Dalton's pregnancy-termination contract with Bayside University Medical Center is and ought to be considered an unmistakable grant of custody of Baby Renata from co-mother Dalton to co-mother Chandler. Additionally, the injunction against Dr. Fletcher and all damages are denied."

The courtroom experienced a strange momentary silence during which everyone tried to arrive at an opinion on the verdict. The spectators had seen two warring factions come together without the force of a court decision. They had just heard the court mimic the private agreement. Whatever personal outlook anyone possessed, it seemed inappropriate to cheer or jeer an outcome that both women so dearly wanted.

At the table, though, Karen and David expressed their own reaction, hugging each other, teary eyes overflowing. Valerie joined in with arms spread wide to embrace them both. Terry stared breathlessly, surprise frozen on his face. Evelyn slapped an arm around his shoulders.

"Hey, kid, you won!"

"Yeah," he said, smiling. "And against such an adamant foe." He slipped an arm around Valerie.

The jury members smiled at the scene. Judge Lyang's grin, tilted with a sardonic edge, spread across her face with easy pleasure.

Someone at the back of the courtroom clapped his hands loudly. The happy litigants turned toward the jarring sound. Valerie's throat tightened upon seeing Ron standing just inside the doorway. He gazed coolly at Johnson, inclining his head ever so slightly in acknowledgment. He clapped again. And again. A few spectators joined. More. Seconds later, the court-room thundered with triumph.

Nobody heard Lyang's gavel. Even the reporters applauded.

Ron pushed his way forward to Valerie.

She turned her back to him to confer with Karen and David for a moment. Ron silently watched her receive nods of assent from the couple.

Valerie turned to Dr. Fletcher. "Can you go with us to the hospital? The three of us would like to see our daughter."

Ron Czernek was an aggressive lawyer and not easily deterred. He followed the quintet out of the courthouse, past the throng of reporters, and into the parking lot. Approaching Valerie there was impossible.

"Mr. Czernek!" a TV reporter shouted. "What's your opin—"

He ducked between two arguing pickets to race toward his BMW. He saw nothing of Valerie and the others until he bullied his way into the infant ICU at Bayside.

The others must have been delayed by reporters, he thought as he stood before the observation window. A lone nurse sat beside the high-tech crèche, reading a thick, dog-eared paperback. Equipment quietly registered Renata's every vital sign. Through the glass drifted the faint, steady sound of a heartbeat monitor.

Ron stepped about for a look at Renata. In all the time he had struggled to gain her custody, he suddenly realized, he had never actually seen her.

Standing on tiptoes at the corner of the window, he managed to peer past the tangle of wires and tubes to see directly into the isolation chamber.

A blond head lay on a stark white sheet. Tiny hands flexed their fingers, testing them out. The head rolled. Renata Chandler gazed toward her father.

She could not possibly have seen him, he realized. He stood in darkness; she lay bathed in light. Her blue eyes, though, seemed to stare at him and through him.

He watched his daughter, unable to fathom the feelings that raced through him. All his life he had been able to make snap decisions, had always been on the go, on the way to a goal. He had embarked on the custody battle with equal zeal.

Now he gazed at a child, his daughter, whose gaze implored him to stop, to think, to consider. There existed no need to rush. Watching Renata, there were no decisions to make, no appointments to keep. She squirmed and kicked and twisted about in the crib like life itself—ever changing, ever ready to contort into some different position and then start anew.

Footsteps scuffled and clacked down the hallway.

Ron turned, looking at the approaching people with guilty surprise.

"Valerie," he said. "We've got to talk."

She gazed through the window before answering. "I think you've said everything already."

Terry glanced at Evelyn, who nodded and quietly escorted everyone else toward the break room.

Alone, gazing at their daughter through the glass barrier, Valerie spoke in a weary, hushed tone.

"Today I gave up Jennifer for the second time."

"It's what you wanted. Both times."

She nodded. "Renata is a lovely name, too."

"She's beautiful."

Valerie pressed her hands against the cool, smooth window. "I'm sorry I lost the case for you."

He shrugged, leaning his hands against the window frame. "I didn't lose. I walked off. It turned out the way you wanted, didn't it?"

"Only the trial."

He glanced over at her for an instant, then looked back at Renata. "I'm sorry about what I did. About the way I've acted." He nodded toward his daughter. "You know, I never saw her until just now."

Valerie's hand moved slowly down the glass to touch his. "Isn't she wonderful?"

His hand grasped hers, held on for dear life. "You don't regret losing her?"

She shook her head. "I lost her eight months ago. I've only just found her." She stood on her toes as high as she could to see more of Renata. After a moment, she lowered herself to face Ron. "She may be Karen and David's daughter now, but we gave her something no one else could. I'll never again take that miraculous gift for granted."

Ron gently pulled her close and wrapped an arm around her. "You gave her that gift twice." He held her tightly as her arms drew him near. "More than anyone, you're a part of her. Now and forever."

Valerie felt the warmth of his body against hers. She turned her head to look through the glass and plastic at the tiny figure inside. She gazed at Renata. And saw the future.

FIRST TRANSOPTION DOWN UNDER

UPI

BRISBANE, AUSTRALIA —Just three months after the well-publicized Baby Renata case in the United States, doctors at Victoria Hospital announced the successful transoption of a six-week-old fetus from one woman to another. Drs. James Whyte and Divaker Ramanan report that they transplanted the fetus—safely recovered from an abortion—into the womb of a 31-year-old housewife from Sydney.

The revelation has caused some public outcry, with calls for legislation to ban or at least heavily regulate the new procedure.

TRANSOPTION DOC LEAVES U.S.

UPI

LOS ANGELES— Despite a grand jury's failure to indict Dr. Evelyn Fletcher on criminal charges in last year's notorious Baby Renata case, the disgraced surgeon departed the United States Tuesday under the cloud of her continued suspension of credentials by California's State Board of Medical Quality Assurance.

BABY RENATA CELEBRATES BIRTHDAY

First Transopted Baby

Times Wires Service

TORRANCE—Renata Chandler, whose birth last year caused a legal upheaval when it was revealed that she had been transplanted from one woman to another while still an embryo, celebrated her first birthday amid the glare of TV cameras and photo strobes.

A blond, blue-eyed charmer, Renata showed off her two front teeth in a happy grin as her so-called genetic mother and father—Valerie Dalton and Ron Czernek—joined with "transoptive" mother Karen Chandler and her husband David for the festivities.

Also on hand was Dr. Evelyn Fletcher, who pioneered the controversial medical procedure. Now conducting her practice at a clinic in Brazil, Fletcher used the opportunity to consult with her attorney regarding reinstatement of her medical license in the United States.

LOCAL BISHOP PRESSES FOR PAPAL DECISION ON TRANSOPTION

Opponents Say Would Mock Virgin Birth

Associated Press

BOSTON—Bishop John Robert Shriver today expressed dismay at the Pope's refusal to comment on transoption.

"In the last two years," the bishop said, "over four thousand transoptions have been performed around the world. Many of the donors and recipients have been Catholics." In light of the Church's opposition to abortion, Shriver said, "many view transoption as the only moral alternative. While the Church has not spoken against transoption, it also has not spoken in favor of it."

Bishop Shriver's attempts to gain a papal audience have been futile, he said, and so he has gone public with his request "in the hope that Catholic women will make their opinions known."

MAN GIVES BIRTH TO OWN SON!

UPI

LOS ANGELES—A San Francisco man gave birth today to his own son in what doctors call a revolutionary medical miracle.

Derek Edwards, a 25-year-old northern California resident, was in LA with his wife, Jane, six months ago when she was fatally injured in a traffic accident. Before she fell into an irreversible coma, she pleaded with doctors to save her unborn child. She was ten weeks' pregnant.

When the hospital administration refused to search for a female volunteer, Edwards offered his own body and the threat of legal action if they refused to transopt the fetus. Reluctantly, the hospital agreed to perform what was to be the first above-ground transoption in the United States.

A legal furor erupted when Dr. Evelyn Fletcher was flown in from South America to perform the operation. Administrators at Otis Chandler Memorial Hospital, though, stood by their decision, stating that Fletcher should be treated no differently from any other visiting foreign specialist. Working with a team of surgeons, Dr. Fletcher successfully attached the fetus to a blood-rich section of the outer surface of Edwards's large intestine.

Kept under constant medical supervision, Edwards spent half a year at the hospital until the birth yesterday morning—by Cæsarean section—of the baby boy. Three weeks premature and weighing only four pounds, three ounces, John Edwards is nonetheless healthy despite a surrogate pregnancy described by the father as "absolutely terrifying."

"I woke up every morning with the fear that Jane's only child might not survive her by very long. He's alive and well, though, and my wife's last wish has come true."

The press and friends of the family were able today to visit the father, who gained forty pounds during the pregnancy. Doctors attribute the weight gain to hormonal adjustments made by the fetus.

"Lactation was the strangest side effect," Edwards quipped. "The doctors aren't sure I can nurse, though, so I think I'll use bottles when I get out of here."

FLETCHER ADMITS FREEZING FETUSES

Never Performed Abortions, Doctor Says in Interview

Associated Press

SÃU PALO—In an exclusive interview with the British science magazine *Nature*, Dr. Evelyn Fletcher admitted that she had always planned to develop transoption as a viable alternative to abortion. In her years at Bayside University Medical Center, she said, she preserved every fetus she removed from women undergoing abortions.

"I could have disposed of them in any number of ways," she said from her clinic in Brazil. "I decided to have them cryogenically preserved in the hope that someday a way might be found to revive them and implant them in recipient mothers."

In all, Dr. Fletcher froze 3,618 fetuses, all of which are being stored in secret locations around the United States. U.S. officials, contacted by *Nature*, could find nothing illegal with the unorthodox method of storage.

When asked, Dr. Fletcher admitted that "probably very few" of the fetuses could be expected to survive the freezing and thawing process. "But even one life saved," she said, "would make my effort worthwhile."

TRANSOPTION RING BROKEN BY FBI

"Massive" Operation Nets Eight Young Surgeons, Gold

Exclusive to the Times

LOS ANGELES—Eight young Southland surgeons were arrested Friday by the FBI and local police in a sweep that netted illegal transoption equipment, nearly a million dollars in cash and gold, and information on thousands of transoptions performed over the last five years throughout California, Arizona, and Nevada.

The eight surgeons, described by FBI Special Agent Richard Delacort as "money-hungry kids armed with lasers," operated out of three family-planning clinics in Malibu, Westwood, and Irvine. "They offered large sums of cash to unwed mothers who came in for abortions," Delacort said. "Then they transopted the fetuses into other women who paid astronomical fees for the service."

Also seized in the coordinated raids were containers of cryogenic liquid that led Delacort to speculate that some of the fetuses were being frozen for future use.

"When there's an underground demand for something as there is for transoption," Delacort stated, "there's a tremendous incentive for doctors to violate their ethics and provide it."

Dear Editor:

Your editorial about the Transoption Eight could not have been more short-sighted and uninformed [*"Doctors Should Have Stuck to Abortions,"* July 18]. Simply because abortion is legal and transoption is not places no obligation on your paper to support the persecution of these dedicated medical pioneers. There was a time when "the majority of medical opinion," as you put it, could "see there was no scientific merit" in a doctor washing his hands between dissecting cadavers and delivering babies.

Consider for a moment what the Transoption Eight have done. Without a cent of federal funding, they have freed thousands of women from unwanted pregnancies and the onus of abortion *and* given thousands of other women the gift of beautiful, healthy babies. For this they have been arrested and imprisoned soley because Congress and the president decided to create a new criminal class with the stroke of a pen.

The women who paid fortunes to receive those unwanted babies are not creating "new burdens on a strained society." They can afford to care for the children that might otherwise have been born onto welfare or aborted at taxpayer's expense. And the women who freely gave up their pregnancies are not the "hapless dupes, silenced with blood money," that you describe. Most of them are women who want neither to be pregnant nor be killers.

I should know.

I am one of them.

    [Name Withheld by Request]

SUPREME COURT AGREES TO HEAR TRANSOPTION CASE

Could Be Another *Roe* v. *Wade*, Defendants Say

UPI

WASHINGTON— Five Supreme Court justices today approved a writ of certiorari to review the case of United States vs. Grosscup, in what will be the first high court test of the Rohrabacher–Hayden Act outlawing transoption. Wanda Grosscup, the first of nearly four thousand women convicted for violation of the law, has steadfastly maintained that she is in fact the co-mother of her son and was granted custody by an arrangement with the so-called "first stage" co-mother.

Basing her defense on the highly publicized Dalton vs. Chandler decision rendered nearly a decade ago, Grosscup has enlisted the aid of outspoken transoption advocate Adrianne Dyer. Dyer's Living Alternative Institute, based in Denver, issued a statement that "the U.S. District Attorney's efforts to overturn the jury nullification of [this] genocidal bit of legislation is doomed to failure, if not in the Supreme Court, then in the real world where women vote with their bodies in support of transoption."

Transoption, already legal in most countries in the Western Hemisphere, has found popularity in the United States despite its risky and illegal nature. (See story, Section C, P.37—"Five Hundred Thousand Plus: Officials Sinking in Sea of Transoption Warrants.")

Grosscup, in appealing to the Supreme Court, seeks to overturn a Court of Appeals reversal—on technical grounds—of a federal district court verdict in favor of her innocence. The verdict incited a blaze of controversy six years ago that centered on the ability of a jury to declare certain laws invalid.

TRANSOPTION BAN UNCONSTITUTIONAL

Supporters Hail Verdict

Reuters

WASHINGTON—In a 6-3 decision, the Supreme Court today overturned a lower court ruling, in effect declaring the Rohrabacher-Hayden Act unconstitutional. Associate Justice Wilson wrote, in the majority opinion, that "transoption deserves at least the same status that abortion has," and that the transoptive co-mothers are "protected by the same... umbrella of privacy that covers any woman who seeks either to terminate or initiate a pregnancy."

Chief Justice Connely, in her dissenting opinion, stated that "a fetus is just as much a part of a woman's body as her heart or liver and, similarly, should not be [bought or sold] on the open market like so much meat."

Attorney Terence Johnson, who presented the oral argument for defendant Wanda Grosscup, said "We're thrilled with the outcome. We always maintained that saving a life was not a crime, and after eight years we are finally vindicated."

Dr. Evelyn Fletcher, the surgeon who first developed transoption over a decade ago, was asked to comment on the decision just before her keynote speech at the International LifeChoice Conference in Edmonton, Alberta. The globally-honored physician merely shrugged and said, "You can't stop progress. You can either get on the train or jump aside and wave as it passes. Otherwise, you'll get flattened."

"DESIGNER" CONTRACEPTIVES GET FDA GO-AHEAD

Could Be Available In Two Months

Times Wire Service

WASHINGTON—The FDA announced that it has granted approval for two different injectable contraceptives manufactured by Brunner Pharmaceuticals of Passaic, New Jersey. Ovustat, an ovulation blocker for women and Spermastat, a sperm disabler for men, have been available in Europe, Canada, and portions of South America for three years. Both offer permanent contraceptive action until neutralized by a counteracting injection, after which fertility is permanently restored.

The FDA denied that it bowed to public pressure in its decision. "The drugs are simply safe and effective. Period," said FDA spokesperson Janet Allan. "That we were able to make such a swift decision should be considered a tribute to our recent reorganization."

Both Ovustat and Spermastat work by taking a sperm or ovum sample and culturing its DNA in order to create a custom-designed injection that "switches off" the genetic codes for ovulation or sperm production. The neutralizing compounds Ovugen and Spermagen switch the genetic codes back on. Ironically, both were labeled safe and effective by the FDA six months before the blockers were.

Public demand for the incredibly convenient contraceptive has resulted in a flurry of one-day "vacations" to Canada followed by another one-day "business trip" the subsequent week. One week, of course, is the time it takes to culture the genetic sample and create the designer contraceptive.

What next for Brunner Pharmaceuticals now that the FDA has issued its approval? Dr. Ian Brunner, the company's founder, says, "We're close to the testing stage for Virocidan, the antivirus virus. When approved, we plan to market it separately and in a package with Ovustat and Spermastat."

270

TRANSOPTION CLINIC, FACING NEW AGE, GOES WITH FLOW

Declining Practice Prompts Switch to "Contras"

Exclusive to the *Herald*

SANTA MONICA—Citing the decline in elective transoptions, the president of Life-Switch Prenatal Adoptions today announced that its entire nationwide chain of seventeen transoption clinics will shift emphasis from transoption to genetic contraception. "Transoptions will still be performed," said president and CEO Valerie Czernek, but "we have to adapt to the times."

When she and her husband, Ron Czernek, bought the chain three years ago, "it consisted of six financially strapped abortion clinics. When transoption became legal in the U.S.," she said, "we moved into the market and adapted the failing company to the altered demands of the time. The new millennium, though, brought with it some rapid changes. LifeSwitch is proving that it can once again adapt to new realities."

With the change comes a new name. Says Czernek, "To reflect our shift in emphasis, Life-Switch Prenatal Adoptions will become ContraTemps. We will also have an initial public offering of stock this spring in order to finance an aggressive expansion program."

As unanticipated and unwanted pregnancies continue to decline, ContraTemps may well become a symbol of the changing shape of a new era.

VALEDICTORY SPEECH
IS *BIG* NEWS!
Local Woman Gets World Coverage

Exclusive to the *Times–Observer*

LOS GATOS—Renata Chandler, Los Gatos High School graduating class valedictorian, got more than she bargained for when she delivered her commencement speech yesterday. Under siege of videocams and microphones, her words reached a worldwide audience estimated at over one billion.

Renata is no stranger to the public eye. As the world's first transoptive baby, she has endured eighteen years of public scrutiny. Moving to Los Gatos at age seven, the perky blond kid quickly made friends who have grown up with her and who know how well she has handled her unintentional fame.

"When that TV movie about her came out, she took it in good stride," said classmate Sally Vanderlaan. "She called it 'Womb at the Top' and thought it was hilarious."

Renata's commencement speech, instead of dealing primarily with the challenge the graduating class faces ahead, concentrated on the contribution of previous generations. Her proud first stage and second stage co-parents—Valerie and Ron Czernek and Karen and David Chandler, respectively—were in attendance to give their daughter a hearty round of applause. Also on hand was Dr. Evelyn Fletcher, the Nobel Prize-winning surgeon who performed the first transoption over nineteen years ago.

When commencement ended, Renata dodged reporters to attend the prom with J. Phillip Nobel, Jr., son of the noted Saratoga *News* film critic.

(See page 3 for complete text of commencement speeches.)

Commencement Speech

by Renata V. Chandler

Los Gatos High School Class Valedictorian

"Thank you, Ms. Canrinus, faculty, staff, and graduates. Most valedictory speeches consist of platitudes concerning the bright future we have ahead, the daring challenges we'll face, and the solemn responsibility we have to make the world a better place.

"I stand here today and ask instead that we look back, to thank those in the past who have struggled to do the same. For we are indeed in a world that is a better place. I say that neither with youthful myopia nor comfortable ignorance. I speak as one who knows.

"Though we can all admit knowledge of this fact, I am the only one in my graduating class who can say this from a particular point of view. Next year there will be three. The year after that, a dozen or more. I would not be here, alive and filled with joy at our future, were it not for eyes that looked at the world and saw the need for change.

"One person. What a staggering difference one person, one life, can make. One woman decided that death was intolerable. She saved one life. One tiny, insignificant, nearly invisible life. And through that action millions came to be saved. Saved without the oppression of any other human being.

"As the first of my kind, I've received the lion's share of public scrutiny. Because of this, though, I cultivated an interest in my kindred spirits. I have sought them out, observed them, and I'm pleased to report that they are coming along nicely. I haven't found out about them all, of course, not even a small fraction. But thanks to the love of life and the devotion to principles of a significant few of the previous two generations, the human race has welcomed over twenty-two million extra members to its ranks.

"Twenty-two million is not a great percentage of the eight billion alive today. Every single life, though, matters. I would not be here to say that if one of our elders had not thought so. And every single person can make a difference.

"We entered the third millennium in a headlong rush to correct the problems of the last twenty centuries. Some said that overpopulation was the cause of all our miseries and sought to suppress reproductive choice. But the wise ones realized that the demon was not a glut of humanity but a dearth of respect for the rights of its members. Who were the wise ones? In retrospect, we can see that they weren't the presidents and kings, the powerful and the established. The wise ones were the mothers who conceived us and gave birth to us or who gave us to another rather than kill us. They were the mothers who received us in our defenseless condition. They were the fathers who loved and protected us. And they were the doctors, teachers, relatives, and friends who saw us not as oddities but as mere humans with all the rights and responsibilities such an honor bestows.

"Let us give thanks, then, to those who brought *all* of us to this point today. To those who gave us birth, no matter how. To those who raised us, taught us, instilled in us the values we hold. And as we go forward into the world they made, let us honor them in the finest way we can: by never slipping back from the frontiers they opened; by understanding the nature of the rights and laws they discovered; and by reaching ever farther beyond their grasp to touch new truths, new worlds, and new freedoms.

"To all of you through the centuries and eons who lived,

labored, struggled, and died to bring us to this point, to deliver us to the threshold of the universe, we take our first step into a world bigger than Earth, and say thank you, thank you, and thank you."

Acknowledgments

Writers often refer to their novels as their "babies," with good reason. The labor through which they go to give birth to such creations can often be as traumatic, physically and mentally, as the birth of a human being. Worse, the labor can last for years. The reward, though, is a lovely offspring that has the potential to live beyond its creator and touch other lives in myriad ways.

And, as with babies, the final, full-grown product is the result of many individual influences that combine to make the whole. A writer's experiences, research, and input from friends are the genetic material of the work. What follows is a DNA map of *Solomon's Knife*.

The initial germ of the story came from that veritable fount of ideas, Samuel Edward Konkin III, whose sarcastic offhand comment sparked a helix of thoughts in me. Wendy McElroy, erstwhile editrix of *The Voluntaryist*, wrote a passionate, logical defense of abortion that inspired me to counterattack, with equal fervor, the flaws I perceived in her arguments. J. Neil Schulman encouraged me to write a nonfiction article about a medical procedure that does not yet exist, ultimately convincing me that a fictional treatment offered more latitude in examining the potential of such an innovation. His constant enthusiasm and support brought this work to fruition.

Dr. John E. Buster, pioneer in nonsurgical ovum transfer, graciously and patiently answered hours of questions from an obviously ardent fan. The work he quietly, diligently performs is capable of changing the face of the world in ways none of us can fully imagine.

Virginia Jacobs provided me with valuable information about blood and marrow; she also coined the term *transoption* as a marvelous alternative to my inferior construct *transortion*.

Regina Cobb patiently explained how lawyers work and think, helping me immensely with the courtroom scenes.

Richard Kyle, eponymous proprietor of the best bookstore in the world—bar none—has helped me out of a bind more than a few times, providing tactical and strategic support whenever necessary.

Joel Gotler, who agented this book with Neil's assistance, has believed in me for the past twelve years, aiding me when he could and always expressing a personal interest when circumstances intervened. He helped keep this work afloat when it was merely a "project"—the artistic equivalent of a dislodged ovum.

Ronni Paer, Ricka Fisher, Denise DeGarmo, and Carol Drexler demonstrated an early interest in the book and gave me a glimpse of the more obscure reactions to transoption that might arise.

Robert A. Heinlein and Ray Bradbury inspired me to write, and then encouraged me onward. They both have a million sons and daughters who love them dearly.

Charles Platt, Ed Breslin, and Kent Oswald of Franklin Watts all contributed their energy and their company's money to ensure that this book is in your hands today.

My daughter, Vanessa, understood quickly—despite her age—that there was some causal connection between Daddy's time at the computer and his ability to purchase food, clothing, and surprises. Her recognition of the Koman variant of the Prime Directive is deeply appreciated.

And most of all, my wife—to whom this book is dedicated—

served as birth partner in this three-year gestation, enduring 5:00 A.M. rolls out of bed, stacks of paper atop every horizontal surface in the house, my discovery of caffeine after four decades of abstinence, and my penchant for gleefully describing imaginary medical operations in the most lurid terms possible. Veronica did more than persevere, though, providing days and nights of insight, criticism, inspiration, proofreading, encouragement, and love.

Any wild prophecies or outrageous mistakes contained herein are entirely my own. I labored long and hard to make them, and I deserve to take the credit.

VICTOR KOMAN
Los Angeles, California
December, 1988